D0839766

# Journey to Hope:
# The Legacy of a Mail-Order Bride

# ENDORSEMENTS

It's typically challenging to find a story that combines adventure, challenge, love, and faith with a strong Christian storyline. But *Journey to Hope* checks all those boxes and more. I was enamored with our mail-order bride from page one. As each new character was introduced, the author's skill in captivating each personality so clearly made me want to be right there in the scene with them. This book is a real winner, and I look forward to reading other stories by Mrs. Renalds.

—**Wendy Wallace**, blogger at www.OneExceptionalLife. com, author of *Victory Over Affliction: 30 Days of Mindset Challenges to Motivate You*

Having read Claudette Renalds's first novel, *By the Sea*, last fall, I jumped at the opportunity to read a manuscript of *Journey to Hope: The Legacy of a Mail-Order Bride*. A historical Christian romance, Ms. Renalds's second offering is more adventurous than her first as she ventures from the more familiar setting of the North Carolina Outer Banks to the wild, untamed frontier of early twentieth-century Wyoming. The unconventional romance of Cathleen Doyle, a precocious though somewhat naïve Boston socialite, and rancher Ben Sorenson, an emotionally scarred widower and father of two young children, unfolds with drama that is well-paced and a passion that is sensual but wholesome. As with her first book, Ms. Renalds manages to bring the characters' faith to life in a way that is sincere and grounded in a deep abiding love, which perseveres through trial and heartache. With her first foray into historical Christian romance, Claudette Renalds's story telling truly captures the reader's heart.

—**Robert Christopher Brown**, Licensed Professional Counselor, author of *Coming Terms With The Potter*

Beautifully written and impossible to put down, *Journey to Hope* breaks the genre mold with a heartfelt story of courage, love and God's unfailing grace.

—**Audra Sanlyn**, blogger, author of *Through the Eyes of a Veteran: A History of Winchester.*

Claudette Renalds's delightful tale of the cultural clashes that defined early twentieth-century America's westward immigration tangles us into the lives of Cathleen Doyle and Ben Sorenson, who are plunged together by a covert advertisement for a mail-order bride. Renalds suffuses her sweet romance with the challenges present in this era: east invades west, big city sophistication butts against wild, untamed rural self-determination, meagerness censures abundance. In response to these conflicts assaulting their personal comfort, Cathleen and Ben learn to wrangle with what separates them, bringing about a merger that weds them body, soul, and spirit, making their lives together a partnership of love and mutual respect. You will enjoy their adventures as well as their misadventures.

—**Johnese Burtram**, Capital Christian Writers Fellowship—Board of Directors, writer, speaker, teacher, supporter of Christian writers.

Claudette Renalds's writing captivates the reader from page one until the end. It seemed as though I was walking next to the main character, Cathleen, and experiencing all her emotions and thoughts. I love the playful romance between Cathleen and Ben. Grab a copy of this book for a weekend getaway with a rich young girl from the city who meets a hard-working rancher. It is the perfect story of when two people from different worlds come together. You can see how God walks with them through each road traveled.

—**Adria Wilkins**, speaker, author of *The Joy Box Journal.*

# Journey to Hope:
# The Legacy of a Mail-Order Bride

## Claudette Renalds

PUBLISHING THE POSITIVE

ELK LAKE PUBLISHING INC
Plymouth, Massachusetts

Cover and Interior Design: Derinda Babcock

Editor(s): Judy Hagey, Linda Rondeau, Deb Haggerty

PUBLISHED BY: Elk Lake Publishing, Inc., 35 Dogwood Drive, Plymouth, MA 02360, 2020

---

Library Cataloging Data

Names: Renalds, Claudette (Claudette Renalds)

*Journey to Hope: The Legacy of a Mail-Order Bride* / Claudette Renalds

340 p. 23cm × 15cm (9in × 6 in.)

Identifiers: ISBN-13: 978-1-951970 65-9 (paperback) | 978-1-951970-66-6 (trade paperback) | 978-1-951970-67-3 (e-book)

Key Words: mail-order bride, cattle ranch, Western, second wife, stepchildren, high society, turn of the century

LCCN: 2020939308 Fiction

This story of courage, hope, and love is dedicated to my three granddaughters—Megan and Elizabeth Davis and Anna-Maria Renalds. I am thankful for the godly young women they are becoming. May they continue on the journey God has planned for them.

*I pray that God, the source of hope, will fill you completely with joy and peace because you trust in him. Then you will overflow with confident hope through the power of the Holy Spirit.* (Romans 15:13)

# Prologue

Cathleen Doyle closed her eyes and leaned against the bedroom door. Not knowing what to expect, she feared crossing the threshold. *God, please. I can't face this alone.*

If the night nurse hadn't opened the door with a motion comparable to her age, Cathleen would have fallen headfirst into the dark room. Gaining her composure, she hugged Nadine and eased past the familiar servant. She sniffed the stale air. Had she entered the wrong room? The usual scent of rose petals couldn't compete with the strong acidic smell of medicine and sickness. She covered her nose with her handkerchief and willed the scent of lilacs to settle her stomach.

"Miz Doyle be eager to see you, Miss Cathleen."

Tears wet Cathleen's cheeks when she approached the bedside. Her once robust grandmother almost disappeared beneath the silk counterpane. Neither the mound of pillows nor the heavy doses of laudanum relieved her suffering. Afraid to face reality, Cathleen had avoided the sick room for over a week. If Nana hadn't sent word, she wouldn't have come now. The most important person in her world neared the end of her life, and Cathleen could do nothing to save her.

Weakened with grief, Cathleen clung to the high bedpost and thought about her grandmother's impact on her life. Mary Pearce Doyle took pleasure in filling the void

Cathleen's parents seemed unable to fill. They cared more for their social standing and increasing their wealth than enduring the endless questions from an inquisitive young mind. In contrast, her grandmother allowed nothing to take precedence over her granddaughter.

When Cathleen graduated from the nursery, she spent hours in the company of the dear woman. To ensure her granddaughter became well-versed in all subjects, Nana took charge of her education. The grand lady possessed a keen mind herself and wanted the same for Cathleen. Together they pursued world geography, politics, and math despite the objections from her governess.

"Refined young ladies should not be taught such nonsense. They only need to know the social graces, a few respectable dances, polite manners, and how to manage a household. No woman should discuss issues reserved for men. It's absurd!"

Nana dismissed the prune-faced woman with a wave of her hand and proceeded to teach Cathleen. They read hundreds of books, both classic and contemporary. Perusing the daily newspaper led to hours of political, financial, and social debate. A challenging game of chess kept them strategizing for days. Nana went to great lengths to satisfy a little girl's avid thirst for knowledge and to stimulate her imagination.

For Cathleen's thirteenth birthday, her grandmother insisted Cathleen accompany her on a year-long tour of Europe, Asia, and the Middle East. As they traveled, they studied the governments, history, and cultures of each country, cultivating friendships among the people. Nana never met a stranger. What Cathleen gleaned from that trip enhanced her education and challenged her thinking long after the trunks were unpacked.

"Cathleen, learn something new every day. Don't let that brilliant mind of yours lay dormant." Her grandmother followed her own advice and rarely let a day end without sharing something new she'd heard or read.

But, the most important thing her grandmother taught her had little to do with travel, literature, or the arts. "There's another kingdom, Cathleen, and it's not of this world. You can only see this kingdom through spiritual eyes. Jesus, our Savior, rules there with love, grace, and human kindness. You, dear child, are one of his valued subjects."

Nana talked to God as if they were long-time friends. She searched the Scriptures for knowledge and believed every promise. "Let's see what God has for us today," she'd say as she reached for the big book.

Understanding came with maturity, and over time, Cathleen learned to trust God for herself. Even the disappointments with her parents were bearable knowing that besides her faith, she could depend on the wisdom of her grandmother.

As she moved to the sick woman's bedside, sadness overtook her with the blatant truth. She could no longer depend on the wise counsel and prayer support from her nana. How would she face the uncertain future alone?

"Nana, you can't leave me. What will I do without you?"

Cathleen laid her hand on the woman's chest and felt the erratic heartbeat. As she traced the raised veins on top of the withered hand, she was consumed with love for her grandmother. How many times had these hands soothed her brow, pointed her toward truth, and held her face to smother her cheeks with kisses? Seeing no response, Cathleen slumped into the chair and bowed her head in defeat. Conviction swept over her when she considered her selfish attitude. *God forgive me for thinking only of myself. Give me grace to accept Nana's release from her suffering.*

Cathleen jerked when a cold, weak hand grabbed her arm. Recognizing the familiar touch, she reached for her grandmother. Renewed hope blossomed when the dear woman pulled her closer. "You'll be fine, darling. I want to share a secret with you. It will be all you'll need when I'm gone."

"But I'll never not need you. You're my best friend and the only one who really cares about me."

Her grandmother smiled and patted her hand. "I know, my sweet girl. We've had some wonderful times together. But you need to stand on your own two feet and apply some of that stubborn backbone you inherited from your father." A rattling cough interrupted and racked her frail body.

Cathleen reached for a glass of water, but Nana shook her head. Clearing her throat a few times, she continued in a low, gravelly voice. "You'll have to forgive your parents, dear. I know you sometimes question their love for you, but they do in their own way. Pray for courage. Stand up for what you believe. Not easy, but you won't be alone. Trust God. He has a plan for you. His Spirit lives right here."

Nana placed her hand over Cathleen's heart and continued in short breaths. "The Comforter will guide you. Stay close to him. He'll lead you to your soulmate—someone perfect God has chosen for you."

Cathleen strained to hear the last few words that had faded into a whisper. Her grandmother's breathing had deteriorated into short, shallow pants. A peaceful look swept over the dear woman as she dropped Cathleen's hand and closed her eyes.

Watching the last labored breath depart from the frail body, a deep sorrow filled Cathleen's chest. She fell across the still body and muffled her cries against the familiar bosom that never failed to welcome her. "I will always love you, Nana," she whispered.

With a gentle move, the nurse pulled her away and led her toward the door. "I's sorry, Miss Cathleen. Looks like yor grandmother has taken her last trip. I 'spect we need to call the doctor."

Cathleen choked back an anguished cry when the reality hit—her grandmother had spoken her final words of wisdom.

# Chapter One

Cathleen mourned for several weeks following her grandmother's funeral. Along with the reading of the will, the attorney delivered personal letters from the elderly Mrs. Doyle to Cathleen and her parents. Cathleen's letter only reiterated what Nana had said on her deathbed, but she would treasure those final words forever. She breathed a prayer of thanks she had her grandmother's words of wisdom in her own hand.

She wasn't surprised at the sizable trust fund left in her name or the enormous inheritance her father added to his already significant holdings. Her grandfather earned every penny of his fortune—from his first job delivering groceries to becoming a major investor in the railroad. Behind the scenes, he claimed grandmother's keen financial mind contributed toward his success.

Though Grandfather bragged that his wife understood investments better than most men, only the family knew the extent of her involvement. Women playing a role in the business world wasn't seen as a virtue in Boston society. The "weaker sex" were deemed useful only to manage households and provide heirs. Mary Pearce Doyle's eulogy fell far short of her amazing accomplishments.

Cathleen longed for a time and place where her own abilities would be accepted and appreciated without consideration of her gender or social standing. Her grandmother understood her desires and had warned her—Cathleen's greatest obstacles would come from within her family. From the moment she celebrated her eighteenth birthday, her parents had invited a continuous stream of eligible young men, and some not so young, into their home. After three years of not satisfying either Cathleen or her grandmother, her mother panicked. She feared her daughter would be left on the shelf if she didn't marry before her twenty-second birthday.

The day her family discarded their mourning attire, the parade of prospective husbands resumed but with greater intensity. Although the number of suitors increased, the lure of her sizeable trust fund diminished their quality. Fortune hunters arrived in droves proclaiming their love and adoration while Cathleen wanted to be left alone.

"Cathleen, Mavis laid out a new dress for you to wear tonight. It's a striking jade color that matches your eyes. We have an important guest coming for dinner and your father wants you to look your best. He's considering a business proposition with this young man's family, and if you make a good impression, you could very well be looking at your future. I hear he's handsome and considered most eligible."

"Mother, I don't want a husband based on some business deal or good looks. What about love and compatibility? If he's anything like those you've suggested before, I'm not interested."

"Don't be impertinent, Cathleen. I warned your father about allowing you to spend too much time with his mother. That old woman had the most ridiculous ideas, and she's filled your head with similar notions. Now that she's gone, you can no longer base your decisions on her outlandish opinions. You must listen to your parents if you want to succeed in Boston society."

Cathleen's arguments landed on deaf ears. She'd lost the only voice of reason in the family. Without the support of her grandmother, she'd never be allowed to choose her own husband—a man more interested in her as a person than her money. As she dressed for dinner, she remembered Nana's instructions to pray and trust God. She knelt beside her bed, expecting to sense God's presence like she had when she'd prayed with her grandmother. Instead, she felt only fear and dread.

Without courage or direction, Cathleen rose and wiped away the evidence of tears. She took one last look in the mirror and tucked a few loose strands of hair in her chignon. Confident she was presentable, she walked down the winding staircase and waited outside the drawing room. Instead of meeting a dinner guest, she felt as if she were walking into a den of robbers, plotting to steal her freedom. She didn't understand why she dreaded this evening above the others. In the past, her parents had left the final decision to her. Surely this time would be no different. Hoping for the best, Cathleen adjusted her corset, raised her chin, and marched into the drawing room.

"Come here, Cathleen. Let me look at you." Her mother turned her back and forth until her head swirled and her stomach quivered. "Just as I thought. That color makes the green in your eyes sparkle, and your hair looks like it's on fire. Doesn't our Cathleen look beautiful, William? She's certain to impress that Stanwick boy."

The silk dress blossomed out at the hips and tapered to a hobble skirt below the knees. Even while standing, her black Mary Janes peeked out from under the hem. She knew she presented a picture of style and elegance, but she resented both the occasion and her mother's controlling attitude.

Cathleen frowned and grumbled under her breath as she took a seat near her father. Without another ally within the household, she looked for an opportunity to appeal to the tenderness lurking beneath her father's business facade. He rarely allowed his emotions to surface. She longed for him, just once, to show some consideration. Why could he not understand her feelings?

Before she expressed more than a greeting, however, Jenson opened the door and ushered in the next candidate. All color drained from Cathleen's face when she recognized the oaf with greedy eyes surveying the room.

"Mr. Stanwick, come in." Her father bounded across the room, hand outstretched. "We are delighted you accepted our invitation. How are your parents?"

"They are well, sir. Thank you for asking." Mr. Stanwick shook hands with her father and then moved to her mother. He held her hand a moment before kissing the inside of her wrist. "I'm pleased to see you again, Mrs. Doyle, and honored to be invited to your lovely home." Her mother gushed with pleasure while Cathleen rolled her eyes in disgust of the pompous display.

The man allowed himself another greedy scan of the room before turning his attention toward Cathleen. She covered her low neckline with her hand as his gaze stopped below her neck. He met Cathleen's frown with an arrogant, mocking smile. Did the man have no shame?

Her father cleared his throat. "I don't believe you've met our daughter, Mr. Stanwick. Cathleen, I want you to meet Mr. Geoffrey Stanwick. His parents have recently become good friends."

"I'm happy to make your acquaintance, Miss Doyle. I don't recall seeing you at the last soirée I attended. As lovely as you are, I doubt you'd be overlooked." He sniffed importantly.

Instead of correcting the lie, Cathleen jerked her hand away from the lingering kiss to her fingertips. Laughing at her discomfort, he moved close enough for her to get a whiff of his cologne. The overpowering smell intensified the pressure in her head. If she thought her mother would believe her, she'd use the headache as an excuse to leave.

"Dinner is served, madam."

Cathleen's heart sank when Mr. Stanwick pulled her hand into the crook of his arm and whispered. "I'm not a monster, Cathleen, but I plan to have you. It matters not how you feel about me. We'll do fine together."

Forced to allow the awful man to usher her into the dining room, she recalled what little she knew of him. None of the rumors were complimentary. How could he pretend he hadn't seen her at the McDougal's ball? Her first glimpse of the flirtatious man had disgusted her, causing her to dismiss him each time he looked her way. Mother was right. Geoffrey Stanwick was handsome. But appearances can be deceiving. How could her parents expect her to marry such an obvious cad?

The meal passed with little meaningful conversation. While Mr. Stanwick promoted himself, the conversation consisted of the latest gossip among the social elite. Cathleen longed for a glimpse of integrity and character in her latest suitor.

A momentary pause presented Cathleen with an opportunity. "What do you think about the orphan trains that have secured homes for children out West? I read in the *Globe* the Children's Aid Society recently reported that eighty-seven percent of the placements have been successful."

Mrs. Doyle closed her eyes and drew in a quiet breath. Geoffrey paused with a bite mid-air. Mr. Doyle placed his knife across his plate and cleared his throat.

"Cathleen, that is not something you should concern yourself with. Your interests are here, not out West, and certainly not with those children."

Regaining his composure, Geoffrey interrupted. "Well, good for them. They do us a great service by reducing the number of waifs begging on the streets of Boston."

Cathleen groaned inside at the thought of giving herself to a man who neither loved her nor cared about anyone but himself. They would never agree on anything, especially her faith. How could she endure such a life sentence?

When their guest finally departed, Cathleen left the drawing room in a state of shock. Her thoughts jumped from panic to illogical means of escape. Geoffrey Stanwick had wasted no time in securing permission from her father to court her, intending to ask for her hand in marriage. Unlike other occasions, her father bought into the plan with gusto. Remembering his mandate, she shook with angry fear. "I want your marriage announced before the end of the month, Cathleen."

Why the sudden rush to marry her off without the least regard for her opinion? *God, please help me escape this nightmare.*

As Cathleen made her way toward the stairs, her eye caught the edge of the *Boston Evening Globe* visible under a stack of mail. The conscientious butler had neglected to place the newspaper on her father's desk. Since her grandmother's death, she'd had to sneak into her father's office to read the headlines.

Cathleen's hunger for knowledge outweighed her parent's stifling ideas. Hoping Jenson wouldn't notice, she grabbed the thin publication and hid it between the folds of her skirt. She didn't understand her obsession. Instead of sneaking around to read the latest news, she should be thinking of ways to escape this nightmare of a wedding.

The moment the door to her bedroom closed, Cathleen opened the paper and skimmed the headlines—Explorers Reach the North Pole. She admired the adventurous men, but their frigid conditions didn't interest her. Local politics, letters to the editor, and Boston social life filled the next few pages. Flipping to the last page, she scanned the classified advertisements. At the very bottom of the column, she noticed something so unbelievable she gasped. Her heart raced and the paper in her hands shook until she could barely read. Could this be real? Glaring back at her in slightly smudged black ink—"Successful Rancher seeking a mail-order bride. Woman must be a Christian of good moral character. Inquire at Post Office Box 7, Laramie, Wyoming."

Mail-order brides, she remembered her grandmother telling her, had been popular before the turn of the century. Women were credited for bringing order and civility to the West. She'd heard of such advertisements, but this was the first she'd seen. Why would anyone resort to such unconventional means? The answer to her question sent her reeling. *A desperate person who needed a means of escape.* Could this be her ticket to freedom?

Cathleen paced the floor as she read the words for the third time. Tears marred her vision while she considered the possibilities—a handsome man wearing a dark suit, string tie, and cowboy hat. A tingling sensation started in the pit of her stomach and soared upward. Hope lifted the heavy burden she'd carried since her grandmother's death.

Excited over the prospect of freedom, she ran both hands through her hair. Bobbie pins scattered in all directions, pinging on the wooden floor. She danced and twirled about the room to the music of a show tune playing in her head.

If she couldn't marry for love in Boston, she'd find her own marriage of convenience in the West.

All she'd ever wanted was a man who would love her for herself. Could this rancher be the one grandmother anticipated? *Even now, Cathleen, God's preparing someone special for you. When the time is right, you must trust God to lead you to him.*

At her writing desk, she picked up a pen to respond. Paralysis gripped her hand. Had she lost her mind? This sounded more like the makings of a novel than real life. Did she have the courage to leave the only home she'd ever known and travel hundreds of miles to marry a stranger? What did she know about being a rancher's wife?

She paced the floor and wrung her hands, searching for an answer. At the window, she contemplated the garden. The signs of spring visible in the sunlight were hidden among the shadows of a waning moon. The eerie scene brought her back to the urgency of her situation. If the rancher didn't work out, she'd have to find an alternative.

Leaning against the windowsill, she prayed for guidance. Cathleen grabbed a pillow from the window seat to stifle her desperate cries. Her grandmother wasn't here to advise her, and she didn't know who she could trust. Her prayers seemed to stop at the ceiling until she remembered her grandmother's touch to her chest. *Jesus called him the Comforter and promised that he would guide us.* Grandmother was gone, but she would never be alone.

At the memory of her grandmother's last words, peace and confidence replaced her attack of cold feet. Excitement returned, along with renewed strength. Her traditional upbringing would never encourage such an unconventional act. But what choice did she have? If writing to the rancher failed, she would have to marry Mr. Stanwick. *Ugh!* Despite the lingering doubts, Cathleen returned to her desk and resumed composing the most important letter she'd ever written.

This time when she picked up the pen, she prayed for favor—that the mysterious rancher would choose her above all the other applicants. What could she say that would make her stand out? He wouldn't need to know about her desperate circumstances or that she possessed a huge inheritance. If he was the kind of man who would be interested in her, he'd want to know the condition of her heart. She smiled in satisfaction as she looked back at the advertisement. Since he requested a Christian wife, she'd give him a glimpse of her sincere faith and love for God.

After a fretful night of tossing and turning on the feather mattress, she vacillated between questioning her sanity and excitement about her decision. Regardless, she sprinted from bed resolved to walk boldly past the suspicious Jenson on her way to the post office. The challenge would be to intercept the incoming mail before the butler got his hands on the return letter. The peculiar man refused to distribute even personal correspondence without strict scrutiny. He didn't hesitate to alert her mother if he found something out of the ordinary.

Few patrons were milling about the post office when Cathleen arrived the following morning. Mr. Griffin, the postmaster, examined her letter with a curiosity similar to the butler's. He would have questioned her if not for another customer waiting in line. Cathleen relaxed when she left the building without having to explain.

With the letter on the way, her doubts returned in full force. She bounced back and forth between worry and trust. At her lowest point, she would have chased the letter down if possible. Her presumptuous behavior had her biting her nails and massaging her stomach to ease the burning acid.

The pressure from Mr. Stanwick and her parents to set a date for the wedding brought additional distress. Another week of waiting, and she'd be tempted to board the train without an invitation. She longed to hear from her mystery man, yet she wasn't sure how she'd answer if he invited her to come.

Every morning, she raced out of the house to catch the mailman before he made his way up the walk. After a few such sprints, Jenson looked at her with raised eyebrows. With her lungs near collapsing, she placed the mail on the table in the foyer.

"Are you expecting a letter, miss?"

"No, er … maybe."

"If you'll give me an idea of the origin, I'll save it for you."

"That won't be necessary. I take a walk about this time anyway. Thank you, though."

Jenson frowned at her obvious lie as she rushed up the stairs. She didn't fool him. Rarely did she leave the house without a specific destination. By the time the dog-eared letter arrived with a Wyoming post mark, she'd run out of patience and excuses. Her nerves were shot.

"I see you've received your expected correspondence, miss." The butler watched her sift through the stack of mail, then snatch the longed-for response from the bundle. He huffed in aggravation when she slipped the letter into her pocket before he saw the return address. Turning on his heel, he stalked off, shuffling through the remaining mail on his way to her father's office.

Cathleen wasted no time running up the stairs and escaping into the privacy of her bedroom. She threw herself across the bed and ripped the letter from its envelope.

Miss Doyle,

It was with great pleasure that I read your reply to my advertisement for a mail-order bride. Of all the responses, you impressed me most with your obvious heart for God. After much prayer, I would like to invite you to Laramie as my guest to explore the possibilities of becoming the future Mrs. Sorenson. If either party isn't comfortable with the arrangement, you may return to Boston. Please let me know your decision as soon as possible and I will send you a train ticket. I am sincerely grateful and look forward to meeting you.

Benjamin Sorenson.

That's it? Cathleen turned the letter over to see if she'd missed something. Couldn't the man at least describe his appearance or give some details about his ranch? Did he expect her to travel halfway across the continent with nothing more than a polite invitation? She deserved answers, but time was running out. Pressure from her parents had escalated, while Mr. Stanwick arrived daily wearing a satisfied smirk on his face. Each visit he took more liberties and pressed harder for her affections, refusing to keep his hands to himself.

A knock on the front door interrupted Cathleen's concerns. A few minutes later, there was a softer knock on her bedroom door. She didn't have to guess who'd be waiting in the parlor. No excuse short of lying would work. When she stepped into the room, her mother wasted no time in excusing herself. Ignoring all the rules of polite society, her parents pushed the man on her without the least consideration of her discomfort. Their attitude further confirmed to Cathleen how little they cared for their only daughter.

The door had barely shut behind her mother before Mr. Stanwick pulled her into his arms. Cathleen turned her head to avoid the disgusting kiss.

"What do you think you're doing? Take your hands off me before I call my parents."

Mr. Stanwick laughed at her useless threat. The first time his wandering hands caressed under her arms and moved toward her breasts, she'd slapped him and run to find her mother. Her mother refused to believe anything negative about the man she'd picked for her daughter to marry. She wouldn't help her then, and Cathleen couldn't count on her now.

"I'm simply getting a taste of what will soon be mine."

Cathleen raised her hand to slap the smirk off his face, but he grabbed her arms and pulled her against his body. "Don't you ever strike me again. I want you, Cathleen, and see no need to wait for the formalities."

"If you don't let me go, I'll scream so loud the neighbors will hear me."

Unaffected by her threat, Mr. Stanwick leered at her. He fondled the edge of her neckline and trailed wet kisses from her throat to the bare skin where he'd exposed her shoulder. Overcome by his ardor, his grip loosened enough for Cathleen to duck under his arm and rush for the door. Looking back, she saw her assailant leaning casually against the mantel. He followed her with a satisfied smirk as though nothing had happened. The unscrupulous man sent chills up and down her spine. She turned around so fast, she almost ran into the doorframe.

"You can run for now, but in a few short weeks, Cathleen, you'll be mine, and I will have my way with you."

Safely on the other side of the closed door, she burst into tears. Angry sobs shook her body, bending her almost double.

At the sound of someone on the stairs, she composed herself and checked her appearance in the large mirror. Horrified at her reflection, she wiped her face with the back of her hands, straightened the neckline of her dress, and finger-pressed the wrinkles from her skirt. The few wayward curls that had escaped the loose bun would have to wait. She had no more options.

She made one final appeal to her mother, who she found at her writing desk in the library. "Come in, Cathleen. I'm making a list of people we should invite to your engagement party."

Panic released a flood of protest in Cathleen. "Mother, I can't take this anymore. The man you are pushing on me is a cad. The moment you left us, he tried to kiss me and put his hands all over me."

"What did you expect, Cathleen? You're engaged to be married. You should be thankful he finds you attractive."

"I am not engaged. The man has not asked me to marry him."

"Of course, you're engaged. Everything's been arranged. Just as soon as you pick a date, we'll post the announcement in the paper. If you don't decide soon, I'll be forced to pick the date for you. Don't forget we're meeting with the seamstress tomorrow about your wedding gown. We're running out of time."

Cathleen shook her head. She saw no hope in trying to reason with her mother. Her parents collaborated with the proposed groom as if her opinion counted for nothing. If the arrogant man assumed she'd say "I do" without objection, he had another thought coming. Her only option was at the mercy of a stranger—the Wyoming rancher.

Waiting for a return letter to travel from Wyoming was not an option. She had to leave Boston as soon as possible.

She would purchase her own ticket and wire Mr. Sorenson before boarding the train.

Late that afternoon, she found the gardener's son plucking weeds from the flower beds. Winston was a couple of years younger than Cathleen, but they had played together when they were children. "Hello, Winston. I know you're busy, but do you mind helping me with something?"

Winston's shy grin revealed two dimples. He lowered his head, looked past her right shoulder, and shuffled his feet. "I hear you're getting married. I wish you every happiness, miss. What can I do for you?"

"Thank you. I need some trunks from the attic. I want to start packing some of my clothes."

Since her request sounded logical, Winston agreed and followed her inside. He soon had the trunks sitting open in her bedroom and made a move to leave. Cathleen caught him by the arm. "Can I trust you, Winston?"

The young man stared at the hand holding him captive. Cathleen released him and wiped her hands down the front of her skirt. Winston crossed both arms over his chest, and his eyebrows wrinkled together in suspicion.

"Of course. But I'm concerned about that look in your eyes. What mischief are you planning now?"

Cathleen smiled at her friend. "I can't tell you, Winston, but I need to get away for a while. Do you think you could sneak my packed trunks down the stairs after everyone retires for the night? When I purchase my ticket later today, I will ask Mr. Vance to store them at the station until the train arrives tomorrow."

Winston's mouth dropped open in disbelief. He removed his hat and wiped his forehead with his shirt sleeve. "It looks like you're about to get yourself in trouble, and I'm not sure I should help you. You never were satisfied to do the expected.

Guess that's what made me like you so much. Besides, you always treated me with respect and kindness. One day after we'd played together, I told my mother that I planned to marry you when I grew up."

Winston again shuffled nervously and looked everywhere but at her. "'Course she set me straight right away. We both know I'm too young for you." Her friend chuckled at his teasing. Warmth spread through Cathleen. Right before her eyes stood an option she hadn't considered.

"Thank you, dear friend. You have been nothing but kind and good. If things don't work out for me, I'll take you up on the offer."

Winston threw back his head and snorted through peals of laughter. The young man didn't know that she would gladly marry him over the abusive Geoffrey Stanwick.

When Cathleen sneaked out of the house and boarded the train early the next morning, she felt as if she'd escaped life imprisonment. Her short breaths lengthened into peaceful release as she fell back against the hard seat—the only accommodations available on such short notice. She looked at the other passengers and wondered about their stories. Were they all running from something? Or, were they running toward someone? As for herself, she preferred the latter. Despite all the questions flooding her mind, the unknown looked far superior to the chaotic nightmare she was leaving behind.

## Chapter Two

After days of miserable travel with little sleep, a gentle tap to her shoulder interrupted Cathleen's confusing dream. "We've arrived in Laramie. Do you still plan to leave us here?"

"Oh, yes. Thank you," she mumbled to the porter. To keep her parents from knowing where she'd gone, she had purchased a ticket all the way to California. The railroad employee questioned her several times before she convinced him to change the destination of her trunks.

Confused and undone, she searched under the seat for a missing glove. Her mother would be appalled to see her looking so bedraggled. Thoughts of her mother aggravated the pain shooting through her head and neck. She'd spent the last few days sitting on a hard seat and staring out the window. Her thoughts turned sour after the first few hundred miles. When she remembered the brief letter she'd left behind, she nearly choked on the guilt. How could she have treated her only living relatives so callously? Would they ever forgive her?

Cathleen stood on shaky legs and held onto the seat until she regained her balance. Though the train had stopped, the swaying motion continued in her head making her dizzy and nauseous. Her clothes were soaked with perspiration. *Then how can my mouth be so dry?* Her swirling head reminded her of the indecision she'd grappled with the whole exhausting trip. Should she leave the train and rush to the ticket window for a return passage? Or should she follow through with what she now considered an impulsive decision? How did she find herself in such a quandary?

"Excuse me, miss."

Cathleen glanced behind her at a man waiting for her to move out of his way. Thinking the place more remote, she was surprised to find another passenger leaving the train at her stop. She stepped back to let the man pass. "Forgive me, sir."

When the aisle had cleared, she fumbled to gather her reticule and hat box. While stooped over, she glanced out the window and wondered how she would recognize Mr. Sorenson. Disturbing questions flew at her from every direction. Would he be handsome like the man she imagined? Would she like him? What if he mistreated her? So many questions and no answers.

Praying for the positive, she started toward the front of the car when she noticed a vile-looking man blocking the aisle ahead. His intense stare weakened her knees and almost sent her back to her seat. He reminded her of the cad she'd left behind in Boston. If the man she intended to marry looked anything like him, she should return to her seat and continue to California.

Cathleen straightened her spine and cleared her throat. "Excuse me, sir." When the man tipped his hat and stepped back, she scooted passed him. Her hat box took a beating on the back of each seat as she rushed forward. She didn't stop until she'd reached the porter and handed him her bag. Before descending the steps, she glanced behind her and released a shaky breath when she saw the man returning to his seat.

After the porter helped her down the steps, she handed him a generous tip and picked up her reticule. He bowed and rewarded her with a wide smile. "Thank you, miss. You can find your trunks on the far platform."

Cathleen stood in the crowded station and searched in every direction. Not one person resembled the man she had imagined. Tilting her hat for a better view, she paced the length of the platform. Just when she feared she'd been abandoned, an elderly gentleman with a full head of graying hair approached from her right. "Miss Doyle?"

Cathleen hesitated before taking the man's outstretched hand. "Yes, I'm Miss Doyle. You aren't Benjamin Sorenson, are you?"

"Benjamin Sorenson, Senior, at your service. I believe you were expecting my son, but I'll have to do for now. We've a few miles to cover before reaching the ranch. We should be on our way before the sun sets on us. I promise an explanation on the way." He turned and headed toward the baggage area.

Cathleen stood in place, trying to take it all in. *What happened to her promised bridegroom? What kind of fiancé sends his aging father to meet the bride he ordered? How could she marry someone who had no more regard for her feelings than that? Was her imaginary cowboy no different than the people she'd left behind in Boston?*

Sensing she wasn't behind him, Mr. Sorenson turned and waited for Cathleen. She gazed at the empty tracks, swallowed her self-pity, and held back her tears. On a slow exhale, she studied the kind gentleman who stood with his head bowed. Could he be praying or was he just embarrassed for his son? When she cleared her throat, he glanced at her with concerned eyes. Cathleen smiled and realized that at least one person cared what happened to her.

"Thank you, Mr. Sorenson. I believe I have found a friend in you. My trunks should be on the platform by now. I'll get a porter to load them into your car."

The man put his hands in his trouser pockets and smiled so wide his eyes crinkled. "You won't see too many cars out here, Miss Doyle. Most of us still travel by horse and buggy. Today, I brought the wagon so there'd be room for your luggage."

Cathleen noticed the man's quizzical look as he eyed her three trunks. "I didn't have time to pack everything, but I'll contact my parents in a few weeks and ask them to send the rest. In the meantime, I'll get by with what I brought."

Again, Mr. Sorenson looked her over and then shrugged. Cathleen cringed and tried to smooth her rumpled suit. Was he displeased with her appearance? She had wanted to make a good impression but, instead of preparing to meet her new family, she'd fallen asleep during the last hour on the train.

Reverend Sorenson smiled to himself as the young man loaded the heavy trunks on to the wagon. Thank goodness he had the foresight to bring the freight wagon instead of the buckboard. The young woman wasn't anything like the person he had envisioned when he read her letter. He laughed to himself at the needy, homely-looking creature he'd pictured—too old and too plain to find a suitable mate on the eastern seaboard. Her Christian maturity must have confused him. Did he not think young attractive women could have that depth of spiritual maturity?

Not only was Miss Doyle strikingly beautiful, but her speech, clothes, luggage, and demeanor spoke of wealth and class. She had to be running from something or someone to venture this far west. He scratched his head and wondered what his son would think. Had he made the biggest mistake of his life? How on earth would this pampered, refined young woman manage on a ranch, miles from the nearest town?

Regardless, she had arrived, and he'd have to follow through with his plan.

Guilt tore at his insides as he helped her board the battered wagon. Every day since he'd sent that misleading letter, he'd been on his knees asking God for forgiveness. The weight wouldn't lift until he'd confessed everything, but how could he explain such foolishness?

Cathleen squirmed on the hard bench seat she shared with her future father-in-law. She bounced with the wagon over every bump. The road more resembled two crooked lines meandering through miles of prairie grass. She spotted the occasional chipmunks playing tag in and around the sagebrush border. Despite her irritation, the view more than compensated for the rough ride. From almost every direction, snow-capped mountains filled the landscape. The peaceful setting turned her thoughts toward God, the One responsible for such grandeur.

Since the quiet man beside her hesitated to address her concerns, she broke the silence with a compliment. "Your mountains are beautiful, Mr. Sorenson. I feel God's presence surrounding us."

The man looked everywhere but at her. Something beside the hard seat and bumpy road made him uncomfortable. He squirmed and shifted his weight, making the wagon rock even more. What had him in such a tizzy? Perhaps he had trouble explaining the missing groom.

When he again shifted and cleared his throat, Cathleen raised her hand. "I'm not interested in your stories, Mr. Sorenson. What are you not telling me?"

"Cathleen, I ..." The man paused and pondered his response. "May I call you by your given name, dear? You see, we aren't very formal out here, and since we are to be family, it seems only right."

"Of course. What should I call you?"

"Well, it might be awkward in public to call me Benjamin. You see, I'm the minister at one of the churches in Laramie. Most of my parishioners call me Rev. Sorenson or Brother Benjamin. I'd like for you to call me Papa or Father. Would that be confusing?"

"No, that's fine. My parents have always been Father and Mother, but since they're far away, that should be no problem. Thank you."

"You might change your mind when I confess my actions over the past few weeks."

Cathleen raised an eyebrow, wondering where the conversation would lead. "I doubt that, but is there a Mrs. Reverend Sorenson?"

"Yes, and she can't wait to meet you."

"Good. Because for a moment there, I thought I'd be marrying you instead of your son."

Cathleen's joke lightened the mood and gave the gentleman enough courage to continue. "Cathleen, you must forgive me, but my son isn't expecting you."

"What? But he wrote a letter and asked me to come."

"No. I regret to tell you, I placed the ad and answered your letter. I know what I did was stupid and dishonest, but I didn't feel I had a choice." He shifted on the bench and trained his gaze on Cathleen. "When you have children of your own, Cathleen, you'll understand the pain of watching a child struggle. You want to ease their suffering and solve their problems. My wife, Maggie, and I have suggested many possible solutions since our daughter-in-law passed away four months ago, but our son rejected every one. His wife left behind an infant and a toddler who need a mother's love and care."

"What? He has children?"

"I'm sorry I didn't mention the children in the notice, but I thought an acceptable wife should be the first consideration. Even though Maggie and I help as much as our son allows, the children still suffer. Two teenage sisters take turns keeping house and watching them, but the young girls are more interested in hooking a husband than doing chores. We've often arrived when Ben wasn't around to find the baby crying and both children needing attention. Advertising for a mail-order bride was our last resort."

"I'm sorry, Reverend Sorenson, but if I'd known he had children, I wouldn't have come. I'm not ready to be a mother. I only want a husband."

With her plans going awry, Cathleen couldn't bring herself to call the man "father." Another man had disgusted her with his conniving ways, and she didn't know what to do. She'd thought the advertisement for a Christian wife was the answer and now, the groom didn't even know she exists.

"Are you certain your son knows nothing about your little scheme?"

"Ben knows how I feel about the situation, but I haven't told him about you. Maggie stayed with the children, while I came to pick you up. I expected a return letter from you, and I intended to explain everything when I sent you the train ticket. When I received your telegram saying you were on the way,"—he rubbed his chin—"well, let's just say, you surprised me in more ways than I imagined."

"Well, you surprised me, too. I guess that makes us even."

"You aren't going to tell me why you left without waiting for my ticket, are you?"

Although Cathleen felt she owed the man an explanation, she also felt justified in withholding information she wasn't ready to share. She wanted Mr. Sorenson and his family to see her as a woman of confidence and courage, not some desperate runaway. *But isn't that who you are, Cathleen?* She brushed off her nagging conscience like one of the pesky flies buzzing around the horse. She'd tell her husband when she found the courage, but not a minute before and certainly not his father—that is, if she even had a husband.

"When we get to the ranch, I'll leave you with Maggie, while I talk to my son. One look at you, and I'm sure he'll be sold on the idea."

"Reverend Sorenson, I'm not some livestock he's interested in purchasing. I'd hoped my letter revealed my true character and the person I am on the inside." Cathleen hesitated when she saw the guilty look on the minister's face. "Your son hasn't even seen my letter. Has he?"

"No, he has no idea, but please don't hold my actions against Ben. He needs you. As for your letter, it clearly expressed your heart, Cathleen, and that's why I chose you over the other candidates."

"I don't know how I feel about this. How can anything good come from a lie?"

"I know, and I feel terrible about bringing you here under false circumstances. But at least meet Ben. If my plan doesn't work for either of you, I'll take you home with us until you can secure return passage to Boston. I realize this isn't what you were expecting, but I beg you to give Ben a chance. I sincerely prayed before I placed that advertisement. Despite my misrepresenting the truth, I feel confident this will work. Will you forgive me, and at least give Ben a chance?"

Cathleen saw love for his family shining through the man's eyes, and she wanted to help him. She even wanted to be a part of a family who cared so much for one another, but she worried how his son would receive the news. And the thought of children made her want to return to Boston on the next train. The groom's father should have advertised for a nanny instead of forcing a wife on a reluctant groom. Cathleen wasn't qualified—her experience with children wouldn't complete one sentence in a list of qualifications. They'd do better with the husband-hunting sisters.

The sun painted a portrait of color across the horizon as it descended behind the mountain range to the west. Shadows lined the roadway when the wagon turned off the main road and ventured down an even less-traveled lane. Cathleen looked up at the arched sign. Written in fading letters were the words, Hope Ranch. Tears filled her eyes and unexplained joy rose in her chest. Could this be a sign that she'd done the right thing?

The wagon bounced over ruts and came to a stop before a small frame cabin. Cathleen took in the rugged scene and exhaled with a deep sigh. A large barn, a shed and several long, low buildings stood off to the right surrounded by wooden fences. Other small buildings dotted the landscape around the house and barn. A neglected garden bordered the left side of the house with a water pump standing nearby like a sentry.

The small outhouse she spotted answered her question concerning the plumbing. Her parents accused her of being spoiled, but she had a feeling the next few months would be the most difficult of her twenty-one years. Regardless, she needed to visit the leaning structure … soon.

The elder Sorenson helped her down from the wagon. A dog ran out of the barn barking angrily. Cathleen jumped backward and reached for the wagon for support.

"Stay, Toby. He won't hurt you, but he wants to make sure you know who's in charge around here."

Cathleen moved cautiously toward him. He sniffed her outstretched hand and moved closer to give it a wet lick. Whining with satisfaction, he wiggled excitedly when she rubbed his head and shoulder. "Good boy! You're not a ferocious beast, are you?"

"Looks like you've won Toby's affection. He doesn't usually take to strangers that easily." Mr. Sorenson patted her on the shoulder, and then looked up as if in prayer. "One down, but a few more hearts to conquer," he whispered. The twinkle in the pastor's eyes let her know the dog wasn't the only one on her side.

Out of her peripheral vision, Cathleen noticed a movement near the barn door. Leaning against the doorframe was a younger version of her escort. Unlike his welcoming dog, his eyes sent a disgruntled message. Could this be her uninformed groom? He looked away for a moment, removed his Stetson, and used his sleeve to wipe perspiration from his brow. When he looked again, his intense gaze sent heat rising from Cathleen's neck and across her face. Embarrassed at her disheveled appearance, she smoothed the front of her dress and pushed a few stray curls under her hat.

Cathleen liked what she saw—a handsome, rugged cowboy whom she could easily come to love. But his severe frown made her feel inadequate and unsuitable. She hoped the man would look past her travel-worn appearance and see the heart that longed for love and a family.

Determined to make the best of the awkward situation, Cathleen smiled and lifted a hand in greeting. Instead of returning the gesture, the man's frown deepened, and he turned away. With one last haughty glance, he disappeared into the darkness beyond the barn door.

*What on earth?* Cathleen checked her blouse for stains and ran her hand down the front of her skirt. *What has him in such a foul mood?* Never had she seen such rude behavior. Though he might resemble her imagined prince, his disposition left much to be desired. *God, please don't let him be my intended.*

"I'll take you inside and introduce you to Maggie and the children. Then, I need to have a long talk with my son. Things will work out, Cathleen. I'm almost positive."

Cathleen continued to stare at the vacant spot in the doorway. "I wish I felt as confident as you.

"Before I go inside, I need to visit the … you know." Cathleen stammered while pointing toward the sad-looking building. Her earlier urge had returned with a vengeance.

"You go ahead. I'll wait on the porch."

Cathleen didn't share her potential father-in-law's confidence that the younger Sorenson would accept her. On her way to the outhouse, she walked through an untidy yard where weeds were the only signs of spring. Most of the structures had never seen a paint brush. Her sagging spirit matched the gates and fences. Reality didn't compare to the prosperous Wyoming rancher she'd imagined.

Cathleen gagged on the foul odor radiating from the leaning outhouse. She scanned the distant tree line, hoping to find an alternative along with a breath of fresh air. When she looked back toward the house, the reverend stood watching her with an encouraging smile on his face. She clenched her teeth, "Ugh!" She would not allow one smelly privy to defeat her.

The stubborn door creaked on its hinges when Cathleen yanked it open. Still holding her breath, she grabbed the rough wood to keep from landing on her backside. Regaining her balance, Cathleen stuck her head inside and waited for her eyes to adjust to the darkness. Other than a few spiders making their home near the ceiling and flies buzzing in and around the stinky holes, the outhouse appeared unoccupied.

Cathleen had to lift the droopy door across uneven boards to fasten the latch. The moon-shaped cut near the roof cast a pattern of light across the tiny room. In place of toilet paper, a thick catalog sat between the double-seated arrangement. An outhouse built for two. An interesting concept, but who wants to share such an experience?

Cathleen tore a page boasting farm implements from the handy catalog and wiped the seat before sitting down. She browsed through the pages in search of a softer piece to finish her mission. That sad little outhouse needed a few improvements, and she began making a mental list. When she escaped the small room, a gentle breeze tilted her hat and blew a few strands of hair across her face. She pushed back the wayward curls, straightened her hat, and took a deep breath of the fresh air.

On her way to rejoin the minister, Cathleen thought how drastic her life changed when she stepped off the train in Laramie. The pampered young lady from Boston would be exposed to a life she'd only read about in books. Worried over her uncertain future, she faltered and almost tripped over her own feet. When she regained her balance, she climbed the steps and followed her host into the cabin.

Never had Cathleen entered a house through the kitchen, but here she stood lingering just inside the door. Her shoulders drooped in disappointment when she scanned the room filled with quaint furnishings. A huge, wood stove occupied one end while a large, kitchen table claimed the center. Benches lined the sides of the table with a straight-backed chair on each end. A wooden highchair had been pushed to one corner. Open shelves, stacked around the room, held an unorganized display of mismatched china, crocks, pots, and pans. The spout of a hand pump hovered over a porcelain sink, strategically placed under an open window. Café style curtains danced with the gentle breeze.

A bluebird landed on the sill for a moment before flying to the nearby Bur Oak tree. Cathleen leaned against the sink to watch him hop onto the bird feeder hanging from a lower limb. From a larger branch, her eyes followed two ropes down to an inviting swing blowing in the breeze. Lifting her gaze to the horizon, peace settled around her. Though the house said, "quaint and rustic," the beauty outside the window changed her description to "cozy and comfortable." Granted, she'd have to make a few adjustments, but with time and a trip to the bank, she would turn this cabin into a pleasant, inviting home.

## Chapter Three

The aromas coming from the oven reminded Cathleen of her empty stomach. She hadn't eaten since an early breakfast on the train. Her future father-in-law looked at her with sympathy when he heard her stomach rumble. "Forgive me, Cathleen. I should have fed you in town. Unfortunately, I have a one-track mind when I'm involved in something so stressful."

The reverend checked the room, then disappeared through the only door. Not knowing what else to do, Cathleen leaned against one of the high-backed chairs. She twisted the handle of her reticule into a misshapen warp as she shifted her weight from one foot to the other. Why didn't he have her wait in the parlor?

She spotted one comfortable chair, but before she could take a seat, the man returned carrying a small boy. Close behind rushed an older lady with an infant in her arms. "Please forgive me. I'm sorry Benjamin had to come get me, but I had to change Annie's diaper. You must be Cathleen. We're thankful you agreed to come. If you don't mind holding the baby, I'll finish our supper."

"Cathleen, this is my wife, Maggie. You'll have to excuse her. She's overwhelmed. These two are our grandchildren—Sammy and his sister, Annie."

Cathleen gulped when the woman thrust the baby into her arms. She grabbed the wiggling child under her arms and prepared to pass her back. But Maggie turned to the stove.

Afraid she'd drop the baby, Cathleen turned pleading eyes toward the grandfather. Instead of relieving her, he broke into a wide smile which he didn't even try to hide behind his hand. Cathleen grumbled under her breath expecting the child to burst into tears. To her surprise, sparkling blue eyes studied her with an intensity she didn't expect from an infant.

"Are there any more surprises hiding around here, Mr. Sorenson?"

The twinkle in his eyes made her wonder if he wasn't harboring more information he hadn't shared. Before she could quiz him further, the baby, legs pumping, reached for her face. A strange longing came over Cathleen as she reluctantly pulled the child into her arms. She winced at the wet mouth bouncing against her face but relaxed when Annie cooed in her ear.

The child was impossible to resist. With her free hand, Cathleen caught the tear that slipped from the corner of her eye. How could love blossom so soon—and for the child of a stranger?

The little boy, still in his grandfather's arms, giggled and reached for her. Cathleen shrank into the back of the chair. Forget the love. She wanted to flee the responsibility of caring for two children.

Reverend Sorenson walked her to the rocker and straightened a pillow at her back. He adjusted Annie on her lap and deposited her brother on her other side. Seconds later, Cathleen felt moisture seeping through her silk skirt. She frowned at the boy's droopy diaper. Before expressing her disgust, she bit her lip to keep from frightening the children. *God help me. What am I to do?*

"It'll be okay, Cathleen. I'll be back in a few minutes," the reverend whispered as he pulled her arm around the child and gave her shoulder a comforting pat.

Cathleen felt trapped in a nightmare of her own making. Could marriage to Mr. Stanwick be any worse? The thought sent cold chills running up and down her spine. Her grandmother had warned her to expect a few challenges, and here was the first of many. She stiffened her backbone while whispering under her breath. *You can do this, Cathleen. Since you believe God sent you here, he will give you the strength and perseverance for the task ahead.*

The children must have sensed her distress. Two pairs of blue eyes looked at her. The baby wrinkled her face as if she might cry. Cathleen pulled her closer and gave a little bounce. What does one say to a baby?

Before she found an answer, the little boy held a wooden toy car in front of her face. "See. My car got wheels."

"Yes, your car is nice. Did you receive it as a gift?" Cathleen wanted to correct his English and comment on the condition of his diaper, but she didn't want to upset him. There'd be plenty of time for teaching if she stayed. She shifted the children to a more comfortable position and took the children's book Maggie handed her. Cathleen smiled and helped Sammy turn the pages.

"Shall we read "Mary Had a Little Lamb" together?"

Sammy bounced his head up and down and looked up at her, eager for her to begin. The rhyming words combined with the gentle rock of the chair made her drowsy. If not for the dampness on her leg, she would fall asleep with a little boy and his baby sister sitting on her lap.

Ben stood at the barn door scratching his head and wondering what his father had in mind this time. The man had already brought over every widow and single woman for miles around, insisting his children needed a mother. He loved his parents, but he'd had enough of their attempts to marry him off. His heart protested any woman taking Lana's place.

With this new arrival, he regretted not finding an acceptable nanny to take care of the children. Since his wife's sudden death, he couldn't complete even the simplest of tasks. If not for his capable foreman, his ranch would be in shambles. Even as he praised Dan, he noticed the missing boards in the fences, the sagging gate, and the weeds thriving in the garden plot. So many things were left undone while he grieved and tried to care for his children.

The well-dressed woman who climbed from his wagon reminded him of someone from another time and another place—a place that held terrible memories. He refused to go there again. When he looked up, he saw his father coming down the porch steps and heading his way.

"Ben, I'm glad you're here. We need to talk."

"If you've brought another woman over for me to marry, you might as well take her back where you found her."

His father slumped his shoulders and whispered gently, "I can't do that, son. I ordered her from Boston, and she can't be returned."

"What are you talking about?"

"Cathleen is a mail-order bride. I made a commitment to her on your behalf because your children need a mother. You don't have to love her, just marry her. Those Langland sisters have the gossip mills humming, and I can't allow the scandal to continue. Since you refuse to consider any of the women from around here, I advertised for one back East."

Ben shook with anger. "I can't believe you would do something like this. You've gone too far this time. I'm not marrying that beauty queen or anyone else. I had my fill of spoiled little rich girls when I attended the university."

"At least you noticed how pretty she is; I knew you'd like her. You should see her with Sammy and Annie. I didn't mention the children in the letter, but she's warmed right up to them. I believe they found themselves a mama."

Ben's anger brewed. He kicked a bale of hay and swallowed the curse words on the tip of his tongue. "Why do you keep doing this to me? I've always looked up to you and considered you level-headed, but this is ridiculous. The children had a fine mother, and they don't need a replacement. And I certainly don't need a wife. Why don't you and mother just leave us alone?"

Regret seized Ben, and he knew he should apologize, but the words lodged in his throat. Taking out his anger against his father wasn't fair. He wouldn't have survived the past four months without his parent's support.

His father looked down as if in prayer before continuing. "I know this is hard for you, son, but I want you to pray about it. Here's the letter she wrote after she saw my advertisement in the paper. She sounds like a woman who'd be easy to love. When you read her words, I think you'll agree.

"Spend some time in prayer, then come in for supper. Your mama made a fine pot roast that smells delicious. You don't want to miss out. If you really find Cathleen repulsive, I'll take her to Laramie and arrange her return to Boston. But, if you give her a chance, I believe she'll make you the perfect wife. Please do this for the sake of your children. I'll be praying for you to find God's will."

Ben glared at his father, turned and stalked off to the wood pile where he took out his anger. With every swing of the axe, he ached for himself and his children. He had neglected them, for sure, and the house only looked presentable the few days after his parents visited. They had wanted to take the children to their home, but he couldn't part with them. It would be like losing Lana all over again.

Ben threw down the axe and rested on the stump he'd just abused. He licked his dry lips and tasted salty tears mixed with beads of perspiration. The afternoon breeze hit his sweat-soaked shirt and cooled his back. He looked up at the clouds and hated the person he'd become. Lana would not be pleased. Anger and self-abuse had drained his energy and left him feeling limp like a rope abandoned in the dusty corral.

His father's suggestion that he pray motivated him to return to the empty barn. With his energy drained, he slumped on a bale of hay. Cathleen's letter crinkled in his pocket, and he remembered what had triggered his anger. He straightened his leg and pulled the pink envelope from his pocket. Staring at the address, he smelled the distinct fragrance of lilacs. What kind of woman doused her letter in perfume? He'd had his fill of such women back in Boston, and he wanted nothing more to do with any of them. Such a woman didn't belong out West or anywhere near him, that's for sure.

He traced the perfect penmanship with his finger and remembered another letter—one that had changed the course of his life. Near the end of his second year at the university, the woman he'd wanted to marry had rejected him. Confused and homesick, Ben's spirit rose when a letter arrived from Laramie. He recognized the handwriting.

From the age of twelve, Ben had spent every summer on the ranch with Lance Thomas, a man he loved like his own father. Lance's wife had died in childbirth and left him to raise a daughter alone. Being the same age, Ben and Lana had become fast friends. The girl had taught him every skill needed to work on a ranch—roping, riding, and rounding up beef cattle. They teased and fought their way through adolescence and into high school as if they were siblings. Usually the quarrel ended with her boxing his ears, but occasionally, the fight found them rolling in the dirt. Regardless of their disagreements, she became his best friend, and he would do anything for her.

As Ben read Lana's letter, his already wounded heart felt as if it would explode with grief. Her father, who'd treated him like a son, had died of a massive heart attack. Lana had become an orphan at the age of twenty, and Ben ached for both of them. After sharing the details of her father's sudden death, she begged him to come home and help her run the ranch. The devastating news became his excuse to leave school and escape the life he despised.

Though he wanted to shred Miss Doyle's letter into a million pieces, he stuffed the envelope back into his pocket unopened and unread. A few heartfelt words wouldn't change his mind. His experience with such a woman had ended in heartache. Nothing would convince him to remount that disastrous horse. Pain gnawed at his gut when he thought of all he and his children had lost. He didn't appreciate his father dangling a beautiful woman before him. Ben collapsed into a bed of hay and sobbed. *God help me. What am I to do?*

"Here's a bottle of milk for Annie if you don't mind feeding her." Maggie looked at Sammy and wrinkled her nose. "Looks like you need a diaper change, little man."

Ben's mother picked up Sammy and noticed the wide damp spot on the front of Cathleen's skirt. Both women stared in horror at the ruined silk.

"Oh, my. I am so sorry, Cathleen. I can't believe my husband put that soggy mess on your lap. Neither of us can do anything right. We're so worried for our son and grandchildren we've turned into a couple of simpletons. Now, my husband feels guilty over the way he tricked you into coming. Believe me when I tell you he values honesty and integrity in others and expects no less from himself. I watched him cross the yard after talking with Ben. He walked like an old man—his shoulders slumped in defeat. Right now, he's sitting on the porch with his Bible, praying for God to intervene."

"I'm sorry for what you and your family are going through, but if your son doesn't want me, I can't stay. The children are lovely, but I wasn't expecting them, nor do I feel qualified to be their mother."

Cathleen again looked down at her skirt. "Don't worry about my outfit. The wear and tear of the trip had already ruined the dress—a little moisture couldn't do much more. As for deceiving me, when I left home, I felt certain I was doing the right thing. Though I would have preferred another way, I wouldn't have had the courage to come had I known the whole story. Even if your son rejects me, I will always remember this time with you and your family."

Cathleen wiped the tear that rolled down her cheek. She didn't care about the ruined dress, but she did care that she'd come this far to marry a man so different from her expectations—a man who didn't want her. Only a force greater than her disappointment kept her from returning to Boston on the next train. From the moment she read the notice in the paper, she felt God leading her. She didn't appreciate much of his plan, but a surprising tenderness and sympathy for the children compelled her to stay.

When she heard the sucking of air, she took the bottle from Annie's mouth and watched the baby's eyes close. Wasn't she supposed to pat her on the back after feeding her? Not sure what to do, Cathleen shrugged and watched the motherless baby. She pushed the short blonde curls back and planted a kiss on the child's forehead. Could the children be the only reason she'd come?

Maggie came back from changing Sammy and set him on the floor near her feet. The little boy scooted closer and leaned his warm body against her leg. When his toy rolled out of reach, he crawled to retrieve it and then returned to her side. She chuckled and ran her fingers through the blond curls that matched his sister's.

A verse from the Bible popped into her head. *Children are a blessing from the Lord.* She looked past the spider making his home in the ceiling and lifted a prayer to God. *Thank you for the gift of these sweet children. Please help their father see how much I need them.*

Cathleen didn't understand the strong bond that had formed so quickly. Although she was drawn to the children, she worried over her lack of experience. The responsibility as their sole caregiver made her stomach quiver and her head ache. If their father realized how incompetent she was, he'd never allow her near them.

The delightful smells coming from the cookstove tortured her. Her stomach growled and burned in protest to the increased acid. With her free hand, she rubbed between her rib cage and wondered how much longer she'd have to wait for something to fill the emptiness.

When Cathleen heard the stomping of feet, she forgot her hunger pangs and watched the door with trepidation.

Her heart raced at the prospect of coming face-to-face with the man who would decide her future. The door opened, and the rugged rancher lumbered into the room. He towered over her. Cathleen cowered in the chair.

Mr. Sorenson's eyes and nose were red as if he'd been crying. Grassy debris and dirt clung to his wet shirt and the knees of his pants were dark brown with a questionable substance. For the third time since she'd arrived, Cathleen slipped the handkerchief from her sleeve and held it over her nose.

Glued to the rug, Ben looked from her to the children and back again. She returned his glare, refusing to let him intimidate her. After all, she was the guest here.

Sammy broke the spell when he stood and reached for his father. "Papa."

Cathleen warmed when the man gathered his son in his arms and pulled him tight against his filthy shirt. "Have you been a good boy for Grandma?"

His head bobbed up and down while he turned around and pointed to Cathleen. "Mama read me story."

The burly man glanced around confused. Without finding an answer, he scowled at her. Was he blaming her for his son's declaration? She didn't know what gave Sammy the idea, but if they married, her role would be inevitable. She'd be the only mother he or his sister knew.

Ignoring her, he looked down at his boy. "I'm glad you enjoyed the story."

He turned on his heels, dismissing Cathleen, and greeted his mother with a kiss on her cheek. Though he had no manners for his guest, his affection toward his mother warmed her heart.

"Something sure smells good. Thank you, Mother."

"I'm surprised it's not burned to a crisp while waiting for you to come in. I'm sure Cathleen's famished, and it's almost dark. She probably hasn't eaten since breakfast." Maggie made a face and sniffed. "You look like you've been wrestling a bull—and what is that disgusting smell? Go change so we can eat."

Ben disappeared into the bedroom, and Maggie looked at Cathleen. "Honey, I'm sorry. I should have at least offered you a cup of tea and a little butter bread. I'm a bit distracted. Please forgive my son's rudeness. He hasn't been himself since Lana died. I'll have our supper on the table shortly."

"It's quite all right. I understand. I could help, if someone took Annie."

Ben rushed back into the room, still stuffing his shirt into clean jeans. She'd never seen anyone change clothes so fast. Was he afraid she'd hurt his children while he was out of the room?

He looked down at the sleeping baby. "I'll put her in her crib."

When his fingers touched Cathleen's arm, she looked up into tender, swollen eyes. A strange feeling came over her. Pity? Exhaustion? Why did she have such an emotional response to this family? Ben jerked his hand away as though he'd touched a hot burner. In one swift movement, he grabbed Annie from her arms and disappeared through the open doorway. Was she that repulsive? Would he reject her without even getting to know her? In slow motion, Cathleen rose from the comfortable rocker.

"Don't worry, dear. He's as bewildered as you are, but I know he'll make the right decision. Here, let me show you where Lana kept the tablecloth and napkins."

Cathleen arranged the mismatched, chipped china on the wrinkled fabric, cringing at the shoddy setting. She thought of her home in Boston and the elegance she'd taken for granted. Flickering lights from hand-polished candelabra glimmered on fine china, silver, and crystal. The centerpiece of fresh flowers filled the room with warmth and the fragrance of her grandmother's garden. Here a few bowls of food were scattered haphazardly on the rough table. There an array of delicacies waited in silver chafing dishes on the sideboard. She sighed at the harsh contrast.

Remembering her life of luxury, Cathleen felt sorry for herself. She longed for what she'd left behind and wanted to catch the next train East. Her parents would understand and forgive her bout of momentary insanity. Just as another escape plan took shape, she remembered her reason for running away in the first place—the unscrupulous cad wanting to marry only for her family's money. Only a fool would return to such a sentence. Marrying a stranger and learning to care for his children looked better all the time.

The shabby cabin didn't matter if she could make her disagreeable groom fall in love with her. A long sigh escaped, and she jerked her head toward Ben to see if he heard. She growled under her breath. Not only had he heard, he'd seen her every move as he watched from the bedroom doorway. From the frown on his face, Cathleen could tell he knew exactly what she'd been thinking. If she continued to criticize his home, she'd never gain his affections.

Again, he dismissed her with a haughty look and flopped down on the floor beside his son. That was fine with her because now Cathleen could watch him. The well-proportioned man stretched his long, muscular legs across much of the floorspace. One arm supported his head as he drove a wooden car over the rough floor, mimicking the sound effects for Sammy. She hadn't noticed any automobiles in Laramie when she left the train station. Where had he learned to make such sounds?

Ben's loving attention to Sammy stood in sharp contrast to the looks of disgust and defiance he directed at her. Despite his rude treatment, Cathleen felt sorry for the man. She understood his anger and confusion over his father's subversive plan to get him a wife and mother for his children. His doubts about her suitability were written all over his face. Still, Cathleen sympathized for all he'd lost and the two constant reminders. She convinced herself that God had sent her here, and she hoped she'd come for more than the children. Satisfied at her renewed decision to stay, a smile spread across her face. His children were adorable—she could only imagine the beautiful offspring they'd make together.

Cathleen remembered a recent conversation with her mother and blushed. She'd been embarrassed by the way her mother described childbirth and the physical act between a man and woman. But, taking another look at her handsome groom, she nearly swooned. Cathleen rubbed her hand across her forehead in a futile attempt to wipe the ridiculous ideas from her mind. With all the hurdles standing between herself and her Mr. Sorenson, she doubted she'd ever experience such pleasure. Sighing, she mourned the hopelessness of her dreams.

At last, Mrs. Sorenson called them to the table. Cathleen stood to one side as family members took their seats. The men sat at each end of the table.

"Cathleen, please take the bench next to Sammy."

Sammy grinned and waved his spoon in her direction. Sammy's highchair conveniently separated her from the contrary man on her left. When no one pulled out her chair or helped her with her napkin, she resigned herself to the extreme differences she'd have to accept in her new family. She pulled out the end of the bench and took her seat.

Cathleen's disappointment soon gave way to ideas popping into her head. In her imagination, she replaced almost everything in the room. The rough furniture transformed into fine polished wooden tables and chairs. The only thing she'd keep was the rocker chair—the place where she felt most comfortable. New cushions would brighten the room, along with fresh linens. Her table would entertain guests of the highest caliber, perhaps even President Taft himself.

The house wouldn't be the only thing she'd change. She'd teach the children manners. Her husband might never pull out a chair for her, but Sammy would grow up to be a gentleman. He would stand tall and proud among the greatest of men.

Cathleen returned to reality when Sammy reached his small hand toward her, and Ben's father captured her other hand. He looked around and smiled when his son motioned for him to ask a blessing. All heads bowed and most eyes closed, except Cathleen's. She kept hers half open not wanting to miss anything. Unlike the memorized prayers her father recited, Reverend Sorenson prayed like her grandmother, as if talking with a friend.

Her head jerked to attention when she heard her name. "Guide Cathleen and Ben as they seek your will for their lives. You know the needs of this home, and you know what is right for each person around the table." Had she sought God's will before hopping on a train and heading West? Or, had she taken the first opportunity that came along? Conviction seized her as she looked around Sammy into the eyes of her intended. His hand massaged the back of his neck while he stared at her with a look of bewilderment similar to her own.

By the end of the prayer, exhaustion and confusion had claimed Cathleen. Her appetite fled along with the energy to hold a fork. Only a few bites squeezed past the lump building in her throat. She tried to focus on the conversation buzzing around her as she pushed her food around the plate. The voices sounded like a distant hum of words with no meaning. What did she know of cattle drives or cutting hay? She wanted to discuss the one subject no one else seemed willing to address. Where would she be sleeping? If she didn't find a place to lay her head soon, she'd be face down in beef gravy.

Cathleen pinched her nose, rolled her shoulders, and rubbed her temples. Nothing worked. Despite her efforts, she felt herself slipping into peaceful oblivion. A loud noise interrupted her stupor, and she jerked alert. Sammy threw his spoon and demanded, "Down!"

"I'll put him to bed. You finish your meal." When Cathleen looked up, she noticed that Maggie had addressed her.

"What?" Three pairs of sympathetic eyes stared at her.

"Are you okay, Cathleen? You've hardly touched your food."

"I'm fine, Mrs. Sorenson. Just a little tired. The food is delicious, but my appetite seems to have fled along with my energy. Forgive me."

"I can tell you're exhausted. We need to come to a decision and get this girl to bed. Wait until I come back though. This needs a woman's perspective." Maggie smiled at her and winked before leaving the room with her grandson.

# Chapter Four

Ben stood on shaky legs when his mother returned to the room. If the spoiled city girl thought him stupid, she should think again. He'd noticed her disapproval of the table settings. Even her clothes spoke of wealth and refinement. The over-indulged little rich girl didn't belong here, and they both knew it. He'd met many like her when he attended the university. He preferred a country girl like Lana who was content and satisfied with whatever came her way. No running off to the great unknown in search of adventure.

Now that the gorgeous Cathleen realized the situation, he'd be surprised if she agreed to stay. He didn't want her here, but he had no choice. When he cried out to God in the barn, the answer came as a whisper so quiet he almost missed it: *Ask her, for the sake of the children.* Then, when he saw her holding Annie, he knew what he had to do.

If she accepted his terms, they could expect a shaky future—two very different worlds colliding in a sea of turmoil. He wasn't ready for another woman in his home and certainly not in his bed. Besides, she would never survive this rough, abrasive life. Regardless, he didn't seem to have a choice, and he needed to do something before the woman collapsed headfirst into her plate of food.

"I spent time in the barn praying, as you suggested, Papa, and I feel I should ask Cathleen to stay."

From the other end of the table, Ben heard a long sigh of relief. Looking up Ben read the words on his father's lips, Thank God.

Turning his attention to the woman, Ben glimpsed a shy smile before Cathleen ducked her head. "I'm probably crazy for agreeing to this, but I have no choice. I'll marry you, but I'm not ready to take another woman into my bed."

The smile fled Miss Doyle's face. Before she looked away, her fair complexion turned a bright pink.

"I'm sorry if this isn't what you expected, Miss Doyle, but it's all I can offer. I'll sleep in the bunk house with my men while you sleep in the bedroom with the children. I'm only marrying you for their sakes. They need a mother, and you have already stolen their affections."

Ben watched Miss Doyle's confidence return along with fire flashing from her eyes. She stood and jabbed a finger at him. "No. This is not what I expected. I believed I would find a groom who would propose marriage, one who wanted a wife and a lasting relationship. All you want or need is a nanny for your children."

"You don't have to accept my terms. I didn't invite you in the first place. Just take the next train back to your life of luxury in Boston and leave us alone."

Ben could tell his words stung. She dabbed the corner of her eyes with a lace handkerchief before straightening her shoulders and pinning him with an angry glare. "You know nothing of my life in Boston, Mr. Sorenson. Don't pretend you do. Regardless, I've come this far, and I believe God wants me to stay. Let's get on with this so-called ceremony."

"Fine. If you'll excuse me a few minutes, I'll ask my foreman to serve as a witness"

The groom plodded from the room without another word. He let the door slam behind him, his heavy boots thudding down the porch steps. Cathleen gripped a chair to keep the room from swirling like a carousel. Acid burned her empty stomach and moved into her throat. She felt nauseated and light-headed. Exhaustion coupled with raw emotion sent her reeling from surprise to disappointment to rage. The last stop was hopeless defeat. She held her head and burst into tears.

"Cathleen, I don't know what's wrong with our son. We didn't raise him to be so callous or bitter."

Cathleen looked at the sweet couple and recognized their own disappointment. "I know you didn't. You and Rev. Sorenson have been nothing but kind from the moment I arrived. I should not have had such high expectations, but from a young child I've dreamed of a church wedding with flowers and music and lots of guests. Now, here I am far from home, without my father to walk me down the aisle, and not even a church to hold the guests. Where's the romance? Your son doesn't even want me. I don't know why I thought a mail-order bride should expect her wedding to be different, but I did. I even bought a beautiful dress and trousseau. How could I have been so naïve?"

Disappointment weighed on Cathleen. She leaned her elbows on the table and cried into her hands. Maggie put her arms around her. "It's okay, honey. When you and Ben fall in love, we'll have a church wedding with all the trimmings. You'll see. Tonight is just a formality, so you can live here and be a mother to my grandchildren."

"But I don't know anything about children. I haven't been around them, ever. What if I hurt them or they get sick? I wouldn't know what to do."

"You'll be fine, Cathleen. I have a feeling you'll be the perfect mother in no time at all. I'll come by in a couple of weeks to see how you're doing. That should give you and Ben time to get acquainted and for you to adjust to your new family. In the meantime, I'll finish these dishes while you freshen up. Before we leave tonight, I'll give you a quick tour of the pantry, the cellar, and the springhouse. You'll be an expert before you know it."

Cathleen walked into the bedroom in a fog. She didn't understand much of what the woman said. What does one do in a springhouse? All she knew was she would be marrying the cold but handsome rancher for the sole purpose of providing a mother for his children. She stared into the mirror and cried another bout of tears. Nothing had turned out the way she'd planned.

Pulling herself together, Cathleen looked around the crowded room—no wardrobe for her clothing, only unpainted walls with a few nails along one side. The children's cribs took up one end with a chest between them. To accommodate her three trunks, the dresser had been moved against the double bed. How would she manage to dress in such tight quarters? No point in sending for more of her things; they would only shrink the room further.

*Stop complaining, Cathleen. What other choice do you have?* She continued to reprimand herself as she rummaged through one of the trunks. She relaxed when she found a blue silk gown that had turned a few heads back in Boston. Perhaps the dress would work a little magic on her reluctant groom.

She remembered the newspaper advertisement that had lured her into this impossible situation, and fumed—again. Ben's father should have advertised for a cook, housekeeper, and nanny instead of a wife. That's all his son wanted. Could she have exchanged one bad situation for another?

Opening her reticule, Cathleen found her brush and pulled the bristles through her mass of auburn curls until they glistened. Without the assistance of her personal maid, she struggled to twist her long hair into a low bun at the base of her neck. She washed the travel grime from her skin with water she found on the dresser. The bowl and pitcher gave her pause as she ran a finger over the hand painted floral design. The fine porcelain brought a semblance of beauty to the otherwise dull surroundings.

Satisfied with her toilet, Cathleen changed into fresh undergarments. The silk felt smooth and delicate against her bare flesh and the scent of lilacs sweetened the air in the room. She longed for the wedding night of her dreams. Instead, her groom's cold proposal threatened to send her into another bout of tears—worthless tears that would only streak her silk dress. Would she ever feel the strength of those strong arms or his moist lips touching her own?

A knock at the door interrupted her sad thoughts. "Cathleen, are you about ready?"

Ben stood still as a statue when his mother opened the bedroom door. The vision of blue floating into the room caught his breath. His jaw dropped almost to his chin with a silent "Ah." The stunning woman looked as out of place as a pig in a palace. The longing look he saw in her eyes sent his heart racing. His breath quickened, and his body tingled with desire. How would he keep a vow of celibacy with that kind of temptation living under his roof? This marriage of convenience might be more difficult than he'd imagined.

As Ben continued to stare, a single tear slid down the woman's cheek. Compassion drove away his lustful thoughts.

Beneath all that loveliness and hesitant smile, he recognized hurt and disappointment. How could he do this to her? She wasn't cut out for this harsh life and didn't deserve such treatment. A woman of her beauty and caliber would have no trouble finding a husband back east. Why had she come this far without a good reason?

When the downcast but captivating woman took hesitant steps toward him, Ben met her halfway. He took her hand and whispered into her ear. "You don't have to do this, you know."

Her body stiffened next to his and a determined scowl replaced the sadness. She shook off his hand and stepped away. "Are you trying to talk me out of this marriage? I thought that was settled—I'm to be your housekeeper, cook, and nanny. This excuse for a wedding is to dispel gossip and protect your good name in the community. At least we agree on one thing—we're marrying for the sake of the children."

How could she do that? One minute she's melting him with her tears and the next she's close to boxing his ears. One thing for certain, his father had found him one stubborn, sassy woman. Instead of dreading the future, he found himself intrigued. Eventually, they might become friends, if they didn't kill each other first.

Ben ignored the ceremony until he heard his father say, "to love and to cherish …" The words rolled over in his mind with blatant accusations. His vows seemed dishonest, as if cheating the woman at his side. Because he'd been hurt by that girl in Boston didn't mean he should take his anger out on Cathleen. Though he could never love her, nothing said they couldn't be friends. But could they live as husband and wife without the passion of love binding them together?

His father's words startled him back to the present. "Benjamin, you may now kiss your bride."

*What?* He'd forgotten about the kiss and could kick himself for not asking his father to omit that part. Too late now. During the ceremony, his anxious bride fidgeted from one foot to the other and studied her gloved hands. She'd twisted and stretched the white gloves until they no longer fit properly. He had to strain to hear her repeat the vows and her reluctant, "I do."

At the mention of the word "kiss," Cathleen jerked her head up and looked him square in the eyes. A mischievous grin brightened her face while he squirmed. Was she daring him to kiss her? If the sassy woman thought him beyond passion, he'd give her a kiss she wouldn't soon forget.

Ben pulled Cathleen into his arms and touched his mouth to hers. Her lips parted beneath his, and he felt whispers of sweet air filling his mouth. His emotions took him away. She moved closer and he leaned deeper into the kiss. Forget the vow of celibacy—the passionate woman had found the key to unlock his cold heart. He wanted to rush her into the bedroom and release every suppressed longing he'd squelched since Lana died.

Like a pitcher of cold water poured over his head, thoughts of Lana weakened his passion and stopped him mid-kiss. Despite the longing for his new wife, he couldn't allow himself the pleasure. Reality had won. Lana was gone and he'd never make love to her again. Neither could he let himself surrender to this appealing woman. He'd made himself a promise and he'd grit his teeth to keep from yielding to the temptation. Anger at himself and his situation stymied any lingering passion. He backed away and dropped his head in defeat, sentencing himself to a life of misery.

Cathleen reeled on her feet and almost fell forward when Ben released her. Without another word, her groom disappeared out the door. Was he running away to escape the same fire that burned her insides? She'd never experienced such feelings. Confused, she looked at his parents for an explanation, but they stared at the closed door, as baffled as she. When they turned pitying eyes toward her, she fought to hold back the tears.

Reverend Sorenson cleared his throat. "I'm sorry, Cathleen, but our son must need time to adjust to your presence in the house. Though this day didn't go quite the way I'd planned, I'm confident you did the right thing by coming here."

With tears of grief clogging her nose and throat, Cathleen only shook her head. She stared out the window, hoping for Ben's return.

"Maggie, we really need to leave. I'd hoped to be home before dark. At least we have a cloudless sky and a full moon in our favor. Will you be okay, Cathleen?" She turned toward her father-in-law's voice and noticed the sadness on both their faces.

"I hate to leave you like this, honey, but we do need to get home."

Cathleen coughed into her gloved hand and plastered a fake smile on her face. "I understand. Thank you both for everything. Though I don't know what's happening with Ben, tomorrow is a new day, and I plan to make the best of it."

Cathleen watched the buggy disappear in a cloud of dust. Inspecting the tiny house, she released a slow breath along with the pent-up emotions. Unhindered, tears trailed down her cheeks and dropped off her chin onto the front of her silk dress. *What a fool I've been!*

Her expectations when she'd boarded the train were far different from the reality facing her. The wedding was a farce, the house a shanty, and instead of a handsome prince, she had married an uncouth, insensitive cowpoke. He was more handsome than she'd imagined. But he didn't want her. She might as well have stayed in Boston. At least there, she would be surrounded by the familiar. Here, she felt completely alone in a foreign land surrounded by cows, a dilapidated ranch, and strangers.

Cathleen turned back to the window and wondered what could have gone wrong. Ben had kissed her with a passion she didn't know existed. He'd held her when her knees gave way to the unfamiliar tremble. How could a man turn her to mush with such a brief kiss? Just when she began to see a glimmer of hope, he pushed her away as he would a thief about to rob him of something precious. And then he'd abandoned her without a word.

Looking again at the empty room, she ached at the thought of spending her wedding night alone. That awful proposal warned her to expect nothing, but she'd foolishly thought if he took a good look at her, he'd change his mind. How could she have been so wrong?

Cathleen sat at the table and cradled her head in her arms. The tears became a river of insecurity and despair. She cried for the little girl who'd felt abandoned by her parents, for the loss of her grandmother—the one person who loved her—for the bride without a suitable wedding, and for the husband who didn't seem to care. Amid the pain and uncertain future, she remembered her original goal: to find a husband who would want her for herself—not her money or her outward appearance. *God, please help Ben to see me—the real me.*

Her tears spent, she took the oil lamp into the bedroom and undressed. She rummaged in the trunk until she found the night gown she'd bought for the occasion—the "perfect garment to lure your groom," the salesgirl had claimed. She shouldn't have bothered, but she wanted to look presentable in case Ben changed his mind.

After checking on the children, Cathleen curled on her side and snuggled into the cool fresh sheets someone had thought to provide. Certainly not her so-called husband. She welcomed another bout of tears. How she longed for her grandmother's words of comfort. Weariness took over, and she soon drifted into a restless slumber.

Cathleen's dream turned into a nightmare when she heard the cry of a baby. She grappled in confusion for several moments before realizing the crying came from the crib in the corner. Annie kicked and wailed until Cathleen picked her up and snuggled her against her breast. The baby shivered and wiped her eyes before grabbing a fistful of slinky nightgown. Her temperature felt normal, but what did she know? Perhaps she was hungry and only needed a bottle.

On the way to the kitchen, Cathleen remembered that in their rush to leave, Maggie had forgotten to give her the promised instructions. She didn't even know where the bottles were. After a quick look around the kitchen, her temper flared at her impossible situation. She had no choice but to search for the delinquent husband.

Ben had tossed and turned for hours, replaying their passionate kiss in his head and fighting a battle between two equally formidable foes. He kicked himself for not taking her to his bed, yet doing so would be unfair to Cathleen since he didn't love her. He wouldn't use her tempting body to satisfy his lustful desires. His tired mind and body had finally surrendered when a knock sounded on the bunkhouse door. Wishing the disturbance would go away only increased the knocking. Lest he waken the men, he opened the door with a reprimand on the tip of his tongue.

Instead of the tongue lashing he'd planned, he gasped. Cathleen stood there with his daughter clinging to the flimsy robe she'd thrown over her nightgown. Neither garment succeeded in covering her well-formed body. Annie pulled on the neckline, exposing even more flesh. He grabbed his wife by the arm and rushed her off the porch before one of the ranch hands caught a glimpse of the half-clothed woman. On the way, he pulled her under his arm and walked toward the house.

"What in the world, Cathleen?"

"Oh, Mr. Sorenson, Annie woke up crying, and I didn't know what to do. Your mother forgot to tell me how to take care of her, and I've never been around babies before. Could she be sick? Should I feed her? Where is her milk? You don't have an icebox in the kitchen—and where are her bottles? Do I change her diaper? I'm not sure I know how. How could you leave me in there alone with the children? What if something happened to them?"

Annie stared wide-eyed at her new mama, while Ben wrapped them both in his arms.

"Shhh. It's okay. Annie's fine. Look at her. You're the only one crying."

Cathleen pulled Annie tighter against her chest. "You sweet baby, you're hungry, and all you've got is this incompetent woman pretending to be your mother and a father who doesn't seem to care."

"Don't worry. She often wakes in the middle of the night needing attention. We keep at least one bottle in the cellar for night feedings. Let me show you how to change her, and you can rock her while I get her milk."

Ben showed Cathleen where he kept the diapers and the pail for the dirty ones. When he lifted the lid, her face grew pale, and she gagged. He doubted the finicky woman would survive the night.

"I'm not sure I can do this, Mr. Sorenson. What happens when she does more than this?" She turned her nose up in disgust as she watched him fasten the fresh cloth on Annie.

"You have to take the dirty diaper outside to the pump and rinse it. Don't worry for now. They rarely do their business before breakfast."

Ben noticed the look of horror when he handed her Annie and ushered Cathleen back into the kitchen. As he settled her into the rocker with the baby, he again noticed her skimpy attire. "Cathleen, you must never go near the men dressed like that. Do you realize what that does to a man? And, don't you think it a bit formal to call me Mr. Sorenson."

Cathleen looked down at her gown and pulled the neckline from Annie's grasp. He'd already noticed that his wife's red face meant she was about to lose her temper. He braced himself for the inevitable tongue-lashing and congratulated himself for the insight he'd gleaned in a few short hours.

"It's all your fault for leaving me alone on our wedding night. I need you. I understand I'm not as appealing as your dead wife, but I have one advantage—I'm alive. From now on, if you abandon me like that, I'll go to the bunkhouse and crawl in bed with you. Sleep in the kitchen if you wish, but you will not leave me alone in this house. As for calling you something less formal, I'd say you should start acting like a husband if you want me to respond with a semblance of familiarity."

Ben stepped back and rubbed his hand across his face. *What had he gotten himself into*? He wanted to shake some sense into her, but nearly choked on laughter.

"So, you think I'm funny, do you? Make yourself a pallet, because you'll be sleeping on the floor from now on unless you want to haul over a bed from the bunkhouse."

Ben stopped laughing when he noticed the serious frown on Cathleen's face. If the little minx thought she'd win this battle of the wills, she had a rude awakening. There would be no more feeling sorry for her. If he let her have her way now, he'd be giving in to her every whim for the obvious short stint of their marriage. The spoiled brat seemed determined to make his life miserable.

As he tromped down the stairs to the cellar, Ben mumbled angry words under his breath. How dare she threaten him? Would she really enter the bunkhouse and climb into his bed? He wouldn't put it past the brazen woman. He'd sleep on the bare floor before he gave her the opportunity. He hoped no one had seen her earlier. Why couldn't she have been homely and submissive?

Besides, he didn't need further ridicule from his men. After Dan returned from witnessing the wedding, the description of his bride must have been a doozy. When they saw him sneak into the bunkhouse only moments after his foreman, they couldn't believe his choice of sleeping arrangements. He threatened to cut their pay if they didn't shut up and let him get some sleep. He had a feeling this was only the first of many sleepless nights.

## Chapter Five

Ben made a pallet on the floor while Cathleen fed Annie her bottle. She understood his anger, but she couldn't put the children at risk. Besides, she felt abandoned, disillusioned, and rejected. That kiss Ben gave her just made her want more. She wanted a real marriage, and one way or another she would get it.

When the baby slept peacefully, Cathleen returned her to the crib and pulled a couple of soft quilts from one of her trunks. Ben sat in the rocker holding his head in his hands. "Here"—she thrust the covers at him—"these will make your bed more comfortable."

"I don't want your fancy quilts or your sympathy. Just go to bed and leave me alone."

Cathleen stared at him, unable to believe his unkind remarks or his pout. "I have no sympathy for you. You have a perfectly adequate bed which you refuse to share with your wife. Am I that repulsive?" Tears threatened to choke her as she turned to make her way toward the bedroom. She'd only taken one step, before Ben grabbed her arm and jerked her around.

"You are one spoiled brat, Cathleen Doyle, who'd do almost anything to get your way. Well, it won't work with me. I'm sleeping on the floor a few nights for the sake of my children, but that's all. Do you hear me, woman?"

Cathleen had never been treated with such harshness. She only wanted to love him and feel his arms around her. She pulled away from his hold and threw the quilts in his face. The door slammed a little harder than she intended when she retreated to the lumpy bed. Tears flowed in earnest as she struggled to find a comfortable spot. All the crying she'd done throughout her life didn't add up to what she'd shed since getting off the train only a few hours ago. She wanted to run away and never see Ben again, but she felt bound by the vows she'd made before God and his parents. Although the children were a challenging surprise, she felt responsible for their welfare. They needed her and they'd already moved into her heart. Besides, she needed them.

In the early morning darkness, Cathleen awakened from a deep sleep when she heard a soft knock on the door. "Cathleen, are you awake?"

Without finding her robe, she stumbled toward the door. "Well, I am now. What's wrong?"

"Nothing's wrong. I only wanted to let you know that I'm going out to milk the cow and do a few chores. I'll be back in about an hour for breakfast."

"What time does the cook arrive?"

"What cook? The only cook we have is at the bunkhouse. I can't ask him to cook for us. What gave you the impression we had a cook?"

"I figured your mother let her have the day off yesterday, and she'd return today. My mother never cooked a day in her life. We always had a cook, housekeeper, gardener, chauffeur, and butler." Cathleen paused. "Why are you staring at me like that? I've never heard of anyone not having at least a cook and housekeeper."

"Are you joking? I doubt there is a single butler in the whole state of Wyoming. I'm pretty sure you and I are from different planets. If you expect that kind of service, now would be the time to pack your bags and head for the train."

Cathleen realized her mistake not long into her list of servants. Of course, she'd read books about the Wild West, poor farmers and ranchers, but she had no idea she'd find herself married to one. "Let me remind you, Mr. Sorenson, that you married me a few hours ago, for better or for worse. I'll just have to get by until something can be done. There's always a remedy to these tricky situations. See how quickly I learned to change a diaper and feed Annie? Perhaps I could also learn to cook. Do you have a few cookbooks I might use?"

Ben couldn't believe the woman's presumptions and saw no hope for her as a rancher's wife, but she certainly looked appealing in that flimsy nightgown. She hadn't even bothered to cover herself, but then, the robe was equally revealing. Cathleen seemed oblivious to the effect she had on him. He forced his hands into his pockets to keep from reaching for her.

After their mid-night fiasco, he'd overheard her smothered cries through the thin walls and regretted his harsh treatment. The young woman had left everything to come west and marry him. What was in it for her? She seemed to have everything, while he felt empty and stripped of anything worth giving. Ben smarted at the reality of his conscience. *You're only using her as a nanny and maid.*

The sooner he built the new ranch house, the sooner he could invite Pedro's family from Mexico to come assist

Cathleen. Despite his resistance to her as his wife, he felt certain she'd be around for a while. She didn't seem inclined toward an annulment. He wondered what drove her determination to make the best of a disappointing situation.

In a few short hours, the unsuitable woman had made herself irreplaceable—at least with the children. But how would they survive in the meantime? If she didn't poison him with her cooking, she'd drive him crazy with her alluring body.

"This top shelf is where Lana kept a couple of cookbooks she received when we first married. Here's one that sounds perfect for you—*Cookery for Beginners* by Marion Harland." Ben expected Cathleen to take offense at his sarcastic suggestion, but she reached for the offered book with a smile. She was either extremely naïve or wasn't easily offended unless it concerned his sleeping arrangements.

"Thank you, Ben. I need a recipe for preparing oatmeal for the children. If you don't like what I make, you'll have to eat with the men."

"The new Quaker Oats box has directions on the side. That would probably work for oatmeal. Don't worry about me; I'll eat whatever you make." Cathleen raised an eyebrow, and then smiled in appreciation. When the smile lit up her face, he thought he'd unlocked the mystery of his spoiled wife. She thrived on affirmation. He certainly hoped he'd find something praiseworthy in her cooking.

"What do you know? Here's a remedy for a cantankerous husband. This just might come in handy."

"How about a remedy for a stubborn woman?"

"That's not my problem. I'll stick to the recipes that apply to me."

Ben chuckled as he left Cathleen looking through the cookbook and reading the instructions on the oatmeal box.

While he had his doubts about her suitability, her attitude and sense of humor made him smile. If they could overcome their cultural differences, perhaps there was hope for the future.

By the time he entered the barn, the ranch cookie had almost finished the milking. "Thanks, Clint. It took a few minutes to get my wife settled this morning."

Ben ignored the man's smirk. "I see ya ended up in the house after all. Guess that pretty filly wuz hard to resist."

Ben wasn't sure how to respond so he decided to let the cowboys think he actually slept with his wife. "Guess so. Have you seen Dan this morning?"

"Last I seen of 'em, he wuz headn' to the tool shed with Pedro. Want me to get him for ya?"

"No, I'll find him. You finish the milking, and I'll take it up to the house when I go in for breakfast."

Ben found his foreman in the workroom just inside the barn entrance. "Have you talked to Pedro lately about his family coming next spring?"

"Not recently, but I know that's Maria's plan. She's concerned about the boys finding suitable employment when they get older. Are you thinking you don't need them now that you're married?"

Ben hesitated to make Cathleen look bad, but his foreman and best friend needed to know his dilemma. "Looks as though I'll need their services even more than before. My wife might work out for the children, but I could starve before she learns to cook."

"I wouldn't complain if I were you. Somehow you managed to snag the prettiest woman I've ever seen. If you don't want her, I'll be happy to take her off your hands."

Ben laughed at the tease. "She is easy on the eyes. Guess I'll keep her, but not because of her cooking."

After they discussed their plans for the day, he picked up the milk and returned to the house. The smell of burning oatmeal permeated the air while a heavy layer of smoke smarted his eyes. Cathleen stood at the stove crying. "What's the matter now? Are you hurt?"

"I'm such a failure. I can't even make oatmeal without burning it. I left the kitchen to check on the children. By the time I changed their diapers, the oats had outgrown the pot. Just look at this mess. What am I going to do?"

"It's okay, honey. You go back to the children and I'll take care of breakfast."

"Honey? Do you realize you actually called me by a term of endearment?"

Calling his wife honey had come out of nowhere and surprised him as much as her. "It suits you when you're standing at the stove crying over burnt oatmeal."

Cathleen hit him with the dishcloth she'd used to wipe her tears. "I don't like your reason, but I rather like the term."

"Looks as if we've finally agreed on something. Go on. I'll take care of this."

"Are you sure? You doing my work doesn't seem right when you have your own waiting outside."

"I don't mind. The children need you."

Embarrassed by the unintentional use of an endearing term—and her noticing it—Ben prided himself on pleasing her. He didn't know how long she'd be with him, but despite her fiery temper, she chipped away at his wall of resistance. When he saw her standing there in tears, he wanted to take her in his arms and tell her how happy she made him. Although he had married her for the sake of the children, he felt at peace with his decision.

That morning when he went to his office to find Dan, he finally read Cathleen's response to the advertisement. Her description of her Christian faith helped him understand why his father had chosen her. "I long to draw closer to God and put him first in my life. I look to him to lead me to the man I should marry. I place my life in God's hands."

With so many hurdles against them and a bumpy road ahead, he knew they had one thing in common—they both trusted God. Ben's faith had been shattered when his wife died, and he still wrestled to trust someone who would take a mother away from two small children. Regardless of his recent loss, he had to agree that God must have had a hand in bringing Cathleen to his door.

While Cathleen put the children to bed that night, Ben washed the dishes, straightened the kitchen, and then sank into their only chair—the rocking chair he'd made Lana before Sammy was born. If he ever found the time, he needed to make another one for his new wife. There was no doubt she'd come from money and probably bought anything she wanted. Why she chose to come West was a mystery she didn't seem willing to share.

As he reflected on the disastrous day, the breakfast incident paled in comparison to the other events. Dinner produced meat so dry and tough it resembled cowhide. Supper tasted as though she'd poured a whole bag of salt into the stew. He gulped down a cup of milk followed by two huge glasses of water and still his mouth felt dry as cotton. If he weren't walking on eggshells, he spent a good part of the day putting out fires, literally.

Regardless of her failure as a cook, Cathleen excelled in every other way. She kept the house clean and tidy. While the children napped, she weeded the garden. More than anything, he loved the way she treated Sammy and Annie. She took to mothering as if born to the task, and the children thrived on the attention.

Ben laughed when he remembered Cathleen's attempt to change the first messy diaper. She left Sammy on the bed and rushed to the edge of the porch to empty her stomach. Her cries for help had him racing from the barn.

"I can't do this, Ben. The smell is disgusting, and he's a little boy. Should I be looking at his … you know? Besides, isn't he old enough to take care of this without wearing a diaper?"

Ben roared with laughter while his wife scowled. Experience told him any type of affection would soothe her. He put his arm around her shoulder and walked her into the house without answering her questions. The squeamish woman must also be a prude. Perhaps the boy was old enough to be trained, but no one had bothered—certainly not him. Cathleen glowered from a distance while he changed the soiled diaper.

No matter how angry Cathleen became with herself or him, she never raised her voice at the children. When they weren't in the room, however, he got an earful. Most complaints concerned her lack of cooking skills or that she kept him from his own work. But after he spoke a few soothing words in her ear and gave her a gentle hug, her confidence was restored and her temper subdued. At the least encouragement, she moved into his arms, forcing him into an embrace. The woman became an almost irresistible temptress.

When the door to the bedroom opened, his mouth dropped in disbelief. Cathleen's flimsy nightgown clung to her slim figure, leaving little to the imagination. Her auburn curls reflected the light from the lamp as she moved toward him. Before he could offer her his seat, she slithered into his lap. He rubbed the silky material with his work-scarred hands as she snuggled her face into his neck. Unable to resist, he surrounded her soft body with his arms and kissed her. The longing moved him into a place he hadn't visited in a long time, and he didn't want the kiss to end. But at the height of passion, he remembered where such actions led. He would die before he killed another woman in childbirth. The harsh reality shot him from the chair so fast that Cathleen landed in a heap on the hard floor.

"What in the world, Ben?" With a pain-filled face, she screamed at him, "Are you trying to kill me? What happened to the loving, sweet man with the passionate kisses?"

"He came to his senses. That's what. Go to bed, Cathleen. This was not part of our deal."

Cathleen rubbed her backside and moaned. With a pain-pinched face, she scowled at him, then lowered her head and turned toward the bedroom. He wanted to grab her and take back everything he'd said. But he couldn't give her what she wanted. Uncontrolled passion would only end in heartache.

Cathleen retreated to her bedroom in shame. Ben probably thought her a wanton hussy cuddling up to him like that, but she wanted to be near him. She felt safe in his arms and longed for his affection. Besides, he was her husband. By the way he looked at her with those sleepy eyes, she knew he cared for her, too. But he confused her with his mixed messages. The only time he let down his guard was when she needed comforting. At the first hint of passion, that man disappeared.

Throughout the day, Ben couldn't have been kinder or more considerate. But as the light waned, he used every excuse to avoid her. She didn't know what to think. She hoped she'd figure him out before her father showed up. If he discovered her whereabouts before she and Ben consummated their marriage, he'd force her to return to Boston and seek an annulment. She couldn't let that happen.

## Chapter Six

Every day, Cathleen gained confidence in her role as cook, nanny, and maid. She cringed remembering the first meals she'd served her family. They were either burned to a crisp, tasteless, or too salty. She wasted a fortune in ingredients and days of experimenting before the dish tasted edible. The wood stove became her nemesis. She longed for one of the newer models her mother had ordered for their kitchen in Boston.

The laundry presented yet another problem. Initially, she'd tried to ignore the smell coming from the diaper pail or the mound of soiled clothing that spilled from the hamper in the corner. When Monday rolled around and no laundress arrived, she had a bad feeling.

That afternoon during the children's naptime, Cathleen found her husband. She caught him outside the barn with his foot in the stirrup preparing to ride out on a beautiful stallion. The animal danced as if impatient for the exercise and her heart leaped with him. How she longed to ride away for a few hours. Too bad. She wasn't going anywhere, and neither was her husband until she received an answer to the smelly problem growing inside the house.

With the need to get his attention, she employed a trick she'd learned from Winston. Her mother had nearly fainted when she demonstrated the technique. The proper woman ordered her to never again repeat the unladylike gesture. Perhaps now would be a good time to try her talent on her husband. She put her fingers in her mouth and gave a loud whistle. Ben halted mid-mount and almost lost his balance. She smiled to herself.

"Are you crazy, woman? You nearly scared me to death and look at Prince. He's skittish as a cat."

"Get down, Ben. I need to talk to you about the dirty clothes. When is the laundress coming? The children are running out of clean diapers."

Ben removed his hat and scratched his head pondering a response, then broke into unadulterated laughter. "Where did my Boston bride learn to whistle like that?"

Her fury at his amusement only escalated when he resumed mounting his horse. She inserted her body between him and Prince, and with her hands on her hips, she moved into his space. "You are not going to leave until you answer me, Ben Sorenson. That patronizing smile won't work this time."

Cathleen sensed Ben's anger as he grabbed her arms as if to tear her apart. Before she could cry out, he relaxed his hold and caressed her. He went from anger to soothing calm in seconds. How did he do that? Her own fiery temper often took hours to cool.

"Cathleen, I'm sorry if this is too much work for you, but you know you aren't cut out for this life. If you can't handle the job, I'll be happy to drive you to town any time you want. The marriage can be annulled, and you may return to your servants and life of luxury. In the meantime, I would appreciate your help with the laundry."

Cathleen ignored his offer to put her on the next train. "I guess you mean I'm the washwoman too. I don't even see a laundry shed."

Ben gave her a sympathetic smile and looked about for one of his men. He didn't have to look far. Several cowboys peered out the barn door while others leaned on the corral fence—all eyes and ears focused on their conversation. Her ear-piercing whistle must have summoned them from every corner of the ranch.

"Walt, help Cathleen with the laundry. Show her how we do things out West. As for the rest of you, get back to work."

Ben remounted and rode off, leaving her to the mercy of a cowhand. Without a word, Walt walked her to the side yard and began filling a black iron kettle. When the container was half-filled with water, he brought a load of wood from the woodpile and started a fire.

"While the water hets, shave some lye soap into the kettle and separate the clothes by color and dirt. Take this here paddle and stir 'em good. If you get a stubborn stain that won't come out, you'll have to use a littl' elbow grease and the scrub board. I think you'll find hit in the shed. When they're clean 'nough, rench 'em in this big tub. You kin fill it yourself. I gotta nuf chores without doin' women's work. We got us a pile of dirty clothes in the bunkhouse if you're a mind to oblige."

With that, the uncooperative man disappeared into the barn. If her family were to have clean clothes, it would be her responsibility. Even though she'd never done laundry, she felt certain there had to be a better way. Surely the housemaids in Boston didn't use such rustic methods—or did they? Now that she realized how much physical labor it took to maintain a household, she was ashamed of how she'd treated her father's servants.

Without a laundress, Cathleen determined to come up with a less archaic system. By the end of the day, her back would be breaking along with every fingernail. She remembered reading in a trade magazine about washing machines. The invention was new even in Boston and undoubtedly required electricity. Did some washing machines operate with an alternate fuel? A trip into town couldn't come soon enough.

When Ben returned from his ride, he stopped a short distance from the house and watched his wife and children. The clothesline groaned under the strain of flapping sheets drying in the warm breeze. Cathleen had attached the baby to her back with some odd contraption. Sammy had a rope tied around his waist with the other end fastened to a nearby tree. With a spoon, his boy dipped dirt into an enamel saucepan. Annie cooed in contentment while Cathleen carried on a continuous conversation interspersed with cute little jingles.

"Sammy, what are you making?"

"I make Daddy a choklat cake."

"That sounds delicious. Will you let Mommy and Annie have some too?"

Sammy held the spoon toward Cathleen who danced over and pretended to taste the delicious mud cake. "Hmmm. You'll be a great chef someday, Sammy."

The devoted woman tickled the boy under his chin and went back to scrubbing on a pair of work pants as if battling an enemy. Probably him. Perspiration dripped from her dainty chin, and her hair hung in ringlets about her pretty face. He'd never seen a woman more appealing. Something resembling love attacked his insides. Though he could easily fall under her spell, he wouldn't. She didn't belong here, doing the work of a washwoman with hands red and scarred from the harsh lye soap.

Engrossed with the children and her work, she didn't notice when he rode up, dismounted and approached her from the side. Unfortunately, she took that moment to finish with the rinse water. Before he could stop her, she maneuvered the huge tub to the edge of the rough table and turned it on its side. Instantly, the ground became a mud hole, splattering his leather boots in the process.

Jumping back from the quickly spreading stream, Ben brushed the mud from his chaps with short angry strokes. "Can't you do anything right? We don't waste water out here. The rinse water can be reused on the garden. Look at this mess."

The moment the words left his tongue, he wanted to take them back. She'd slaved all afternoon, and all he saw was a little wasted water along with splashes of mud. Cathleen's face transformed from the contented mother to an angry setting hen. He braced for the torrent of words he saw roiling in her.

"You aggravating man! How dare you criticize me when you leave me here to do all this work. It takes a household of servants to run a home in Boston, and you expect me to do everything without help. I'm not putting up with this another day."

"Now, Cathleen, women have been doing laundry without help for years. You'll soon get the hang of it."

"If getting the hang of it means I have to work like a slave, I'm not interested."

Ben rubbed the back of his neck. "I'm sorry, Cathleen. I'll take you to town tomorrow."

"Fine. I'll be ready right after breakfast."

Cathleen finished the family's laundry but refused to go to the bunk house for the men's clothes. They could deal with their own dirty laundry. She'd done enough with refilling the iron kettle and tub several times. Three times during the afternoon, she'd filled the clothesline, letting the hot, dry air work its wonders. With the last load hanging on the line, she'd gone inside to make dinner. She regretted losing her temper but refused to apologize. The man expected the impossible, and she'd had enough of his unrealistic expectations.

Ben spent a sleepless night, aching with the thought of Cathleen leaving. She was right though. He expected too much. But what would he do without her? She might be out of her element with the cooking and housework, but no one could fault her care of the children. She'd even held her nose and conquered the distaste of changing his son. Sammy and Annie loved her, and she loved them. Unless they were sleeping, she included them and made a game out of everything. How could she think of leaving them?

The aroma of pot roast drew him into the cabin following evening chores. He lifted the lid and inhaled the delectable goodness permeating the air. Even with all the laundry, his wife still managed to prepare a meal. If the food tasted half as good as it smelled, he'd be a contented man. She'd learned fast with little complaint, until today. He didn't mind helping with the children or even with the cooking, but he had yet to do the laundry. Before Cathleen, Ben had saved that chore for his mother and the Langland sisters.

Ben watched Cathleen struggle through the meal. Whether from sadness or exhaustion, he couldn't tell, but he'd never seen her so quiet. As soon as the dishes were put away, she went to her room. The last weary look she gave him only made him feel guiltier. He didn't blame her for leaving, but how would he survive. The woman had inched her way into his heart. Thankfully, he hadn't surrendered to her nightly visits to the kitchen.

Cathleen seemed even quieter at breakfast than she did the night before. What happened to the bubbly personality who bent over backward to please him? Even the children sensed her frustration. Sammy turned over his milk, and Annie cried to be free of the sash that tied her to the high chair. Without a word, Cathleen cleaned up the mess and released Annie. When the child refused to be put down on the quilt, Cathleen finished her meal with one hand while holding Annie with the other. The only sound the woman made was the soothing reassurances directed toward his daughter.

Would she really walk out on the children? His only hope lay with begging her to stay, but he knew that wouldn't work. They'd both agreed to her departure right after breakfast. The way she rushed through the meal, she couldn't get away fast enough.

"When you're ready, Cathleen, I'll get one of the men to help load your trunks."

"What are you talking about? We're only going to town. I can't imagine why I'd need my trunks."

"I thought ..." Ben stopped while they exchanged confused looks.

Cathleen broke into a laughter that sounded more like frustration than happiness. She stood from the table with her hands on her hips. "Ben Sorenson. You think a little work will chase me off, do you? I need to go into town on a personal matter. While I'm there, I plan to investigate an easier way to wash clothes. I can't take another exhausting day like yesterday."

Ben breathed a sigh of relief. He wanted to grab her and kiss her senseless, but if he could convince her he had a plan to make her life easier, maybe she wouldn't be so temperamental. "If you can survive until after the roundup, I'll have the money for the new ranch house. With fewer cattle to manage, the men and I can devote most of our time to the project. When we move into the new house, Pedro plans to bring his family from Mexico. The cabin will need expanding, but Maria and her daughter will assist you with the cooking and chores. I'm sorry the work is so hard, Cathleen, but I'm glad you're staying. You've made yourself indispensable. Even the men like having you around."

"I doubt they all feel that way, but I appreciate your encouragement."

"Now that that's settled, are you sure you need to go to town today?"

"Of course, I do. Nothing changed since last night as far as I'm concerned."

Ben was more confused than ever but didn't want to admit it. He'd have to waste a whole day of work to make his wife happy, and he didn't mind at all.

## Chapter Seven

Cathleen enjoyed the buggy ride with Ben and the children. Sammy sat on the seat between them while she held Annie. She'd never seen her husband in a better mood. When he misunderstood her intentions and thought she was leaving on the next train, he moped around as if afraid to speak.

The man frustrated her to tears at times, but she'd never consider leaving him. Every day she awakened with a renewed desire to please him and make him happy. Being with him and the children felt right, and though he didn't love her, she loved him with enough passion for them both. As for the children, they had stolen her heart that first day.

"Do you have business in town as well, or do you plan to visit your parents?"

"No, I thought I'd help you since I'm familiar with the local stores."

"I'd rather you didn't, if you don't mind."

Ben stared at her, then lowered his eyes in disappointment. "Whatever you want, Cathleen. I only wish to make you happy."

"That's the sweetest thing you've ever said to me, Ben Sorenson. I'll explain more later, but for now, I need to take care of this alone. Could you drop me off at the general store and pick me up in about an hour? Better make it an hour and a half, if you don't mind."

Asking her husband to trust her without giving him the least bit of information would be difficult for any man. Worry lines tightened Ben's forehead. He turned away without responding. After their misunderstanding over the laundry, he seemed afraid to question her further. Withholding information wasn't any way to build trust in their marriage, but her instincts told her that Ben would not be pleased if she told him everything. The less he knew, the better off she'd be until she knew for certain how he felt about her.

The day she stepped off the train in Laramie, Cathleen had been so consumed with her own circumstances she'd paid little attention to her surroundings. What she saw now looked much different from the rustic storefronts and dusty streets she first imagined.

Modern brick buildings lined the street of the main business district. Ben pointed out a public library, the courthouse, and several small businesses. She was surprised to hear about the University of Wyoming, which had been founded in 1886, four years before the territory became a state.

"Are you sure you don't want me to go with you? I could drop the children off and come back."

"No, no. That won't be necessary. Spend some time with your mother, and then pick me up around noon."

Ben's curiosity proved too great. He dropped Cathleen off and watched her enter the general store before driving the wagon to his parent's home. He took the children inside, left them with his mother, and shouted to the surprised woman, "I don't have time to talk now. I have to meet Cathleen."

A few minutes later, he guided the horses into a parking area a few blocks from the general store. He jumped from the wagon and sprinted down the street in time to see Cathleen heading out the door. He followed her at a distance and watched her march into the National Bank of Laramie with a look of confidence he rarely saw in a woman. Since she didn't want him with her, he turned toward the mercantile, slowed his pace, his confidence at an all-time low.

"Hey, Ben. I see you got yourself one of them mail-order brides. Looks like you hit the jackpot. She's sure a pretty little thing. Smart too. You gonna let her do business at the bank without you?"

"How are you, Harvey? Guess you told her how to get there."

"Yep. She just walked in here with her long grocery list and insisted on directions. I told her you wouldn't approve of her ordering so many supplies—that you seldom ordered even half that much. She told me not to worry. She'd pay her own bills. Then she wanted to know if you owed anything at the store. I said you had a small account you always paid in full after the roundup."

Ben didn't like his business affairs discussed behind his back, but he wasn't sure who should be the target of his anger—his smart wife or the owner of the general store. Apparently, he and every other person in the store had been privy to his business and his wife's first appearance in town.

"Yep, she's a pretty little thing all right and feisty too. She said I should tally your account with hers and she'd pay them both when she picked up the groceries and other items. Then, she wanted directions to the bank and insisted I make my catalogs available for her when she returned. She's not planning on robbing the bank, is she?"

"I'm pretty sure she doesn't plan on that, but you never know about these mail-order brides, Harvey. I need to go check on the children. When Cathleen returns please ask her not to rob you while I'm gone."

Cathleen entered the local bank with an equal mixture of confidence and indecision. Every head turned as she made her way toward the cubicles in the corner. She ignored the curious stares and walked to the receptionist's desk. The mousy-looking man greeted her with a welcoming smile. "How may I help you, miss?"

"My name is Mrs. Benjamin Sorenson, Jr., and I would like to meet with your bank president."

"Mr. Jacobson is a busy man. Might I ask the nature of your visit? Perhaps one of the clerks could assist you." The receptionist frowned and looked suspiciously at Cathleen.

"I'm sorry, but I prefer to speak to Mr. Jacobson in private."

The man shuffled his papers and sniffed in importance. "I will see if he is available."

When the receptionist closed the door to the adjoining room, Cathleen paced the area near the man's desk and prayed she was doing the right thing. Up until now, she'd taken her access to money for granted. Without justification, her grandmother's accountant had supplied more cash than she ever needed.

This trip to the bank could complicate her life in more ways than one. In addition to not wanting Ben to know the extent of her resources, she needed more time before her father found her. Though she'd brought some money with her, she didn't think she had enough. She needed more cash, but what she was about to do might have unintended consequences. Just as Cathleen had decided to leave, the receptionist returned.

"Mr. Jacobson will see you now, Mrs. Sorenson."

Cathleen saw the timing as a sign she should continue with her original plan and eased past the receptionist into a small but well-furnished office. A tall, thin man stood with his hand outstretched. "Mrs. Sorenson, please come in. I had no idea Ben found himself a wife. When did this happen?"

"We were married week before last, but this is our first trip to town since the wedding. Thank you for your interest, but that's not why I came. I have this letter from my accountant in Boston with my bank numbers and other pertinent information. I'd like to transfer some funds."

Cathleen waited for the man to check the document she'd laid on his desk. "First, I would like to open accounts for the children's education and then transfer the remainder into my husband's account. I have the amounts written on this piece of paper." She placed the pink stationery on the desk.

"Could you change my husband's account to a joint account, accessible by either party?"

"I can't give you access to Ben's account without his permission."

Cathleen raised her eyebrows. "Mr. Jacobson, are you telling me Ben is so wealthy he would be concerned about my use of his funds when I'm transferring thousands of dollars into the account?"

The banker took another look at the paperwork and raised his own eyebrows. "I see. How about we let Ben's account remain as is and open an additional account for the two of you to share. The next time he comes in, I'll have him sign the papers.

"Do you want both your names on the children's accounts as joint owners?"

"Yes, please. I doubt we need all these accounts, but if that's the best you can do, I understand. Could you also pay off the loan on the ranch as soon as the money becomes available?"

"That's a considerable amount of money, Mrs. Sorenson. Are you sure you want to do that?"

"Absolutely. I doubt you'll be paying us in interest what you charge for the loan."

Mr. Jacobson smiled indulgently. "You're a smart woman, Mrs. Sorenson. As soon as everything's in place, I'll mail you a copy of the paperwork. Let me write up an agreement concerning Ben's loan and I'll pay it off as soon as the money is transferred."

Cathleen stood and shook the man's outstretched hand but stopped before turning to leave. "Instead of mailing my copy, could you hold it for me? I'll drop by in a couple of weeks."

"Of course. It's a pleasure doing business with you, ma'am."

Cathleen rushed from the bank, hoping to finalize her business at the mercantile before Ben returned. In her hurry, she almost missed a small shop with children's clothes in the window. The ruffled pink dress on display caught her eye, and she knew it would be perfect for Annie. She grabbed the item and took it to the clerk.

"Do you happen to have a suit to fit a little boy? He's almost three but he's probably large for his age." The clerk went to the back and returned with a dark blue suit that looked perfect for Sammy.

When the woman tallied the bill and began wrapping the items in brown paper, Cathleen knew she'd made a mistake. Too embarrassed to halt the transaction, she ridiculed herself for the frivolous purchase. She should have never stopped at the upscale store. The normal rancher's wife didn't have this kind of money, and Ben wasn't stupid. He'd suspect something as soon as he saw the outfits. Cathleen groaned at the time displayed on her watch brooch. Taking the small package, she thanked the clerk and hurried down the sidewalk.

Mr. Harvey met her inside the mercantile door with crossed arms and a disagreeable frown. "Your husband came by and said for you not to do something crazy before he comes back. You want to have a look at those catalogs now?"

"I'm not sure what crazy thing he expects me to do, but I'll be happy to browse through your catalogs. Thank you."

The owner ushered Cathleen to a long table designed to measure fabric. A yardstick had been nailed to one edge. Mr. Harvey brushed aside a bolt of fabric and a pair of scissors, then pulled out a high stool and set a dog-eared catalog before her.

"Here you go. Just write the number on this paper so I can order what you want."

"Thank you, Mr. Harvey." The man stood over her, reluctant to leave. Cathleen waited until another customer called him away before opening the book. Flipping to the back and slowly paging forward, she searched through tools and farm equipment until she arrived at the household merchandise. She found the section with washing machines. Most required electricity. A mechanical version still required manpower to rotate the dasher and operate the wringer. Even that would be better than stirring and squeezing the clothes by hand—anything to make laundry day less strenuous.

She wrote the number down and turned to the section with modern woodburning stoves. The advertisement touted them as "efficient and easy to use." She also found one fueled by coal oil which looked too small for their use. She recalled Ben's promise of a new ranch house and decided to wait on the stove. "Sassy Sally," her name for the finicky contraption, had been a nuisance, but with practice, Cathleen had figured her out. Besides, she'd already spent more than she'd planned, and she didn't want to upset Ben by making too many changes at once.

Cathleen selected a few small items for the house, then turned to the front of the well-used book and scanned the section with children's clothing. There she found everyday outfits for each child and three dozen diapers. The stained, ill-fitting clothes her children had been wearing were unacceptable.

"Could you order these items for me, Mr. Harvey?"

"Just Harvey, ma'am." Mr. Harvey smiled when she handed him the list. Seeing the many items, his mouth drooped into a frown. "No, I can't. I promised your husband I wouldn't do anything until he returned."

"Mr. Harvey, that is about the most ridiculous thing I've ever heard. Is that another of those explanations as to how business is conducted around here? Most proprietors would be happy to make a sale. What is your problem?"

Cathleen had hoped to finish her purchases and complete the transaction before Ben returned and questioned her. Knowing her husband, he would be too proud to let her pay and he'd be embarrassed she'd spent more than his budget allowed. "Men," she grumbled under her breath. If only Ben would express his love before he discovered her financial situation. Otherwise, she should prepare for battle.

Why had she insisted on going to town so soon? Not only would she displease her husband, but the minute the bank in Boston received the request to transfer funds, her father would discover her exact location. He'd be on the next train West and who knew what else he'd do.

# Chapter Eight

Cathleen had her fill of Mr. Harvey. No argument budged the disagreeable man. She stood, hands on hips, with the list of items to be ordered when a familiar voice joined her at the counter. "What seems to be the trouble, Harvey? Is my wife giving you a hard time?"

"Glad you're here. Maybe you can set her straight. She wants me to order all this stuff and won't let me put it on your account. I told her she'd have to get your approval."

"Poor Harvey. Without the benefit of a wife, you've never learned you can't argue with a woman. Give her whatever she wants but charge the balance to me."

"Ben, I'm trying to pay the man in cash. I don't want us to rack up a huge bill you'll have to pay after the roundup. Please let me settle with Mr. Harvey now."

"I'm sorry, Cathleen, but you are my responsibility, and I plan to take care of you and the children. We'll discuss this later. Mother's expecting us for dinner, and I would like to be home before dark."

Cathleen would let the man have his way for now, but she dreaded the day of reckoning. She hoped before Ben got the bill she'd have time to convince him that the money could be a blessing.

When Ben finally convinced Cathleen to accept his terms, he helped Harvey load her purchases into the wagon. He didn't understand why the man was so upset. She hadn't ordered many more groceries than usual. A few unnecessary items and a couple of extra boxes wouldn't make that much difference. Perhaps Harvey's concern stemmed from the catalog order. He'd find out soon enough. For the time being, he only wanted Cathleen happy and content. Any thought of her leaving left him hollow inside.

His mother met them at the front door and hurried them into the dining room. "Dinner's ready to serve as soon as you're seated." Sammy sat on one of his grandfather's books. Maggie had him tied to the chair with a long sash. Annie babbled into her grandfather's ear. The baby shrieked and reached for Cathleen as soon as she saw her.

"Annie, have you had fun with your grandpa and grandma? I missed you." Without skipping a beat, she turned to Sammy. "And what have you been doing, sweet boy?"

"I help make cookies."

"You did? Did you save one for me?"

Sammy smiled and nodded while tapping on the table with his spoon. Ben noticed Cathleen admiring his mother's table setting. The setting represented his mother's best china. *Probably too simple for her high-toned tastes.* Sammy's place setting remained empty except for the spoon. Otherwise, the boy would be wearing the bowl on his head.

When Ben pulled out Cathleen's chair, she extended a surprised smile. "Thank you." Her whole face beamed with pleasure. Did she think him some backwoods hick with no manners? Ben winced when he remembered how awful he'd treated her during their first meal together. No wonder she thought him ill-mannered.

The meal progressed around thoughtful conversation. Cathleen held Annie on her lap and fed her sweet potatoes she'd mashed with her fork. Occasionally, she managed to put a small bite into her own mouth.

Ben waited to compliment his mother on the delicious pork roast, but Cathleen didn't give him a chance. "Thank you, Maggie. This is the best meal we've had since the last one you cooked for us. Do you think you could teach me to cook like this?"

"Of course. How about I come out in a couple of days, and we'll get started? In the meantime, would you consider calling me Mother?"

"I would love that. Thank you."

The women continued discussing the basics of cooking and proper seasoning.

"Poor Ben. My first attempts were either overcooked, under cooked, or over salted. I'm surprised I haven't burned the house down."

Ben didn't disagree with her but sat in silence admiring the way she interacted with his parents. She confessed her cooking mishaps with amusement while urging Sammy to eat and breaking off small bites for Annie. Warm pleasure and desire niggled at his inner core.

Ben would love to know his father's thoughts as the man looked from Cathleen then back at him with a mischievous grin. Obviously, Papa hadn't missed Ben's look of longing for his wife.

"Ben, I noticed you have yet to bring your wife to church. My parishioners keep asking about her. Do you think you might join us on Sunday?"

Cathleen didn't wait for him to refuse. "Of course, we'll be there. Now that I've done business with a few of the town's people, they will think Ben is ashamed of me if he doesn't bring me to church."

First the tempter, now the manipulator. Ben hadn't been to church since Lana died and didn't look forward to going now. But his spoiled wife had him at a disadvantage. She certainly knew how to get her way. Surprisingly, her methods didn't bother him.

When Cathleen stepped out of the bedroom with the children the following Sunday, she looked more fit for the foyer of a fine mansion rather than the rustic two-room cabin. Strands of wayward curls escaped the loose bun beneath her stylish hat. She complained about having to dress without the assistance of a maid, but what she considered imperfections looked good to him.

She made such a pretty picture he didn't have the heart to ask her to wear something less extravagant. Although Laramie had prospered since the turn of the century, most of the members of his father's church were ranchers and farmers with limited incomes. The banker and his wife were probably the most successful parishioners. Most of the women wore simple homemade dresses or shirtwaists and skirts made from flour sacks or coarse wool. Ben sucked in a deep breath and returned to the moment. His fancy wife would stand out regardless of what she wore. He only hoped no one took offense.

"I can say one thing—I certainly have a fine-looking family."

"Why, thank you, Mr. Sorenson. You don't look so bad yourself."

"Me got new suit, Papa."

"You certainly do have one, and you look handsome, Sammy." The suit was one of those unnecessary items along with the fancy dress worn by his baby girl. Annie's blonde head peeked out from rows of pink ruffles and bows. He'd never seen anything comparable, and certainly not at Harvey's. Had Cathleen stopped at another store before returning to the mercantile?

The buggy ride into town turned into a study of the vegetation and scenery they passed. "Ben, look at those little white flowers. What are they called? And look at those. What's the name of that mountain range? May we go there sometime?"

As his wife bubbled with excitement, Ben answered her questions as best he could, and marveled at her interest in the smallest detail. Cathleen craved knowledge like a thirsty man in the desert. She made his dull answers sound interesting when she repeated them to the children. Even Annie seemed captivated by her new mama. No cause for worry about the children's education with Cathleen around.

When they walked into the small church, every eye turned toward them. Ben felt proud as he held Annie in one arm and escorted his gorgeous wife with the other. With her free hand, she held on to Sammy. The confidence Cathleen exuded made him feel taller, richer, and a better person. She looked each congregant in the eye and smiled as he ushered her toward his mother who sat on the front pew.

Ben's father walked down the aisle from the back as the congregation sang the processional hymn with Mrs. Spence pounding out the rhythm on the upright piano. "Come Thou fount of every blessing. Tune my heart to sing Thy praise ..." The old hymn moved Ben to count his blessings—among them his father, the instigator who'd brought Cathleen to his home.

Tears of gratitude filled his eyes. He coughed into his hand to dissolve the lump lodged at the back of his throat.

Following the opening hymn, his father smiled at them. He cleared his throat and asked them to stand. "I'd like to announce the marriage of my son, Ben, to Cathleen Doyle. They were married on the fifteenth out at the ranch. Maggie and I are delighted to welcome Cathleen into our family. They'll be standing at the door with us following the recessional. Please greet our new daughter-in-law and make her feel welcome."

Cathleen beamed as she turned her kind eyes on each person. He'd never met anyone who could capture a crowd so fast and with such little effort. Too bad she didn't run for office instead of choosing to marry a cowboy. She certainly possessed the smarts.

Ben remembered little of his father's sermon. Instead, his thoughts turned to Cathleen and the mystery surrounding her arrival in Laramie. People would want to know her story, and he had no answers. The few times he asked about her past, she'd dismissed his query and changed the subject. Eventually, the truth would come to light, and when it did, he prayed her secret wouldn't embarrass the family.

When they joined his parents at the back of the church, the locals stood in line to meet the newcomer. The men teased Cathleen and commented on her good looks while jesting with him about his lucky find. The women warmed to her charm as they discussed her outfit, how she styled her hair, and how she liked ranch life. Not one person thought her overdressed.

They had a good laugh at the mercantile owner's expense when he came through the line. The twinkle in her eye assured Ben his wife had something amusing on the tip of her tongue. "Why, Mr. Harvey, what a delight to see you again.

Have you forgiven me for trying to pay for my purchases instead of being an obedient wife as you suggested?"

"Now, Mrs. Sorenson, you're not going to let that little incident keep us from being friends, are you?"

"Of course not, as long as you don't accuse me of robbing the bank."

When Mr. Jacobson stood before them, he looked intently at Ben before he spoke. "It's good to see you, Ben. I had the pleasure of meeting your wife a couple of days ago. Could you stop by the bank the next weekday you're in town? We have some unfinished business to discuss."

The banker then turned his attention toward Cathleen. "Mrs. Sorenson, I am honored you chose us for your banking needs. I should have those papers ready for you sometime next week. I enjoyed our little visit on Thursday."

"I'm sure you did, Mr. Jacobson." Cathleen smirked and turned toward the woman at his side. "And this must be your wife. Hello, Mrs. Jacobson. Please call me Cathleen. I understand you're in charge of the Women's Guild here at church. Please let me know when you'll be meeting again. If my husband can watch the children, I'd love to participate."

"You've made quite the impression on us, Cathleen, and you'll be welcome to join us whenever you're free. We meet at my house the first Friday of each month for a covered dish luncheon. You must call me Louisa."

Ben thought he might burst while watching his wife work her magic on every person who greeted them. His stomach growled as the last person made their introduction, and he nudged her toward the parsonage next door. They'd have another of his mother's delicious meals before returning home. The children had left earlier with his mother and were probably already fed and down for an afternoon nap.

Cathleen snuggled on his arm as they strolled toward his parents' home. "That was incredible, Ben. Why didn't we go to church before? Were you ashamed of me?"

"How could I be ashamed of you? It's not enough that you've captured the affection of my family and ranch hands, but now you have the whole town under your spell. If anything, I'm jealous."

"Ben Sorenson, stop your teasing. You and the children are the only ones whose affection I seek. Tell me the truth. You haven't been to church since Lana died, have you?"

Ben hung his head as he realized how much this woman understood him. Not only did she capture the affection of every person she met, but now she held a grip on his heart. With her brilliant mind and sensitive spirit, perhaps she would understand if he explained why they would never share a bed.

"You're right. I've been angry with God and even my parents. I didn't want to be in a place that held so many memories. You and God are healing me, Cathleen. I do believe I'm falling in love with you."

Cathleen pulled him close and snuggled her face into his neck. Her sweet perfume assaulted his senses, and he felt his body responding to her closeness. "Oh, Ben, how I've longed to hear those words. Do you really mean them?"

Behind them, Ben heard someone clear his throat. "Okay, you love birds. Do you want to have the gossip wheels turning again? I'll have to say, though, I've never seen such a loving couple."

"If you recall, Papa, you're responsible. How can I ever thank you?"

"You can thank me by moving the conversation inside. I'm hungry."

When the talk around the table turned to the sermon, Cathleen squirmed in her seat and felt her cheeks grow hot with embarrassment. She remembered similar after-church discussions with her grandmother—her grandmother quizzing her on the pastor's message. Today, she didn't remember the first point of her father-in-law's sermon. Her mind had wandered from Laramie to Boston, covering all problems, both real and imagined. In the future, she'd have to pay more attention.

Cathleen realized she'd been caught woolgathering when all eyes turned toward her, waiting for her answer to her mother-in-law's question. She'd been so busy reprimanding herself, she missed the question.

"I beg your pardon?"

Her new family smiled patiently while Maggie repeated herself. "What are your thoughts on the sermon, Cathleen?"

"Umm. I'm afraid my mind wandered considerably this morning. Please forgive me. So much has happened, I can't seem to focus." Would she ever learn to stay in the moment? What must Reverend Sorenson think of her?

"Of course we forgive you, Cathleen. You've had a lot of adjustments to make over the last few weeks."

"Do you mind telling us what had you so distracted." Her father-in-law had a frank way of delving into an issue. Now, she wished him less astute. She didn't like being put on the spot.

"After singing that first hymn, I felt thankful for the divine intervention that brought me to this town—for the wonderful people and especially my new family. Then, I regressed a bit when I remembered how different and difficult life can be out here. I'm embarrassed to confess I have a long list of things I want to change. I suppose you think I should first focus on changing myself."

"Actually, today's sermon, in addition to encouraging us to trust God, stressed the importance of contentment in whatever situation we find ourselves."

"Ouch! Perhaps I should have listened. Contentment doesn't come easy for me. When I'm confronted with a situation I don't like, I want to correct the problem and make it more agreeable."

"For the record, Cathleen, I happen to like you just the way you are." Maggie patted her hand as she rose from the table and began removing the dirty dishes. "Would anyone be interested in apple cobbler with whipped cream?"

That night Cathleen twisted and turned on the uncomfortable mattress while thinking about her first Sunday at Laramie Community Church. On the arm of her handsome man, she felt pretty, accepted, and loved. Although she'd met some wonderful people, she longed to find someone she could call a friend. Someone who would understand her.

Despite the happiness she felt with her family, Cathleen wasn't satisfied. Was Ben telling the truth when he said he loved her? He treated her with respect and love throughout the day, but when nightfall approached, and they could spend time together, he disappeared. Most nights, she was in bed long before she heard him making his pallet on the floor. Even during the day, he wouldn't enter the bedroom when she was there.

What could possibly be his problem? When he did come in early enough, she paraded herself before him and took every opportunity to lure him toward her bed. The man resisted as if made of stone. Would they ever experience the physical love between a husband and wife? That little romantic interlude earlier in the day was the closest thing to romance she'd seen besides the two mushy kisses. Each kiss had ended with him fleeing in regret. Something had to be done before her father tracked her down and forced her to return to Boston.

As she changed positions again, thoughts of her absent husband frustrated her. Unfulfilled longing gripped her inside and made her crazy. She had to do something to make him love her. Pulling herself from the bed, she knelt on the cold rough floor and placed her desires before the Lord. A few minutes later, she heard the door open and Ben returning from the barn. Though her amorous thoughts escalated when she heard him removing his clothes, the making of his makeshift bed did the opposite.

Light from the dim lamp bathed the room in shadows. She noticed her Bible lying next to the lamp. She'd been so busy with her new life—the Holy Book had remained unopened since she placed it on the dresser the night of their wedding. The story of Ruth and Naomi popped into her mind, one of the last stories she'd read with her grandmother.

Naomi's husband had died, and a few years later she lost both her sons. When she decided to return to her homeland, her daughter-in-law, Ruth, returned with her. Because the two women were poor and needed someone to care for them, Naomi suggested something that would be considered immoral in polite company. Boaz was a distant relative who would accept the responsibility for their welfare if he realized their situation. At her mother-in-law's suggestion,

Ruth washed herself, dressed in her best attire and used her most appealing perfume. She then went to the wealthy man where he and his labor force were spending the night on the threshing floor. He became her kinsman-redeemer as she curled into a ball at his feet and placed her future in his hands.

Cathleen had loved the story since her grandmother read it to her years before. Dare she follow Naomi's advice and be that bold with her husband? Did she have the nerve? She started for the door several times before she finally crossed the threshold.

# Chapter Nine

Ben tossed and turned on the hard floor and wondered how long before his wife would let him return to the bunk house. He didn't want to go. He wanted to climb into that lumpy bed with her and show her how much he loved her. But the potential heartache wasn't worth the few nights of pleasure.

He'd almost accepted his fate when Cathleen waltzed into the room. From the slits in his loosely closed eyes, he watched her stop near his feet. She hesitated. *What scheme lurks inside her manipulative head?* After standing in the same spot for a couple of minutes, she took a deep breath and knelt on the floor beside him. Another deep breath, and she rolled her body against his, spoon style.

The seductive woman wouldn't be satisfied until she'd captured him—spirit, soul, and body. Well, he'd teach her to play with his emotions. He put his arm around her and pulled her closer. She moaned with pleasure when he began nuzzling her ear and whispering words of love and affection. "I love you, Lana."

Big mistake. In one swift move, she pulled herself to the edge of the pallet with her left arm and punched his nose with her free elbow. It happened so fast he didn't have time to react. His eyes watered and blood gushed from his nose. If he intended to remove her from his pallet, he more than succeeded.

"Benjamin Sorenson, you can't fool me. You were wide awake when you called me by your dead wife's name. Don't ever do that to me again. I am not Lana. I will never be Lana. You said you loved me. How can I love someone who treats me so cruelly?"

Cathleen rushed back to the bedroom in tears. Ben started after her, but by now blood trailed down his face and onto his undershirt. He stumbled to the sink, where he grabbed a dish cloth, and then sat with his head resting on the back of the rocking chair.

Her curiosity must have forced her to take one last look. She moved to his side and whimpered.

"Oh, Ben. What did I do? You have blood all over your shirt. I thought to motivate you toward something good, but instead, I've injured you. I'm so sorry. Please forgive me." She wet a cloth and held it over his gradually swelling nose.

"It's okay, honey. The bleeding's stopped. I shouldn't have teased you like that. I'm the one who needs forgiveness."

"Are you sure you're okay?"

"Come here." Ben pulled her onto his lap. His arms encircled her as he placed soothing kisses on the side of her neck. "Cathleen, I need to tell you why I'm afraid to make love to you. It's unfair, and I should apologize.

"When Lana died, I promised myself, I'd never marry again for fear of getting my wife with child. I couldn't stand the thought of being responsible for another death. When you agreed to a marriage of convenience, I thought I could handle the pressure. But almost from the start, I was physically attracted to you. After getting to know you and seeing how you fit into my family, I can't imagine life without you. I want to love you, Cathleen, but I don't want to lose you."

"Oh, Ben. I understand why you'd be afraid, but you must trust God. You were not responsible for your wife's death. She wanted the children as much as you did."

"I know that in my head, but my heart doesn't want to endure more heartache. Between your reminder and Dad's sermon today, I understand I have a trust issue. I need to trust you and I need to trust God. Just give me time, please.

A few weeks later, Ben sat on the front porch repairing leather harnesses. Cathleen had yet to venture far from the house without the children in tow. "Ben, would you mind listening for the children while I take a walk. When we were down by the creek last week, I noticed wildflowers blooming near the bank. They were so pretty. I'd like to dig up a few and replant them near the porch. Do you mind?"

"Not at all. I have enough work here to keep me busy the next couple of hours. Take your time. If they wake up before you're back, I'll take a break and keep them entertained until you return."

Excitement filled Cathleen as she tied the strings of her bonnet and headed out the door. Swinging a pail containing a small shovel, she made her way down the path toward the creek and mulled over the past few weeks. Even with her husband still sleeping on the floor, she'd never imagined such happiness.

Instead of complaining, she relinquished her expectations and prayed for her family. Exchanging her discontent for a grateful heart, God gave her peace. She determined to face the future with courage—no matter the circumstances.

Cathleen felt blessed to have ended up with a husband like Ben. He had unrelenting patience while instructing her in the simplest tasks—skills that country girls were taught from their youth. With his mother's guidance, she now served decent meals. But, regardless of the outcome, her husband never complained. He buttered a hard biscuit and declared it delicious or smothered the dry meat with lumpy gravy.

On laundry days, Ben helped carry the heavy loads and watered the garden with the rinse water. After he examined her make-shift cloth contraption she'd made to hold Annie, he turned a piece of leather into a carrier that proved more comfortable for the baby and her. They took long walks with Annie riding in the new carrier on her father's back and Cathleen running ahead with Sammy. An adventurous child, he delighted in discovering bugs hiding under rocks, watching grasshoppers jumping in their path and listening to birds singing in the trees.

When her mind returned to the present, she looked around and felt overwhelmed at the beauty. A warm wind from the east brought the smell of freshly mowed hay. She scratched her nose and sneezed. Wildflowers were scattered over the grassy knolls, but they were small in comparison to the ones she'd found thriving near the creek.

Glancing toward the horizon, Cathleen admired the distant mountain peaks still covered with snow above the tree line. She shivered at the thought of being confined to the small cabin during the cold winters. She'd read about the dangerous blizzards and the months of freezing wind bearing down from the north. Kicking at a small rock, she sighed in frustration. Why couldn't she enjoy the beauty of the moment without worrying over something months away?

Looking toward the creek, she heard frogs croaking over the sound of water rushing over the rocks. Adjusting her eyes to the shadowed area, she noticed a movement under the trees. Her heart raced at the thought of something or someone lurking in the shadows. Should she turn around and head for the cabin? She wanted to be brave, but she wasn't prepared to face a dangerous wild animal. While hesitating, her hearing picked up the mumble of human voices. Two people came out of the woods and walked toward her. The man looked like a cowboy, but the woman had long dark braids and wore a leather beaded dress. He heart skipped a beat.

"Indians. Help! Ben!" Cathleen let out a piercing scream, dropped her pail, and turned around so fast she nearly lost her footing. With her heart about to explode in her chest, her feet pounded a path through the tall grasses.

When she reached the porch, her breath came in short gasps, and she struggled to speak. Ben grabbed her and held her as she panted and pointed toward the creek. "Oh, Ben, I'm so scared. There are Indians coming up from our creek. Get your gun before they hurt us."

Ben looked up and smiled. "Hello, Myriam and Jim. Nice day for a walk."

Cathleen turned and stared at the two strangers Ben had greeted with polite familiarity. "Honey, meet our neighbors from across the creek which isn't ours alone. We share the water with the Hensons." Ben cast a teasing smile at Cathleen. "This pretty lady who's afraid you might scalp her is my wife, Cathleen."

"It's nice to meet you, Mrs. Sorenson. Imagine our surprise when we returned from our trip south and heard that old Ben here had found himself a wife." Mr. Henson, who seemed a little older than Ben, grinned as he settled one foot on the lower step.

Although she'd made an honest mistake, Cathleen felt like a fool. Heat rose from her neck and turned her face to scarlet which only added to her embarrassment. Mrs. Henson looked exactly like the pictures she'd seen of Indian women.

The bodice of her leather dress was decorated with colorful beads. Fringe ran up the sleeves and surrounded the edge of her skirt. The light-colored leather contrasted with her dark, smooth skin. Her black braids were tightly woven with additional beading. The lovely woman more resembled an Indian princess than a Wyoming rancher's wife. The woman stood at her husband's side eyeing Cathleen with glistening black eyes.

Cathleen had to clear her throat, before she could speak. "I am so sorry. Please forgive me for letting my imagination run wild. Of course, you aren't about to *scalp* me." Cathleen hit Ben as she emphasized the word scalp and reached her hand toward the intriguing woman.

"Ben, get Mr. Henson a cup of coffee and you two can chat out here on the porch. Mrs. Henson and I will have tea in the kitchen. I have a feeling we're going to be the best of friends."

Ben shrugged his shoulders and shook his head at the other man as he headed toward the kitchen. "I'll join you in a moment, Jim. It seems my wife has given me an order."

Cathleen took Myriam by the arm and ushered her inside. "Tell me, Mrs. Henson, where did you find that beautiful outfit?"

The woman smiled up at her hostess as she took a seat at the table. Her movements were graceful and deliberate. Cathleen sensed a peace about her that contradicted the stories she'd read about Indians. The hint of gray around the woman's temple left Cathleen wondering about her age along with a slew of other questions.

"Since we are to become friends, please call me Myriam."

"What a beautiful name, and you must call me Cathleen."

Myriam looked down at her dress with a hint of a smile. "We returned a few days ago from a trip to Texas where

Jim purchased a new line of beef cattle. On the way home, we stopped at the reservation in Oklahoma to visit family members who live there. The dress was a gift from my sister. She's very talented."

"She certainly is." Cathleen admired the fine stitching and bead work as she placed a cup of tea in front of her guest. "Does she sell them? I'd love one like it if you don't mind."

"Not at all. I'll write her with your request, but I doubt she'd accept payment. She sews them for special people. Surely she'd make one for my new friend." Myriam gave her hand a gentle squeeze.

"If she doesn't let me pay, I'll think of some other way to reward her."

"There are always needs on the reservation. Jim and I help out when we can, but ..."

Myriam shook her head and changed the subject. "I'm sorry we weren't here when you arrived. I can't believe Ben married while we were gone. Tell me. How did you meet?"

Cathleen hesitated, not knowing how much she should share. Friends shouldn't keep secrets from one another, but she couldn't reveal something she hadn't even told her husband. She caressed the chipped teacup for a moment before taking a sip of the hot liquid. In this kind of weather, she should be making iced tea, but where would she find ice? So much to learn about this unfamiliar place.

When she could delay no longer, Cathleen sighed and gave an abbreviated version of her venture west. "I answered an advertisement for a mail-order bride, and Ben turned out to be my intended. Let's just say, God led me here to be Ben's wife and Sammy and Annie's mother."

She didn't want to make her father-in-law look bad, so she left out his part in the story. Neither did she want to expose the selfish ambition of her parents. Myriam raised her eyebrows as if expecting more, but Cathleen had told her all she could for now.

Cathleen redirected the conversation toward her new friend. "Tell me how you and your husband met. He looks more like a cowboy than an Indian."

"Jim was an officer in the army assigned to keep the peace on and around the reservation. I fell in love the first time I saw him. I watched as he knelt before my sister's little boy and gave him a piece of candy. The few words he spoke were in our own language, and I marveled that he conversed so easily.

"Unlike the young bucks on the reservation, Jim looked at me with tenderness and respect. It took him a while to see me as someone other than the chief's daughter, but after a few visits to our camp, he found the nerve to ask my father if he could court me. At first, Father was furious and threatened to report him to his superior officer, but Jim persisted. He spent hours sitting in my father's tent and discussing everything from horses to solutions to the violence between the white man and Indians. Finally, Jim convinced my father that, in addition to him being a worthy suitor, the courtship could be considered a wise political move. It hasn't always been easy, but we've been married over twenty-three years and I couldn't be happier."

"Do you have children?"

"Two boys. They're back with our foreman working with the new cattle our drovers brought up from Texas."

"Did you experience any prejudice when you were down south?"

"There's prejudice everywhere, Cathleen. Especially where people aren't willing to follow Jesus."

The conversation continued along those lines, until the men came inside. "Myriam, would you be available to help

Cathleen occasionally on wash days. She's not accustomed to doing laundry, and the task is even more difficult with two small children. I've been helping, but with the roundup coming, I won't be as handy. I'd be happy to pay you."

"You will do no such thing. I'd love to help Cathleen. That's what neighbors do. Is Monday your wash day?"

When the couple left, Cathleen knew she'd made her first close friend since moving West. Outwardly, the two women had little in common, but in the places that mattered, they were in total agreement. Although Myriam appeared closer to the age of her mother, their kindred spirits discovered their mutual love of nature, their commitment to God, and their desire to reach out to others. They both had a desire to change the world around them for the better.

## Chapter Ten

The next afternoon Cathleen worked in the garden while the children slept. Soon after she arrived, Ben showed her how to pull weeds and made sure she recognized the difference between a vegetable plant and a noxious weed. Several young plants suffered the consequences before she mastered the skill. The weeds became her nemesis. She couldn't walk by one without yanking the offensive plant from the ground. After a few hours of the monotonous work, an army of weeds marched through her head every time she closed her eyes. How she longed for a gardener like Winston's father.

Ben came out of the barn with Prince saddled and ready to ride. Removing his hat, he wiped his forehead with his shirt sleeve and walked close enough to observe her work.

"Do you still worry that I might destroy your garden?"

Ben threw back his head and laughed. "No. I like watching you. Regardless of what you're doing you seem happy."

"I am happily frustrated with these pesky weeds. Why do they appear heartier than the vegetables? Is there something we can purchase to help them along?"

Ben shook his head. "Do you think money can fix everything? The vegetables have all the nutrients they need with the compost I turned into the soil."

"Where did you get the compost?"

"From the barn. Do you even know what compost is?"

"Of course, I know—compost is cow manure."

"Ours is mostly horse manure. It's better than any fertilizer you can buy."

Cathleen grimaced, shook the dirt from her hands and wiped them on her apron. "You mean we eat vegetables that grow in manure?"

"That's right, even city gardens use compost as a natural fertilizer. It won't hurt you."

"Are you sure? You shouldn't have told me. I don't think I will ever eat another green bean without feeling sick."

After Ben's reassurance, she continued the weeding. She knew he thought her spoiled and not a suitable wife, but she'd come too far to surrender now. Despite his reservations, Cathleen respected him for his patience and understanding. She longed to please him in every way. Her cozy feelings about the man only lasted until she remembered his cutting remark regarding money.

"I don't think money can fix everything, Ben, but a little extra would certainly make life easier around here."

Ben kicked at a clod of dirt and headed for the barn. Once again, she'd hurt him with her sharp tongue. Why did she have to spoil their time together? She hurried after him.

"I'm sorry, Ben. You know I didn't mean anything by that remark. I love you, and I'd rather have you and the children than all the money in the world. Will you forgive me?"

"Of course, I forgive you, but I feel inadequate knowing you're used to much nicer things. Since you've chosen to be my present and my future, I'd appreciate a glimpse into the life you left behind in Boston. If you would just tell me why you answered an advertisement for a mail-order bride, perhaps I could understand you better."

"I know you have a right to know, but I need more time. Please be patient with me."

"Nothing you tell me could make me love you less, but I'll wait if that's what you want."

Ben gave her a gentle hug before mounting his horse and riding west toward the creek. He looked good on the chestnut. The only thing better would be to admire him from the back of her own horse. Longing for a few hours of pleasure wouldn't rid her garden of the noxious weeds. She groaned as she returned to the back-breaking task.

Toby looked at her and whined from his spot in the shade where he'd made himself comfortable. "Are you whining along with me, Toby? We should be ashamed of ourselves. We are blessed with a wonderful home and family. Who could ask for anything more?"

Humming under her breath, she turned her discontent into gratitude and felt the warmth of God's peace. As she loosened the soil around the growing plants, she felt thankful for her simple life on the ranch, far from the turmoil and problems of Boston.

Cathleen ignored Toby's first growl. The dog objected to any intrusion, including the small rabbit that visited daily to nibble the carrots. If not for her intervention, the sweet bunny would have been stew by now. She reminded Ben of his remark about sowing extra seeds for the birds. Their garden visitor also deserved his share.

When Toby's growl turned into a sharp bark, out of the corner of her eye she spotted unfamiliar boots walking her direction. Her racing heart pounded in her head. Standing on shaky legs, she wiped her hands on her apron and weighed her options: run or confront. The peace and security she'd felt only moments before had disappeared as fast as the rabbit hopped away from Toby.

Without acknowledging the man, she looked toward the barn and bunkhouse, hoping to spot one of the men. Most of the cowboys had ridden out early to check and repair fences, but Ben usually left someone behind in case of an emergency.

"I already looked, little lady. There's no one here but you and that pesky dog. If you want him to keep breathing, you'd best shut 'im up."

Cathleen moved carefully toward Toby and put her hand on his head. He licked her fingers and rubbed against her legs. "What do you want? Since my husband isn't here, you should come back when he can help you."

"I didn't come to see yor husband. I heered ole Ben ordered hisself one of them mail-order brides, and I come over to check you out. Looks like he done hit the jackpot. You shore are pretty."

"I appreciate your compliment, sir, but I'm not the least interested in what you think of me. My only interest is in my husband."

"I beg to differ. It ain't fair for him to have you all to hisself. I think he needs to share."

With that, he jerked Cathleen by her arms and pulled her against his dirty shirt. The smell of his unwashed body caused her stomach to rumble. When he pulled her head toward him, she gagged at his foul breath. Dreading what he planned to do, Cathleen whimpered and slumped. She felt so weak and defenseless against the brute holding her. *God, save me from this wicked man.*

Cathleen remembered the children sleeping inside the house. Rage at what he might do to them brought strength to her legs. With a blood curdling scream, she kicked the man's shin with a force so strong she almost lost her balance. He cursed her as she turned to run.

The man grabbed her from behind and yanked her against his lustful body. A dirty hand came over her mouth and nearly suffocated her. She twisted against his hold.

"Now, you listen to me, you little bitch. I'm gonna have you whether you like it or not. If you be good and quiet, you might find out I'm a better lover than yore ole Ben."

Cathleen grieved at the thought of this wicked man taking her virginity before she'd experienced physical love with her husband. Tears trickled down her cheeks and she choked on the mucus building in her throat. *God, please don't let him do this to me.*

With her last hope of saving herself, she bit down hard on the filthy hand covering her mouth. At the foul taste of blood and dirt, she pushed her assailant with all the strength she had left. He struck a numbing blow to the side of her head. Another scream moved Toby into action.

The dog grabbed the man's leg in his jaw and yanked until he released his grip on her. She landed on her backside, scrambled to her feet, and turned to run. Before she'd gone far, Toby yelped. Then a hand grabbed the back of her shirt. *God, help me.* With a strength Cathleen didn't know she possessed, she turned around fast. The momentum smashed her fist into the culprit's hairy face. He staggered backwards. She ran for the barn. *God, please show me what to do.*

Searching the empty stalls for something to defend herself, she stumbled over Clint, bound and gagged on the floor. He brightened at the sight of her. She yanked the dirty bandana from his mouth.

"Thank God, you're okay, Miz Sorenson. Ben would never forgive me if I let something happen to you."

Quickly, Cathleen undid the ropes binding his hands. Then he took over. He untied his feet and grabbed a shovel.

Motioning for her to stay in the stall, Clint moved toward the open door. "Don't you worry, ma'am, I'll take care of that buzzard."

"Come back, pretty lady. I only want a few kisses." Cathleen quivered at the thought of the man touching her again.

Praying that Clint would not be injured, Cathleen watched between the slats of the stall as Clint's shovel came down hard against the man's head. She slumped against the rough boards. Tears of relief trickled down her cheeks.

When she had gained her composure, she stood on shaky legs. "Oh, Clint. I don't know what I'd have done if you weren't here."

"Are you sure you aren't hurt? Ben's gonna have my hide fur letting that polecat get a jump on me."

"Don't you worry about Ben. I'll tell him how brave you and Toby were today."

At the thought of the dog, Cathleen started toward the door. "Toby?"

Rushing out of the barn, she found Toby lying on his side near the place where the man had attacked her. Dropping to her knees, she rubbed her hand over his chest and relaxed when she felt short, panting breaths. Thank God, the man hadn't killed him.

"Clint, Toby's hurt, and I don't know what to do?"

"Let me take him into the barn. I have a feeling he's only unconscious from a swift kick to the chest. When I checked the buzzard over, I didn't find a weapon."

Clint gently lifted the dog and carried him into the barn. Before he found a soft spot in the hay, the dog had regained consciousness and kicked and twisted in protest. Toby leaped from Clint's arms and struggled against his hold as if anxious to get at the intruder and finish him off.

Cathleen stroked his back and whispered calming words in his ear. As Toby recognized her voice, he whined and scooted toward her. "What a brave doggie you are, Toby. If not for you and Clint, who knows what that bad man would have done. I'm sorry he hurt you. Please let Clint see if you're injured."

Cathleen turned toward the house. "I need to check on the children. Shouldn't you do something to restrain that man before he wakes up? Poor Toby. I hope he's going to be okay."

"I'll take care of that buzzard and don't worry yourself about Ole Toby. He's goin' to be fine. I don't think he'd appreciate your calling him a doggie, though." Clint snickered as Cathleen left the barn.

Clint met Ben at the barn door when he returned that afternoon.

"What happened to you, Clint?" He unbuckled the back cinch. "Bump your head on something?"

"You might say that. I ran into a piece of wood wielded by a no-good drifter. The buzzard laid me out cold, tied me up and left me for dead while he went after yor wife."

"Dear God." Ben threw down the harness and sprinted toward the house. Without wiping his feet or washing up, he found Cathleen standing at the stove. Releasing his breath, he gathered her into his arms.

"What on earth, Ben? Has something happened? Calm down before you frighten the children."

Ben raised his voice, frustrated with her casual demeanor. "Has something happened? Clint told me you were attacked by some drifter. Thank God the man didn't kill you. He didn't, uh, you know?"

"Besides disgusting me with his foul odor and a little manhandling, I didn't give him a chance." Ben fell against her while releasing a slow breath. Cathleen laid a reassuring hand on his and kissed his cheek. "With the help of Toby and Clint, I managed to escape. Thank God they came to my rescue."

Ben pulled away and gaped at her. "I can't believe your calm attitude. Tell me what happened."

Cathleen related the story, minimizing the danger and praising her guard dog and the cowhand. He'd have to question Clint to get the real version and figure out how someone trespassed on the property without anyone's knowledge. "I'm thankful you weren't hurt, honey, but I am enjoying an excuse to hold you."

Teasing her relaxed him enough to feel her heart beating against his own. How could she downplay what could have been a terrible crime? The man might have violated her or even killed her before Ben overcame his fears and shared a bed with her. He pulled her closer and kissed her cheek, her eyes, her neck. Just as he moved to her lips and her body molded to his, the screen door squeaked open. He looked up and saw Myriam standing wide-eyed, afraid to move. Ben felt his face growing hot with embarrassment.

"Excuse me for interrupting, but Pedro told me what happened, and I wanted to make sure Cathleen's not injured."

Ben turned Cathleen toward their visitor. "See for yourself, but she seems fine to me. Though I can't say the same for her attacker. I'm proud of her for defending herself against that piece of garbage."

"Careful, Ben. Our little boy watches every move you make and doesn't miss a word."

Sammy stood in the doorway. Ben grabbed his hat from the floor and beat it against his pants. He picked up his son and darted out the door in one swift movement.

"Oh, Myriam. I'm so happy to see you. How did you know I could use an understanding friend?"

Myriam hugged her and took the chair Cathleen offered. "I'm glad you're okay, but I do believe I embarrassed your husband."

Cathleen laughed. "Of course you did, and he deserved it."

Over a cup of tea, Cathleen told her friend a more realistic version of the attack. "I've never been more frightened. That man seemed determined to have his way with me, but I was equally determined to resist his advances. Toby gave me the chance I needed to escape. That dog deserves his own steak tonight, cooked to perfection—no scraps for my hero."

"I'm thankful your strategy worked this time, friend, but you need a better way to defend yourself than a bite on the hand and a well-placed punch to the face. Though, I must say, you were impressive for such a refined lady. Still, you should ask Ben to teach you to handle a gun. This can be a dangerous place for a woman alone. With the roundup approaching, you'll be here several nights without a husband or any of his men."

"Oh, Myriam, I haven't seen that refined lady since Boston. God's mercy and my fiery temper saved me. Remembering my precious children alone in the house motivated me to fight back. I'm not sure Ben would survive another blow if I let something happen to his children."

Cathleen's hands shook as she relived the story with her friend. "I detest violence and guns, but I understand the need to defend myself and the children."

She gathered the cups. "You want to stay and eat with us?"

"Thank you for the invitation, but I promised Jim fried fish. If I don't get back to the river and claim my string, I wouldn't be surprised to find a bear or raccoon helping themselves to our supper."

"Really? A bear? This close to us?" Cathleen's earlier bravado gave way to concern. "Does that happen often?"

Myriam brushed off her concern with a teasing laugh and rushed out the door. Perhaps she should consider a gun.

Then, as though her friend and husband had conspired together, Ben burst into the house. "Cathleen, honey, I need to teach you to shoot a gun so you can defend yourself when none of us are around. After breakfast tomorrow, you'll have your first lesson in marksmanship."

## Chapter Eleven

All through breakfast, Cathleen made her case against firing a weapon. "Ben, what if I accidentally shoot one of the children?"

"That's why I'm giving you lessons. Once you learn, shooting will come as natural as breathing. After you get the children down, meet me in the field behind the house."

"I'm not shooting toward the house, am I?"

Ben rolled his eyes and growled as he left the house on the run. Cathleen mulled over her dilemma. Of all the things he taught her since coming west, her husband had never asked her to do something so repulsive. As she shook the dishwater from her hands and dried them on a towel, she remembered how frightened she'd been the day before. What if someone tried to hurt the children? She would do everything in her power to protect them. If that meant shooting something or someone, so be it.

Ben stood in the middle of the field, hat in hand, appraising a pyramid of tin cans sitting atop a bale of hay—her makeshift target. Glancing back toward the house, his expression changed when he noticed her walking toward him. His bright smile and twinkling eyes made her want to dance away the remaining distance separating them. The man was a charmer.

"Yeah! I thought I might have to come get you." He bowed with his hat low to the ground. He reminded her of Sammy when he ran to her with his latest discovery. How could she not love the man?

After a quick adjustment to his "target," Ben met her halfway up the hill. He carried a rifle under his right arm and a pistol in his belt. Cathleen recoiled at the sight of the firearms and inwardly protested the idea of dangerous weapons around children.

"Honey? You're shaking like a leaf. There's nothing to be afraid of. You may never have to use a gun, but I want you to be prepared. Please try to remain calm."

Ben placed the guns on the ground and rubbed her shoulders. He kissed her neck until she felt waves of passion washing over her. She wanted to forget the lesson and stay in Ben's arms.

"What a great idea, Ben. We should kiss instead of shoot."

"Oh, no. I'm not letting you out of this. Shoot now, kiss later." He stepped away from her and picked up the smaller weapon.

"We'll start with the pistol since you can easily carry it with you when you leave the house."

Ben explained the mechanisms of the firearm. "Here, hold it. Notice its weight. Keep this lever in the locked position to keep the gun from firing accidentally."

She imagined shooting herself in the foot and avoided looking at the gun Ben placed in her hand. He turned her to face the target and continued to spout instructions. The more he talked, the more confused she became. When he released the safety, Cathleen gritted her teeth and willed herself not to faint. *I can do this.*

Ben held his hand over hers, and she relaxed enough to aim the weapon. She closed her eyes and pulled the trigger.

The force pushed her backward into his arms and threw the gun to the ground. If he hadn't been there to catch her, she would have landed in a heap.

"What was that! The thing nearly knocked me off my feet."

"I forgot to warn you about the kick."

"Kick, huh? That pretty much describes it. I don't think I can do this." She started toward the house. Ben grabbed her by the arm and fixed the gun back in her hands.

"Of course, you can, but you need a little more practice. Let's try again. This time brace yourself. Lock your knees and keep your eyes open. You should at least look at the target if you expect to hit anything. You'll get used to the force."

This time when Cathleen pulled the trigger, she had no trouble remaining upright; however, she purposely dropped the gun and fell back into his arms.

"That, my dear, was quite the performance. Not only did you hit the hay bale, but you used that weak kick as an excuse to throw yourself into my arms." He gave her a quick kiss, and Cathleen responded with a playful jab.

After several more attempts, she heard the ping of the bullet hit one of the cans. She did a happy dance before jumping into Ben and nearly knocking him over. "I did it!"

"See, I told you with a little practice you'd get the hang of it. A few more lessons and you'll be an expert. I wish we had more time today, but I need to ride out with the men."

Ben again scanned the area near the creek before relaxing in her arms. "I see Myriam crossing the creek. Are you expecting her today?"

"No, but we can always do laundry if she can stay."

"Good. After yesterday, I'd feel better with her here with you."

Jim and Myriam had been a lifeline for Ben during those first days after his wife died. He'd been overwhelmed with all the food and offers to help from the town folk, but his neighbors came every day whether he wanted them or not. Myriam took over the house and cooking while his mother cared for the children. Jim and his father worked with Dan to manage the ranch. Ben only sat by the creek and stared into the water.

He remembered watching a leaf floating downstream and thinking how much he identified with that simple leaf. Neither had any ambition or control over their circumstances. They drifted along wherever the current took them. Though embarrassed at his inability to function, he couldn't pull himself out of the stream of grief and sorrow. He'd been unable to care for the children, much less manage the day-to-day operation of the ranch.

A few weeks before Cathleen arrived, he had learned to mask his pain and pretend to cope. Regardless of the pretense, the ache remained, especially at night when sleep eluded him. During the day, he drifted from one task to the next with little accomplished. He despised the sympathetic looks from his parents and friends, but he tolerated them for the sake of the ranch and his children.

From the moment Cathleen arrived, everything changed. She did what no one else could—she gave him a reason to live. Never would he stop thanking God for his mail-order bride and his interfering father who brought her to him. Losing her to that intruder would have sent him over the edge. Again.

"Hello, Ben Sorenson. How are you feeling these days?"

"Good morning, Myriam. I feel better every day. Thanks for asking."

"That sweet wife of yours seems to have worked wonders on you where everyone else had failed. I've never seen you so relaxed and happy." He looked down at Cathleen and felt her snuggle into his side.

"Yes, and I'm grateful, but that little scare yesterday has us all on guard."

"Next time something like that happens, I'll be prepared. Ben taught me to shoot a pistol this morning," Cathleen proudly exclaimed.

"Good for you. We will all feel better when we know you can defend yourself. Biting, screaming, and kicking might not work next time."

Ben looked down at her with a questioning frown. "I see you left out a few details. I'm hoping there won't be a next time, but I need to have all the facts just in case. We'll discuss this later."

Ben gave her two tight squeezes before releasing her to walk toward the house. He gathered the guns and ammunition belt before returning his attention to Myriam. "What do you have in your basket, Myriam? Do I smell your famous tamales?"

Myriam laughed as she slapped the hand that lifted the cloth. "You can wait. I have a bag full in my knapsack for you to share with the men. That way, Cathleen and I won't have to interrupt our work to cook dinner."

"Did I ever tell you how much I appreciate what you and Jim did for me after Lana died? I couldn't have survived without you and my parents. Now, you're helping Cathleen. I really appreciate your friendship."

"We're happy to help. That's what neighbors and friends do. Besides, who wouldn't want to spend time with Cathleen?"

"Well, thank you for coming today. After that problem yesterday, I've been afraid to leave the area. I need to work the remainder of the fence line with the men, and I can't spare a hand to guard the ranch. Hope you have your gun handy."

"Right here under my flap, and I know where you keep your rifle. I'm glad you're teaching Cathleen to handle a gun."

"She did well with her first lesson, but she needs more practice. During a crisis like yesterday, there's no room for hesitation or timidity. I won't worry though, knowing you're here, but I do need to get going. When are you giving me my treat?"

Myriam chuckled as she handed him the sack of spicy food.

"This is enough for an army and I'm glad. Otherwise, I'd have a riot on my hands. No one turns down your tamales and I can't wait to try one of them. Thank you. Will Jim join us for supper?"

"He will. He doesn't like me walking home alone. He says you never know what might be lurking in the shadows."

"He's right, and I appreciate his thoughtfulness. Otherwise I would have to walk you home instead of being with my family."

Ben saddled his horse while Myriam joined Cathleen around the iron wash pot. Most of the men had already left, but he'd helped Clint load the wagon before Cathleen's lesson. He'd dreaded the thought of leaving her alone until he saw Myriam crossing the creek. Thinking of his neighbor reminded him of the smell of tamales and the heat generating from the bag. As soon as he rode out of sight, he'd sample a few while they were still hot.

Although Cathleen's cooking had improved, he often left the table wishing he had an excuse to eat with the men. He didn't dare let her know how he felt or that he secretly envied his friend Jim. But that didn't keep him from wishing his wife would take a few cooking lessons from Myriam. No matter how much Cathleen tried, her cooking remained substandard, either hit or miss. He never knew what he would get when he sat down at the table. One meal deserved high praise while the next tasted like sawdust.

Myriam, however, combined the cooking techniques of three different cultures, along with her native understanding of herbs and spices. His saliva glands worked overtime just thinking about the spicy morsels inside his knapsack.

Ben forgot his obsession with food when he heard the women laughing and teasing one another. They tackled the mound of dirty clothes like children playing a game. At the first cry from his baby girl, Cathleen disappeared into the house and returned a few minutes later with Annie on her back and Sammy holding her hand.

He lingered a moment relishing the sight of his family. Cathleen secured Sammy to the tree and knelt in the dirt until she interested him in making roads for his car. Annie rubbed her wet hand down her mother's hair affectionately. Without hesitation, Cathleen grabbed the saliva-saturated hand and pretended to be taking a bite. Toby ran in circles, excited with the familiar company. Ben's heart expanded at the way Sammy and Annie responded to their new mother. Never could he have found a woman more devoted.

Cathleen blushed with pleasure when Ben made his way over, kissed her cheek and nuzzled his daughter. When the baby reached for his hat, he tickled her chin and pulled mother and child into a tight hug. Releasing his girls, he plucked Sammy from his play and gave him a toss so high he squealed.

"Have a nice day, ladies. I should be back in time for supper."

Cathleen felt blessed by her affectionate husband, but sometimes his rough treatment frightened her. Didn't he see how fragile the children were? Despite her concerns, they giggled at his attention. As she watched Ben put Sammy down and ruffle his curls, she thought how much the son looked and acted like his father.

Ben took his time leaving. When he finally mounted the chestnut and rode out, she noticed him scanning the area around the house and barn. He stretched his long legs in the stirrups to get a wider view. Yesterday's incident had shaken him more than she realized. She'd done her best to downplay the attack, but the intruder had left them both on edge and cautious.

Cathleen heard another bucket of water splashing the sides of the iron kettle. Her shoulders relaxed and her fears eased in anticipation of spending the day with her friend. Surely two women and a dog would be able to defend themselves against whatever dangers lurked beyond the tree line. Cathleen shuddered, hoping to shake the incident from her mind. She wanted to enjoy Myriam without being subjected to constant fear. Besides, together they'd free her house of the disgusting smell of soiled diapers.

"I've never seen Ben so happy—even before Lana died."

"I'm glad. I know I'm happy, but I wish I didn't feel so discontented. I'm often wishing for the impossible such as an invention to make laundry day less taxing. One possibility is to get Sammy out of diapers. That alone would reduce the workload considerably. Any suggestions?"

"Knowing your upbringing, I won't tell you how my people handle the situation. Sammy's a smart boy. He'll figure it out for himself. Just keep encouraging him."

"Now you've got me curious. You have to tell me."

Myriam laughed. "I'm warning you. You'll consider their method uncivilized."

"Come on, you never know what might work."

"The mothers take off the children's clothes and let them run around nude. When they feel the urge to go, no problem."

Cathleen grimaced. "I don't think so. Is that the way you trained your boys?"

"I confess, I was tempted. When I discussed the idea with Jim, he looked about as shocked as you did just now. Since they were boys and he objected to my method, I turned the toilet training over to him."

"And, how'd that work?"

"The training took a while, but we were pleased with the outcome."

Cathleen detested putting her hands into the bucket to rinse the diapers. She took the full pail to the outhouse and poured the water down one of the holes, using a stick to hold back the diapers. She'd learned the trick after her first experience left two at the bottom of the hole. After rinsing the diapers again, she dumped them into the hot water and used the long paddle to stir.

Cathleen watched Myriam fill the laundry tub with rinse water and stopped to admire Sammy's handiwork. She breathed a silent prayer of thanks for the gift of her new friend.

"You seem so peaceful, Myriam. What is your secret?"

"When I look back over my life, I know God walked with me through every situation, no matter how difficult. He brought Jim into my life and gave us this wonderful place to live and raise our cattle. If not for Jim, I'd be living in a teepee or a shack on the reservation. I have so much more than I ever expected—a beautiful home with every possible convenience and two handsome, smart boys. How can I not be peaceful and happy?"

"It's true for me as well. God led me to answer that mail-order bride advertisement and brought me here. I should be ashamed of myself for wanting more. Thank you, Myriam."

The women took a break at noon to enjoy Myriam's tamales. Since the tasty pies were a little spicy, Cathleen warmed vegetable soup for the children. Myriam mashed the potatoes and carrots for Annie and then held her while she drank a bottle of milk. The children loved her friend as if she were another mama. The way Myriam looked at them, Cathleen knew the feeling was mutual.

When Annie whined and rubbed her eyes and Sammy went into slow motion with his spoon, Cathleen wiped them off and put them down for their afternoon naps. She didn't know how much longer Sammy would continue the routine, but not having the children underfoot certainly moved the laundry chore along. Without the babble from Annie and the questions from Sammy, she and Myriam could work and carry on an uninterrupted adult conversation.

"How did your family come to live on the reservation?"

"In 1831 my grandparents were forced from their home in Tennessee to live on the reservation in Oklahoma." Myriam stopped a moment and dabbed the corner of her eyes. "They were newlyweds and had just purchased a farm near my great-grandparents' plantation. Government soldiers drove them from their homes, treating them like herds of cattle.

My grandfather wanted to fight back, but grandmother begged him to forgive and submit to the authorities along with the desires of their white neighbors. The people could take little with them. The journey was especially hard for young children and the elderly. My great-grandmother died during the trip, and Grandmother miscarried her first child."

"Are your parents still living on the reservation?"

"No, they passed away not long after Jim and I married. Papa had trouble accepting my white soldier at first. Before he died, though, he told me he was glad I had Jim to take care of me. I had longed for my father to approve of my husband, and when he told me that, a heavy weight lifted from my heart."

Cathleen thought of her own parents and how happy their approval of Ben would make her. To avoid a discussion of her own story, she continued to question Myriam. "Do you have siblings other than your sister who made the dress?"

"I do have one brother who moved to Canada years ago. He and his family live off the land in the Yukon. They occasionally visit Jim and me, but we've only been up there once. The trip is long and best done in the summer when the weather isn't so cold. But, as you've learned, that's our busiest time on the ranch."

"Thank you for sharing about your family, Myriam. You know, when we first met, I judged you because of our culture differences. Many stories have circulated back East about the Indian lifestyle, the wars and the violence on both sides. Getting to know you and the gracious person you are has given me a different perspective. Please forgive me for my condescending attitude. There's no excuse for such behavior. I know God placed you in my life for a reason, and I am grateful. Thank you for overlooking my flaws and being my friend."

Myriam had been holding one end of the wet sheet while Cathleen pinned the other end to the line. Her helper dropped her end back into the basket and wiped the perspiration from her brow. Reaching for her, the older woman trapped the wet sheet between them. When the dampness saturated Cathleen's blouse, she spit out the two clothes pins she held between her lips and yelped.

Myriam laughed before answering. "Of course, I forgive you. I hope the wet sheet on this hot day feels as good to you as it does to me. I think we should check on the children and have a drink of cold water."

They hung the last piece of laundry and headed for the house. With no sounds coming from the bedroom, the women continued their conversation over a slice of coffee cake Cathleen had made that morning. They fanned themselves with pieces of cardboard and rubbed the moisture from the glass against their hot skin. A cup of coffee would have enhanced the cinnamon flavors bursting from the pastry, but the cool water refreshed their parched throats.

"Since coming West I've had time to think about the prejudice I grew up with, in myself and in others. Back home, people found many reasons to categorize themselves. They were divided by their ability to accumulate wealth, their class, color, ancestry, church affiliation and education. Much of the way people thought had been passed down from their parents and grandparents. You associated with those within your own class and culture and looked down on anyone who didn't quite measure up to your standards.

"Do you know that when I became a teenager, I could no longer associate with the little boy I had played with almost every day of my younger years? My mother thought the child of our gardener too beneath me. Even though we had the same color skin and ancestry, his family were servants in our home. Winston came from the serving class and didn't meet my mother's standard for appropriate friendships. She couldn't look beyond his position to see he was a far better person than the man she'd chosen for me to marry."

"You were supposed to marry someone else?"

"I shouldn't have mentioned that. I haven't told Ben about why I came here. Please forget I said anything."

Cathleen saw Myriam's unspoken question in her narrowed eyes and furrowed brow. Thankfully, she resumed talking about her own family. "Our people have their prejudices, too. Long before we were fighting the settlers and military, tribes battled one another. Sometimes over territorial rights but often over something trivial. Many battles were fought because the chief's daughter fell in love with the son of a rival chief. As long as sin remains in the world, we will have prejudice. Thank God for the missionaries who taught me the way of love and forgiveness."

The conversation continued until Sammy appeared in the doorway and they heard Annie's babble coming from the bedroom. Cathleen changed the children before returning to the laundry. Both had soaked their clothes and their bed linens.

"Sammy, you are getting to be such a big boy, but there's one thing that big boys do not do. What do you suppose that is?"

He eyed her intently as she removed his wet diaper.

"Big boys don't wear diapers. They use the chamber pot or the outhouse when they have to go pee-pee."

Sammy's eyes grew large as this new idea took shape. "Me a big boy like Papa."

"Yes, you are. But big boys do not wear diapers, and they don't wet their clothes. Would you like to start acting like a big boy?"

"Like Papa?"

Remembering what Myriam had told her about Jim and their boys, Cathleen knew exactly what to do. "What a great idea, Sammy. Instead of wearing a diaper like Annie, you'll wear big boy underwear like your Papa. When Papa comes home, he'll take you to the outhouse and teach you something big boys know how to do."

Sammy examined the new underwear and trousers, patted himself, and grinned at Cathleen. She wondered if she wasn't making more work for herself, but at least they'd be outside in case he had an accident.

The women were soon back at work but at a slower pace with the addition of their little helpers. Despite Myriam's teasing, Cathleen kept up a banter of silly songs and constant monolog to entertain the children. Their smiles and giggles only increased her animation. She danced around the yard, enjoying the children's reaction. Annie bounced to the tune while her brother sang along with words of his own. Every little bit, she noticed Sammy remembering his new underwear and giving himself a pat.

Because the laundry took the better part of the day, the two women rushed to finish the evening meal. Cathleen had a beef stew cooking at the back of the stove, but they added a few vegetables and opened a jar of green beans. The remaining coffee cake would be their dessert. Jim arrived only moments before Ben returned with the men. Cathleen met her husband outside with Sammy in tow.

"Ben, could you take Sammy to the outhouse and show him how big boys relieve themselves instead of wetting their clothes. He's wearing big boy underwear now, but he needs a … er … demonstration." Cathleen blushed as she motioned toward Ben's crotch and stumbled through the speech she'd practiced in her head. Ben furrowed his brow and scratched his head.

"What?"

"Big boys don't wear diapers, Ben. He needs to go now"—she cocked her head in the direction of the outhouse—"and he'll understand better if you ... you know, show him." Cathleen batted her eyes and smiled wide as she put the boy's hand in his father's.

"I can see you're enjoying this." Ben shook his head as father and son made their way to the leaning structure.

Cathleen went back inside and helped Myriam put supper on the table. A few minutes later, Sammy ran into the kitchen. "Mama, guess what? Papa taught me to shoot."

"Ben Sorenson, you were supposed to teach your son to use the outhouse, not shoot a gun." Ben beamed.

"Since we're in polite company, wife, I'll not go into the details. But think about it. The idea of shooting seemed the best way to teach him the basics." He chuckled as Cathleen caught on. The word pictures running through her mind, embarrassed her further. She hid her face behind the dish towel she'd been holding.

Cathleen bubbled inside as she listened to the conversation bounce back and forth from the women and children to topics more interesting to the men. Sammy reminded them of his accomplishment. He kicked his feet and received the praise with a wide grin.

After Myriam and Jim left, Cathleen made a significant discovery—she would no longer dread laundry day. This day had been pleasant from start to finish.

## Chapter Twelve

A few weeks later, Cathleen sat on the porch snapping the green beans she'd picked that morning. Her mind wandered to her husband and his concerns about sharing her bed. Though she understood, her heart ached to know him intimately. Fanning herself didn't quench the fire burning inside her when she saw Ben walking toward her with two horses in tow.

"Put those beans down and come ride with me."

Cathleen hadn't ridden since leaving Boston, and she missed the exercise. "What about the children?"

"Clint promised to watch them for us. Since he has a few harnesses to mend, he'll work on the porch. It's not the first time I've had to call on him."

"Let me change." Before Ben could object, she took the pan of beans into the house and rushed for the bedroom. At the bottom of one of her trunks she found the smart riding outfit she'd purchased in Boston. In between pulling on the pants and donning the blouse and vest, she shook the long skirt to remove a few of the wrinkles. She groaned at the crumpled image she saw in the mirror.

Cathleen dismissed her appearance when she remembered that neither horse sported a sidesaddle. Her mother would be appalled, but she wouldn't let that keep her from sitting atop a fine animal. Even before she'd purchased the new outfit, she dreamed of galloping over the hills with a handsome cowboy. Of course, at that time, she didn't know there were children involved. Cathleen groaned and shook off her conflicted feelings. She headed for the door while pulling on her gloves and fastening her hat under her chin.

Cathleen recognized Prince, Ben's chestnut stallion, but next to him stood a regal light-gray mare. The shiny black mane stood out against her light coat. As she approached the horse with her outstretched hand, the horse sniffed, lowered her head and closed the distance between them. Cathleen rested her head against the animal and rubbed the side of her neck.

"She's gorgeous. What's her name?"

"The Henson's called her Lady, but you can change the name if you prefer something different."

"No. Lady suits her. Thank you, Ben. It's been ages since I've been on a horse. You bought her from the Henson's?"

"Yes, I made the deal last week and picked her up this morning." Ben stood back, watching her reaction. "I'd been looking for a suitable mare. When I saw her in Jim's corral, I knew she belonged to you."

Ben moved to her side and ran his hand along the horse's withers. "Jim and Myriam brought her up from Texas. They wouldn't sell her until I told them why I wanted her."

Cathleen would have prolonged the hug she gave Ben, but the anticipation of the ride filled her with excitement. "Oh, Ben. Thank you! Remind me to thank Myriam and Jim. You couldn't have given me a gift I would have loved more. Lady is perfect. Help me up—she's pretty tall."

Ben cupped his hands for her to straddle the horse and then mounted Prince. Sitting astride felt strange at first, but she soon realized the comfort and security of her legs wrapped around the animal. The two horses walked side by side over the hill behind the house. When they crested the peak and started down the other side, Cathleen gave Lady her head and coaxed her into a mild canter. Ben followed close behind.

They picked up the pace. Cathleen felt the lift as the brim of her hat pulled against the forward motion. Exhilaration took over and she felt like a kite carried with the wind. She stood tall in the stirrups letting unfettered laughter break free. When the creek came into view, the horses slowed to a walk. She again lifted herself in the stirrup and turned her body to look at her husband. The grin on his face matched her own.

"I do believe my wife knows how to ride."

Cathleen giggled at his compliment and watched her horse take careful steps over the low creek bank and wade into the water. Lady's head bounced up and down in approval after the horses had quenched their thirst in the slow-moving current. Cathleen clicked her tongue to encourage Lady to climb the bank and follow Prince toward the rise of another hill. Near the top of the knoll, Ben brought his horse to a stop and dismounted.

"Why are we stopping?"

"This is what I wanted to show you." Cathleen looked around as Ben helped her from her horse. That's when she noticed the stakes in the ground connected by thin rope.

"What am I looking at?"

"The footprint for the new ranch house. What do you think of the site?"

Cathleen shifted her gaze from the marked off area toward the crystal-clear sky. Not a cloud could be seen. Despite the chinstrap, a slight breeze played with her hat and blew the curls loosened by the fast-paced ride.

The creek, downhill from where they stood, meandered through the trees and made its way over rocks and around boulders. A peaceful feeling wrapped her in warmth and love. She raised her sight toward the horizon and took in breathtaking views in all directions. The grandeur of the mountains reminded her of the Scripture she'd read that morning in Psalm 121:1, "I will lift up mine eyes unto the hills, from whence cometh my help."

Tears filled her eyes. "Oh, Ben. The mountains are magnificent. Just think. This will be our view when we look out the windows. We will have windows, won't we?"

Ben chuckled in his rich baritone. "Of course, we'll have windows and doors and porches and balconies and even a gazebo, if you'd like. Do you think you'll be happy here?"

Cathleen huffed. "I could be happy anywhere as long as I had a husband to share my bed."

When Ben's head dropped to his chest and he turned away, she knew she'd hurt him. Again. "Forgive me. Why do I keep doing this? I am so blessed to have you and the children, and I know you love me. You want to build me a beautiful home and take care of me, but I'm never satisfied. What's wrong with me?"

"It's not your fault, Cathleen. I should be the one asking forgiveness. I should have never married you until I overcame this crippling fear."

"And have me miss out on these last few months. Never."

Cathleen sniffed at the tears as Ben helped her back on the horse. She'd ruined the moment for both of them. They rode in silence back to the cabin.

After he helped her dismount, she grabbed him by the arm to keep him from moving away. "Please forgive me, Ben. I've turned your wonderful surprise into my own selfishness. I'm so sorry. Please pray for me to be content instead of wishing things were different."

Her husband gave her an abbreviated kiss on the lips and turned her toward the house. "Go check on the children. I'll put the horses away."

The following week, Cathleen saw a freight wagon pulling into the yard. Myriam had just started filling the kettle to wash clothes. "I wonder what Mr. Harvey's delivery boy has on that wagon. Did you order something?"

Cathleen lowered her head and cringed. It had been over three months since she'd made that embarrassing catalog purchase. A few items arrived within weeks, but she'd hoped the new-fangled washing machine had been lost in transit. Weeks had passed since her first visit to the mercantile. She'd almost forgotten about the order.

"I brought your new washing machine, Miz. Sorenson. Where you want it?"

"You might as well unpack the crate out here, Lucas."

Myriam came over and waited with her. "You realize we don't have electricity in the country. Right?"

Cathleen threw a dirty sock from the pile of laundry she'd been sorting. Myriam ducked and laughed. Her black eyes grew larger as the white enamel machine made an appearance.

"I made the frivolous purchase before you came to help me with the laundry. How will I explain my foolishness to Ben?"

The machine had looked much larger in the catalog. Cathleen doubted the tub would hold more than a few items at a time.

"Let's try it out."

Myriam filled the tub with hot, sudsy water from the iron kettle and added a few of the children's clothes. Cathleen turned the crank to make the dasher move the clothes around. After a few minutes, she turned another crank and ran one of Sammy's shirts through the wringer.

Grinning, Myriam caught the shirt before it landed on the ground. After examining the piece, she commented. "The wringer squeezes out much of the water which should shorten drying time. Maybe we should use it for the last rinse."

"I can't believe I thought this would ease some of the workload. My arm's about to fall off, and I only washed one tiny shirt. I'd send the contraption back if I wouldn't have to face Mr. Harvey."

By the time, Ben rode in, the women had abandoned the new toy. They had wasted time and energy trying to utilize the worthless purchase.

"What have we got here, ladies?" Cathleen watched Ben examine the new machine. He looked at her with a curious expression.

"I can explain. You know that first exhausting day I did laundry? I had hoped to find some way to make the task easier. Unfortunately, the mechanical washing machine takes more manpower and time than I imagined. I'm sorry, Ben."

Cathleen hung her head and waited for Ben to explode. Instead, she heard a snicker, then a snort and then a full guffaw. When she looked up, Ben had bent double with laughter. The relief she should have felt didn't surface. She didn't appreciate his amusement at her expense.

Ignoring him, she returned to the clothesline to finish folding the dry laundry. Myriam disappeared inside the house.

The laughter stopped and she soon felt Ben's arms surrounding her. "It's okay, honey. We all make mistakes.

I'll take it to town first thing tomorrow and ask Harvey to return it."

Cathleen stared at Ben with tears glazing her eyes. "How did I get so lucky?"

A few weeks later, soaring temperatures trapped the afternoon heat in the small cabin. Longing for a breath of fresh air, Cathleen decided to take the children for a walk. With Annie in the sling, they left the house and walked down the hill toward the creek. Sammy ran ahead, picking wildflowers and overturning rocks in search of critters. A slight breeze tickled her neck where a few ringlets of hair escaped the tight bun. Annie giggled as Cathleen skipped along to the silly song she composed on a whim.

"Annie and Sammy and Mama, too.

Out for a walk when the skies are blue.

The flowers are blooming, the birds are singing and oh, what a beautiful day!"

When Sammy lost interest in his discoveries and took off after a butterfly, Cathleen ended her song and picked up her pace. "Sammy, come back. You're too close to the water. Remember what your father said about holding hands."

Sammy turned around in protest, "Butterfly."

"The butterfly's looking for a sweet flower. Come back and take my hand and we'll walk to the creek together."

Sammy studied his options but looked again toward the creek. "Mama, bear!"

"What? Sammy come to Mama, now." Cathleen watched the huge bear sniffing around the trees near the creek. Her heart raced when the beast turned his attention toward Sammy. She rushed to her son, scooped him into her arms and headed toward the house. The hill felt more like a mountain as she struggled under the weight of two children. Hindered by the long grass and her full skirt, she heard the bear gaining on them. Every step shook the ground under his heavy weight.

"Mama, will bear eat us?" Not if I have anything to say about it, Cathleen thought. She hated the fear she heard in her son's voice.

"No, Sammy, but we need to pray."

Moments later, her dress caught on a thorn bush and she tumbled headfirst into the soft grass. With Sammy between her and the ground, she worried that she'd crushed him, but felt helpless to do anything about it.

"Sammy, I know that hurt, but we must be very quiet."

Unaware of the danger, Annie had enjoyed the ride before the abrupt tumble in the grass. Now she whimpered. Afraid for the child, Cathleen pulled her beneath her. "Shhh, Annie. Mama's sorry."

How did one play dead with two small children? At the halt of heavy footsteps, Cathleen realized the bear stood over them. His rank smell made her nauseous as he sniffed her clothing and clawed at her shirt. She whimpered as pain ripped through her back. The beast left her no choice. She had to protect the children.

When her hand reached out and touched a medium-sized stick, a plan formed in her mind. "Sammy, I know this will be hard, but I want you to pick up your sister and carry her to Papa. When I say, 'Go,' don't look back, just get your sister to the barn."

Sammy struggled to lift his baby sister while Cathleen prayed for God's strength. She thought of David in the Bible who claimed God had delivered him from the lion and the bear. *Help us, God, just as you did David.*

"Go, Sammy!"

Cathleen jumped to her feet and turned around, screaming at the top of her lungs. She waved the insignificant stick in the bear's face and growled at him. He backed up as if confused by the crazy woman. A series of gunshots split the air. The bear fell face down at her feet while she fell backward. She scooted on her rear end—out of his reach.

Ben's heart raced when he simultaneously heard Cathleen scream and the distinct discharge of two rifles. He rushed out of the barn in time to find Sammy struggling to carry Annie up the hill. Where was Cathleen?

"Papa, a big bear eat Mama."

"What?"

Ben looked farther down the hill and saw Myriam and Jim approaching a huge bear. His wife lay on the ground a few feet away. "Dear, God. Please."

He snatched Annie from his son and called Dan to come get the children. By the time Ben reached Cathleen, Myriam and Jim were hovering over her. His wife was curled into a fetal position, shaking uncontrollably, and crying in anguish. When he pulled her into his arms, she cried out in pain.

"Be careful, Ben. The bear clawed her back. I'm going home to get an ointment to ward off any infection. I'll meet you back at your place."

Gingerly, Ben lifted Cathleen from the ground and headed toward home. "Walk with me, Jim. I'd like to know exactly what happened here."

"Are you sure you want to hear the details? They're pretty scary."

When Ben insisted, his friend continued. "That's the bear we've been tracking. He's the same culprit who's been helping himself to our calves. Myriam just happened to be fishing when she noticed Cathleen coming with the children. Before she reached them, the bear spotted Sammy and lumbered after him. Cathleen scooped the boy up and took off running.

"When your wife tripped and fell, I figured I had a clean shot. I cocked my rifle and prepared to fire. Then Sammy crawled out from under his mother, picked up Annie and headed up the hill. I almost dropped the gun when Cathleen turned around waving a stick and screaming at the top of her lungs. We had no choice, but to shoot. I didn't even see Myriam, but thank God we both got a good shot at the bear instead of your wife."

"I don't know whether to laugh or cry at my crazy, courageous wife, but thank God you and Myriam were nearby. This woman is going to be the death of me."

At the house, Ben took Cathleen into the bedroom and removed her blouse. Since the scratches on her back were not deep, he wondered why she'd fainted and remained unconscious. He looked over her body to see if the animal injured her somewhere else.

Myriam arrived moments before he took off her skirt. "The bear only scratched her back, Ben."

"It doesn't look that bad. Why is she still unconscious?"

"She's probably in shock. Here, let me cover her with this blanket. Do you have smelling salts?"

After only one whiff of the obnoxious smell, Cathleen's eyes opened. Panic-stricken, she grabbed Ben's shirt and screamed into his face. "The children, Ben. Where are the children?"

"They're fine, honey. The children are with Dan in the barn."

"What happened to the bear? One minute I was fighting him off, and the next minute, I heard a gunshot, and he almost fell on top of me."

"You can thank our sharpshooting neighbors for that."

"You shot him, Myriam?"

"Jim and I both shot at the same time. I didn't even know Jim was there until I heard his rifle report."

"I suppose you had to kill him. I only planned to frighten him off so the children could get to their father."

"And you planned to scare him with a stick?"

"The idea seems a little ridiculous now that it's over, but at the time, I didn't know what else to do. Thank God you and Jim came along when you did."

"I brought this cream to help heal those scratches. Your back will be fine in a few days, but I think your shirtwaist is ready for the rag bag."

"Better my blouse and my back instead of one of the children. I'm so glad I reached Sammy before the bear did."

After Myriam rubbed the ointment on Cathleen's back, she left to walk home with Jim.

Ben knelt by the bed, rubbing the salve into the claw marks. "You are one brave woman, Cathleen. How can I ever thank you for protecting my children?"

"They're my children, too. I'd do anything to keep them safe."

Ben wrapped her in his arms, carefully avoiding her injured back. Moving from one tear stained cheek to the next, he kissed and hugged and whispered comfort and love. "Thank God, you're not hurt. Forgive me, but I should never let you out of the house."

That evening on the pallet, Ben mulled the afternoon incident. He berated himself for not continuing the shooting lessons with Cathleen. Not once had they confronted a bear this close to their property. His current wife seemed danger prone. If not for their neighbors, he'd be planning a funeral for three.

Ben took a few minutes to thank God for Myriam and Jim. Countless times they'd arrived on the scene and worked together to help their friends and neighbors. After years of hardship and prejudice from the world outside their neighborhood, their love continued to grow in mutual respect and affection.

Myriam had long given up on acceptance within certain circles, but she bravely entered his father's church every Sunday morning with Jim. She rarely missed the opportunity to raise her voice in song and her heart in worship. He saw some of the same characteristics in Cathleen. She proved herself strong, courageous, and determined against all odds.

Since Ben had shared his fears with Cathleen, she had discontinued her late-night walks into the kitchen. He should feel relieved, but he missed the sight of her gorgeous nightgowns shimmering in the moonlight, her long hair flowing about her face, and the sensuous smiles meant to set his blood on fire.

He knew she felt rejected and questioned his love for her, but he couldn't overcome the fear of her dying in childbirth. Her run-in with the bear frightened him even more. To protect her from the hazards of this harsh land, he wanted to put her on the next train east. He couldn't bear the thought of his world collapsing like the night Lana died.

Now he had another wife he ached for—a wife daintier than Lana. Cathleen would never live through the birth of a child from his loins. If the size of the baby didn't kill her, the lack of adequate medical care would finish her off. Ben twisted and turned on the hard floor, seeking relief from the throbbing pain. Even the tiredness from the long, busy day didn't soothe his longing for the beautiful woman in the other room.

After two hours of useless tossing, he rose from the hard pallet and filled a glass with water to moisten his dry mouth. When his thirst was quenched, he paced the floor near the bedroom wishing he had the courage to enter.

Ben turned at the squeak of the hinge. "Cathleen, are you okay?"

"No, I'm so sick, Ben. My head hurts and I ache all over. What do you suppose is wrong with me?"

He pulled her into his arms. Her body heat assaulted him with a double dose of fear. *God, please, don't let something else happen.*

"Honey, you're burning up with fever. Let me help you back to bed while I get some aspirin and a wet cloth. Roll over on your back so I can see if those bear scratches are infected. I'll send one of the men for the doctor."

"I don't think the doctor's necessary, Ben. Just the medication will be fine."

"I'm not taking any chances, Cathleen. I can't lose you."

Cathleen placed her hot hand on his cheek as he adjusted the covers around her. "My dear, sweet husband, my fever is probably from a slight cold or stress over that frightful incident. If I can survive a bear attack, you're not going to lose me to a simple fever."

After he gave her the aspirin and left a wet cloth across her eyes, he rushed to the bunkhouse to awaken one of his men. If she was fine, he wanted to hear the words from the doctor's mouth.

He returned to find Cathleen tossing about and whining in her sleep. When she didn't respond to his touch or the whisper of her name, Ben felt his world crumbling around him. He replaced the warm cloth with a cool one and slipped beneath the covers. He pulled her hot body into his chest and released the tears of agony he'd held at bay. *God, please have mercy.* He couldn't lose her—not now, when he couldn't imagine life without her. Ben wiped at the tears that had wet her hair and moistened her neck. He'd rather see her return to Boston than to bury her in the little cemetery at the top of the hill.

A couple hours later, Ben heard the wheels of a buggy bouncing over the rough road and coming to a halt near the house. He pulled himself away from Cathleen and went out to meet Dr. Morgan. "What's this I hear about a sick wife, Ben. She's not having a baby, is she?"

"No, but she's delirious with high fever, and she sounds congested. I gave her some aspirin before I sent Dan to get you, but nothing has helped. A bear chased her earlier today and left scratches on her back, but they don't look infected. Cathleen's not used to all the hard work. Do you suppose this life is too much for her? I can't lose her, Doc."

"I'm sure she'll be fine. Let's have a look."

The doctor stumbled over the makeshift bed and looked at Ben in confusion. "Tell me you aren't sleeping on the floor, Ben."

"Don't bother me about that when I've got another wife near death's door. Please help her if you can."

Ben didn't need someone questioning his sleeping arrangements at a time like this. Thank God, the good doctor wasn't prone to gossip. Otherwise, his marriage arrangement would be all over Laramie by morning.

Cathleen regained consciousness while the doctor examined her. She coughed several times between hoarsely protesting the doctor's visit. "I'm sorry you had to come out in the middle of the night, Dr. Morgan. I told Ben I'd be fine, but he worries too much. Do you happen to have a cure for worry, Doctor?"

The doctor chuckled. "I'm happy to come, Cathleen, and I'm glad you have a sense of humor. Ben's long overdue for something to make him smile."

"He's a difficult case, sir, but I'm working on him. What do you suppose could be wrong with me? I've never been this sick before."

"I'm not certain, but you have some rattling in your chest. Have you had this cold long?"

"I didn't realize I had a cold. My throat felt scratchy this morning, but as the day wore on, I didn't think any more about it. You don't think it's anything serious, do you?"

"Not if you'll take care of yourself. Perhaps Ben can find someone to help around here for a few days and give you time to recover. The best remedy for this sort of thing is bed rest and lots of fluids. I'm leaving you with medicine to take every four hours until the bottle's empty. Drink lots of liquids and no hard work for a while. Understand?"

Cathleen understood perfectly, but the reality of resting with two small children and a house to manage wasn't possible. Agreeing reluctantly, she knew she'd be good for nothing if she didn't at least try to follow the doctor's advice. The look coming from her husband assured the doctor that she would comply.

While Ben walked Dr. Morgan to his buggy, Cathleen surrendered to a drug-induced sleep. Somewhere in her subconscious, she heard Annie and tried to release herself from the cover and heavy arm surrounding her.

"Stay still, Cathleen. I'll get her." She smiled when she realized her husband was the force confining her to the bed.

"Mama." Annie's cries didn't cease when Ben picked her up. Annie reached for her as Ben carried her from the room.

"Bring her here, Ben. She doesn't understand."

"I'm sorry, honey, but Dr. Morgan gave me strict orders to keep the children away from you. He doesn't think you're contagious, but he's not sure. They'll survive a few days without your attention."

"Oh, Ben. I hate to see my baby suffer."

"And I hate to see my baby sick. Try to go back to sleep and get well."

When Annie finally settled down, Cathleen relaxed into a light stupor. She felt the bed move as Ben snuggled against her back and put his arm around her as if he'd been sleeping with her every night.

"Does this mean you've given up your fears?"

"No, I've only exchanged one fear for another. I love you, Cathleen. Please don't leave me."

"I'm not going anywhere, but I would've faked illness weeks ago if I knew a little drama would bring you to bed."

"You wouldn't dare, and you know it. This isn't easy for me even with you sick, but I need to be near you. Feeling your shallow breaths and the rise and fall of your chest makes my own breathing easier."

"Forgive me, Ben, for making light of your fears."

Cathleen wasn't afraid for her life; she already felt better. But her husband had a problem greater than any disease. She didn't know a remedy for his fear, but she knew God had the answer. "Prayer and patience," she mumbled as sleep reclaimed her.

With the doctor's return to town, word of her illness spread quickly. Cathleen had never experienced such generosity and kindness. By nine o'clock in the morning, friends and neighbors slipped in and out, leaving pots of soup, freshly baked breads and desserts. Though the smell of cinnamon seeped into the bedroom, Cathleen had no appetite and no strength to greet her guests.

Ben's parents came that afternoon with more food and a suitcase for Maggie. Two of the cowhands brought a bunk over and placed it in the spot usually occupied by Ben's pallet. Even with Ben's mother in the house, he refused to leave her.

Cathleen worried about Ben's neglect of the ranch. "I'll be fine, Ben. If I need anything, I'll call your mother. Don't you have work to do outside?"

"Nothing is more important than getting you well, Cathleen. Dan and the men can handle the ranch."

Cathleen turned toward the wall so Ben wouldn't see her crying. She didn't deserve such a sensitive, caring husband. Despite her inability to cook, her fiery temper and her unwillingness to share her past, Ben loved her and would do everything possible to see her well again.

In her more lucid moments, Cathleen felt guilty for keeping so much of her past from him. If she truly loved him, she should trust him and tell him everything. Until the fever left, she could do nothing but lay in his strong arms and sleep.

Ben hovered and worried over her day and night. He put his face against hers to check her temperature. Until she felt cooler to his touch, her cough had diminished, and her breathing returned to normal, he received little rest. Only then did she see him relax.

## Chapter Thirteen

Cathleen never had the opportunity to talk to Ben about her life in Boston, but, as the days passed, she experienced a happiness greater than she'd ever imagined. Feeling her husband's arms around her at night was worth a few days of fever and chills. Her mother-in-law had left after breakfast that morning. Still weak from the fever, nevertheless, Cathleen resumed her chores. Ben insisted on working close to the house in case she needed him. Myriam had visited a couple of times to help his mother and had promised to return the following day.

After the children were down for their morning naps, Cathleen sat at the table with her Bible open to the Psalms. "Bless the Lord, O my soul: and all that is within me, bless his holy name" (103:1). Gratitude filled her heart even while tears puddled in her eyes and dripped on the open page. She pulled out her handkerchief to blow her nose and considered how far she'd come since she last read the Scriptures with her grandmother. God had been with her—even in the times she felt most vulnerable. He had brought her to this place and even used her sickness to let her see how much her husband loved her. She thanked God for members of the community who'd helped Ben during her illness. His parents and Myriam—what a blessing they'd been.

Cathleen looked out the window at the mountain view and thanked God for her new family. A few months ago, she wouldn't have dared catch a train to the unknown and marry a stranger with young children. Now, she wouldn't know what to do without them. The sickness wasn't nearly as devastating as the forced separation from the children. Though she understood the doctor's restrictions, she'd missed the little ones. Her heart had ached at their cries, knowing she couldn't hold them. Ben brought Annie to the door once, thinking that seeing her mother might help. The child screamed and reached for her. Cathleen cried along with the baby. Thank goodness the doctor lifted the ban at his last visit.

Cathleen's reminiscing ended with the sound of a carriage pulling into the yard. Thinking a friend might be visiting or perhaps someone for Ben, she remained seated and wiped the moisture from her face. The abrupt knock brought her to her feet. Only strangers would knock with such persistence. She straightened her hair and removed her apron before going to the door. Her breath caught at the sight of her father. She clutched the door frame to keep from falling.

"Father? What are you doing here?"

"I could ask you the same question, daughter. Do you realize the pain and worry you caused us by running away to this God-forsaken place? Get your clothes. I'm taking you home."

"I'm not going anywhere, Father. I belong here with my husband and children, and I have a marriage license to prove it.

"Now, Cathleen. I understand why you thought you had to run away, but let's put that in the past. From now on, we'll let you make your own choices."

"You aren't listening to me, Father. I have already made my choice. Though you forced me to leave Boston and marry a stranger, I've come to love him, and he loves me. Thank goodness I didn't stick around for that awful person you and mother wanted me to marry."

A bad feeling swept over Ben when he saw the carriage pull into the yard. He recognized the conveyance as a rental from the livery in town but didn't know the driver. When he opened the door, Cathleen, pale and weak, stood stoically before a stranger. The gentleman carried an air of importance in his dark, expensive suit. Though his beard and light-colored hair held streaks of gray, he appeared younger than his own father. Ben looked from the man to Cathleen and recognized the same determined look.

When Ben moved to Cathleen's side and pulled her against him, the man raised his eyebrows. "So, you're the unscrupulous scoundrel who lured my daughter out here to rob her of her fortune. She's coming home with me, and I'm getting this ridiculous marriage annulled."

"I have no idea what you're talking about, sir, but there will be no annulment. We are legally married, and I will fight you to the finish."

Ben smiled at his wife and knew he'd said the right thing. "Cathleen, I want you to lie down while your father and I have a little talk."

Ben didn't wait for her to move toward the bedroom but picked her up and took his time settling her beneath the covers. She clung to him as if afraid to let him go. He'd never seen her so upset. He kissed her softly and pushed her hair away from her eyes. "Don't worry, honey. Everything's going to be all right. You're my love, and I take care of those I love."

In the kitchen, her father had taken a seat at the table. He looked up when Ben handed him a cup of coffee.

"What's wrong with my daughter?"

"Cathleen has been sick with fever and a cold the last few days, but she's gradually recovering. I'm her husband, Ben Sorenson, and I would like for us to have a friendly conversation. My wife hasn't shared anything about her past, or why she chose to answer a mail-order bride advertisement. I didn't need an explanation before, but your arrival makes it necessary."

"She didn't waste any time transferring money into your account, Mr. Sorenson. You can't tell me you knew nothing about that?"

"I know she made a trip to the bank the second week she arrived, but I haven't been to the bank, and she hasn't shared the details. She didn't want me to accompany her, and despite the bank president's persistence to the contrary, she has discouraged my visit. I should have suspected something when she tried to pay for her order at the mercantile. I told her I took care of my family and didn't want her using her own funds. For her to come this far seeking a husband, I didn't consider her funds amounted to much."

The man huffed in disbelief before taking a sip of his coffee. How could Ben make him understand when they had nothing in common? Ben scratched his beard, searching for an answer. They did have one thing—they were both fathers. "The main thing is, sir, I love your daughter. When she first arrived, I wanted nothing more than a marriage of convenience. My first wife died a few months ago and left me with two small children. I needed someone to take care of them. Sammy and Annie warmed up to Cathleen immediately, and now we wouldn't know what to do without her."

"I see your dilemma, young man, but my daughter isn't cut out for this kind of life. I didn't raise her to live in a shack and be somebody's housemaid and nanny. Her destiny is to dress in fine clothes, oversee a household of servants and marry into a wealthy family of the highest pedigree. Can you provide any of that?"

Ben saw the disgust on Mr. Doyle's face as he examined the room and took stock of the way his daughter had been forced to live. He took a sip of coffee and considered how to respond to the pompous man's question.

"I realized that early on, sir, and I tried to send her home, but she refused. Now, it's too late. I'm in love with her and can't imagine life without her. She doesn't mind what my house looks like or how much money is in my bank account. Cathleen loves me for who I am, and I couldn't ask for a better mother for my children."

"Hogwash! You seem to think you can live on love but I'm telling you, it takes more than romance to make a marriage. Love won't pay the bills, and in the long run, you'll fail to make my daughter happy."

"I realize a strong marriage takes a lot of work, but when two people commit to one another, they can trust God to meet the needs of their family. I've never met a woman like your daughter. She's convinced that coming West was God's idea, and I'm beginning to believe her. Cathleen's different from the other Boston women who need money and social standing to survive. She might not have shared much of her past with me, but I would venture to say my wife wants affirmation and acceptance for the person she is, not for what she looks like or the things she possesses."

Cathleen's father raised his eyebrows as if questioning Ben's knowledge. "What would you know about Boston and its women, Mr. Sorenson?"

"I've been there, sir. Let's just say the slap of prejudice didn't sit well with me."

Ben stood and paced the limited space between the table and the sink. The subject left a sour taste in his mouth. Running his tongue over his teeth, he poured a little water into the pump to prime it. After rinsing the dregs of coffee grounds, he filled his cup to the brim with fresh well water.

While looking out the window he gulped down the cool liquid and flinched at the memory of that distasteful year and the family who caused such heartache. A sadness filled him to realize that his father-in-law displayed yet another example of someone more interested in his fortune and social standing than the welfare of his own daughter.

When Ben remembered how sick Cathleen had been and the thought of her being alone during the roundup, he wondered if Mr. Doyle's arrival might be a solution. He hated the thought of sending her back to that kind of climate, but at least she'd be free of the heavy workload. "I would like to ask a favor, Mr. Doyle. Since she's been sick, I don't want Cathleen returning to the strain she's been under the last few weeks. Would you consider taking her home with you for a month or so? Just until my men and I round up the cattle for market and have time to build the ranch house. One of my workers from Mexico wants to bring his family here. His wife and older daughter have agreed to work for Cathleen, but they will need a place to live before they come. Your daughter has worked hard since the day she arrived, but it's too much for her to do alone."

Ben saw the wheels turning in the man's head. He was probably thinking he could take Cathleen home and talk her into an annulment once she returned to her privileged life. But he knew his wife, and he didn't have anything to worry about, except maybe persuading her to go.

"What do you say, Mr. Doyle?"

As soon as Ben closed the door to the bedroom, Cathleen kicked off the covers and made her way to the door. She cracked the door open and sat on the floor, straining to overhear the conversation.

Cathleen couldn't believe her ears. What was her husband thinking? Did he no longer want her? That couldn't be right. Although they hadn't consummated their marriage, he professed his love. She knew he meant well, but he didn't know her father, and she didn't care if she ever got to know him. The courage that had evaporated when she saw her father standing on the porch returned. She pulled herself from the awkward position, opened the door and burst into the room.

"What are you doing, Ben Sorenson, trying to get rid of me? Well, it won't work. You're stuck with me forever. I know I'm a lousy cook, minimal housekeeper, and frustrated laundress. But you know I'm a good mother. You can return to Boston with Father, but I'm staying here with my children."

"Cathleen, you don't have any children. You've only been away a few months. Come home with me like your husband suggested. You've been ill. Dr. Landon is better qualified to treat you than some country quack. Under his care, you'll be well in no time. Your mother has been crying constantly since the day you left and she'll not be happy if I come home without you."

"I'm sorry she's unhappy, but not once did either of you think of *my* happiness. All you wanted was to marry me off to the highest bidder. Well, I'm married now, and you'll have to accept the man I've chosen."

When she looked over at Ben and smiled, she recognized that look of love and desire smiling back at her. If her father wasn't glaring at them, she would have run into her husband's arms. Thoughts of her romantic husband dissolved when she remembered something from her grandmother's letter. *You'll have to forgive your parents, Cathleen.*

Cathleen hated leaving Ben, even for a few weeks, but she regretted the way she'd left Boston. At the time, she felt she'd done the right thing, but had she dishonored her parents in the process? Sympathy and love for them made her wonder if her husband's suggestion might bring about reconciliation. If she didn't go, she'd never know.

"Perhaps Ben is right, Father. Maybe I should return to Boston for a few weeks. That will give us time to talk about my leaving and reconcile our differences. I'll go with you, but only if the children go with me. They were miserable while I was sick, and I'll not put them through that again. Though they'll miss their father, they're my responsibility. No one cares for them like I do. If you don't want the children to come along, Father, I won't leave them."

Ben gave her a questioning look, filled with concern. "Are you sure you feel like dealing with the children on the train? That's a long trip, and they can be a handful. They could stay with my parents in town while you're gone."

"That won't be necessary. Your mother was here while I was sick, and my babies still cried for me. I can't hurt them again. Leaving you will be hard enough without leaving them behind too."

When Ben saw Cathleen's face turning red and her hands pressing against her chest, he pulled her into his arms. "It's okay, honey, you take the children, but please get some help. You're going away to regain your strength and avoid the heavy workload, not wear yourself out."

"The children will have plenty of attention once my parents become accustomed to being grandparents." Cathleen looked over at her father with a mischievous smile. The newly-designated grandfather puckered his mouth as if he'd bitten into a sour lemon. As his plans for his daughter unraveled, he stood for one last appeal.

"Now, Cathleen. You should listen to your husband. You don't need the responsibility of someone else's children."

"My husband said nothing of the sort, as you well know. When I married their father, the children became my children, and I love them like I would my own flesh and blood. Nothing will convince me to leave them behind. They'll be awake shortly and when you meet them, you'll understand. In the meantime, relax while I put the dinner on the table. The roast has been in the oven all morning."

"Let me, Cathleen. You sit and visit with your father." Mr. Doyle shuffled his feet behind his chair as he watched Ben seat his daughter on the bench near him.

"Are you sure?"

"I'll manage. You're the one who needs to relax." Ben gave her shoulder an encouraging squeeze before turning toward the stove.

Mr. Doyle finally took his seat and began a rather awkward conversation with Cathleen. Ben listened while removing the roast and vegetables from the oven and thickening the gravy. Glancing at his wife occasionally, she seemed more interested in smoothing a wrinkle in the tablecloth than absorbing her father's rendition of the social and financial climate in Boston. When he mentioned her mother and how upset she was, Cathleen's attention returned to the conversation.

"Cathleen, your mother and I were devastated when you disappeared and left that horrifying note behind. I went from anger, to embarrassment for your mother and me, to disgust with myself for forcing you into so drastic a decision.

"If anything, your departure reminded me of some of the things your grandmother had taught me during my childhood. As you know, we always attended church, but I didn't remember the last time I'd sincerely prayed about a matter. After I read your note and realized I'd driven you away, I fell to my knees for the first time in years.

"We meant well, but our insistence that you marry that Stanwick boy only drove you away. Your mother feels terrible she didn't listen when you came to her about his despicable behavior. We both should have been more considerate of your feelings. Please forgive us and return home where you belong. Even your husband sees how unsuited you are for this wild land. I promise to never put you under that kind of stress again."

"Of course, I forgive you, Father. I hated to leave you like that, but Geoffrey was determined to have me, and I couldn't possibly marry such an unscrupulous person. I realize how difficult this is for you to imagine, but I love my life here. The people have become my family and the open spaces give me a peace I never felt in Boston. I'm surrounded by God's creation. You must've noticed the mountain views on your drive from town."

"Yes, the countryside is beautiful, but I wouldn't want to live here, and I don't want you living so far away. We'll never see you."

"You'll see us often enough. I've decided to keep grandmother's house in Boston. That's one reason I need to return. As you probably guessed, my husband knows nothing about my finances. At first, he resented the wealthy social class, and I was afraid to tell him my own situation. Besides, I wanted someone to love me for myself, not my money or the way I looked."

Ben winced as Cathleen described him perfectly. He'd made no attempt to hide his bitterness about anything to do with Boston. "I'm in the same room with you, Cathleen. I wish you had shared your fears with me that night I bared my soul to you. Nothing will make me stop loving you. You should know that by now."

Cathleen rose from the table and made her way into her husband's embrace. "Oh, Ben, I know that now, but you have to admit, we got off to a shaky start."

"Yes, we did. One minute I thought I'd starve to death and the next, I felt helpless to resist your charm." Cathleen gave him a playful swat and snuggled under his arm.

"This is ridiculous," her father interrupted. "I know you think you belong here, Cathleen, but you're used to so much better. Just look at this place. In no time at all, you'll be longing for your old life in Boston."

"I'm sorry to say, but you never really knew me, Father. The only thing I liked about Boston was Grandmother. When she died, I felt I had nothing left. You and mother have always enjoyed social events while I preferred to read or walk in the park. The men you brought around weren't interested in discussing the latest book or the bluebird I spotted on my windowsill. Ben understands me and appreciates my knowledge and opinions. He makes me believe in myself even when I serve him the worst meals ever. No, Father, you can't take this away. If you want me in your life, you'll have to accept my new family and the life I've chosen."

Ben watched Mr. Doyle's reaction. He'd stood along with his daughter and put his weight on the back of the chair. With his index finger he traced the veins protruding from his other hand. When the man returned his attention to Cathleen, Ben recognized the look of love and admiration. Moisture glistened in the man's eyes and a slight smile touched his lips.

"You are one stubborn girl, Cathleen. I hate to admit it, but I see you two belong together. You remind me of the love my parents shared. Growing up, I wanted that kind of love too, but something happened to me in college. I forgot about everything except making money. Instead of marrying for love, I married to increase my holdings, and I expected you to do the same.

"My happiness has obviously been misplaced, and now I'm trying to force the same on you." Ben saw genuine repentance as the man lowered his head and wiped the corner of his eyes.

"I'm embarrassed to admit it, Cathleen, but I never really gave your mother a chance. I should go home and work harder at loving her. We married for the wrong reasons, but that doesn't mean there isn't hope for us yet. Perhaps you're the example we need."

"Well, if you want to know the truth, Father, I married Ben to avoid the cad you and mother wanted me to marry. Ben married me because he needed a cook, housekeeper, laundress, and babysitter for his children, but I fooled him. Even though I didn't know about the children at first, my only success has been as their mother. I love being Mama to Sammy and Annie.

"Speaking of which, I hear those sweet little voices now."

The sound of "mama" came from the bedroom along with little feet running across the floor. Cathleen opened the door and pulled her son into a tight hug. "Did you have a good rest, Sammy? I have a surprise for you and your sister. Go see Papa while I get Annie."

Cathleen changed Annie's diaper and thanked God for the miracle occurring in her family. Her grandmother must be rejoicing in heaven to see her son's change of heart. She hummed the hymn they'd sung at church and let the words settle her mind, "Count your blessings. Name them one by one."

When she returned to the room, Sammy had already made friends with her father. The little tow-headed boy sat confidently on the older man's knee, showing him a picture book. She was surprised at how readily her father accepted the intrusion.

"I see you've met your grandson. I'd like you to meet our Annie."

Ben stood back watching his wife as she pushed the children on her father. The man took to them quicker than he would have imagined. He saw Mr. Doyle wince when Annie joined her brother on his lap. Cathleen looked his way with a wide grin. His wife seemed to be enjoying her father's discomfort. The children giggled when the man bounced them playfully.

"I hate to admit it, but you're right, Cathleen. The children are a delight. If your mother can swallow her pride, she should quickly warm to these two."

While Ben put the food in serving bowls, Cathleen set the table. Shiny new dishes and a tablecloth with matching napkins magically appeared from the corner cupboard. What else did his wife have hidden away? He had noticed new clothes on the children when they attended church on Sundays. When his threadbare underwear showed up in the rag bag, he had to bite his tongue to keep from demanding an explanation. Before the drawer became completely empty, brand new replacements filled the space.

Ben dreaded asking Harvey for the bill at the mercantile. He'd do almost anything to make his wife happy, but there had never been money for fancy dishes or unnecessary clothing. Lana didn't seem to care, but Cathleen would never be content with the bare minimum. Without asking, she went about making subtle changes throughout the house. Even the outhouse showed signs of improvement. Along with the usual catalog stood a roll of toilet tissue sitting on some sort of wooden dowel. The most noticeable change was the way the place smelled. The scent of pine and the outdoors camouflaged the disgusting odors. A small bouquet of wild flowers sat on a shelf next to a painting of a bird sitting amid the flowers of a cherry tree. The words captured his attention, "His eye is on the sparrow." Where did she find something so inspiring, and why would she put a painting in the outhouse?

Now he understood why Cathleen approached life as though she had an endless budget. What he didn't understand was why her parents insisted she marry someone who made her unhappy. He didn't know all the details, but he had heard enough to know that she didn't want the man. Ben should be furious with her parents. Still, God had used the situation to bring her to him. *Thank you, God.*

But an heiress? That would take some getting used to. Now that he understood her fears, Cathleen's attempts to dissuade him from visiting the bank were rather comical. She insisted on accompanying him on each trip into town and kept him so busy he didn't have time to think of the bank. Since the mortgage on the ranch wasn't due until after the cattle drive, he ignored the banker's suggestion he stop by. With these latest developments and his curiosity stirred, a visit with Gil Jacobson would be a priority the moment his wife boarded the train for Boston.

Cathleen might love her new life here, but he had no doubt that she'd bring a bit of Boston home with her when she returned. This business about keeping her grandmother's house also had him scratching his head. Would there ever be an end to the things he didn't know about his mysterious wife?

# Chapter Fourteen

After the meal, Ben took the children and his father-in-law for a walk, leaving Cathleen behind to rest. Though her health had improved, the last visit from Dr. Morgan wasn't as encouraging as he'd hoped. Her lungs continued to give off a weak rattle, and she moved about like an old woman instead of the bubbly person he'd married.

"I agree with Cathleen. This is beautiful country. What's the acreage?"

"A little over a thousand. The creek over the next hill marks the western border. Our friends, the Henson's, have a good-sized spread on the other side. Our cattle share the grazing land in addition to several hundred acres of open range to the north. The next couple of weeks, my neighbor's cowhands will join forces with my own to round up the steers."

Mr. Doyle leaned toward Ben and interrupted. "What becomes of the animals after you round them up?"

Ben stopped and cocked his head. A short time ago, his father-in-law saw Ben forcing his daughter into poverty. Now, he seemed genuinely interested in this "God forsaken place."

"The cowhands separate the cattle by owner and brand the calves. At the end of the roundup, we will drive the steers to the train station in Laramie where they will be loaded onto railroad cars and shipped to the stockyard in Chicago.

Meat packers from the east and even overseas will take them from there."

"Sounds interesting, but do you realize a profit?"

The dollar signs returned. Did his father-in-law doubt his ability to provide for his daughter? "Ranching can be quite lucrative, but it's not without its hazards. Cattle rustlers, drought, blizzards, floods, and wild animals are our greatest challenges. Then, there's the market price for beef which tends to fluctuate with the economy, plus supply and demand. Like any other venture, ranching isn't an absolute."

"I'll have to say I'm impressed with your knowledge of financial matters. You're sure you knew nothing of Cathleen's inheritance when you married her?"

In frustration, Ben made a tight fist and released a slow breath before answering. "Nothing until you came along. I suspected she came from money by the looks of her clothes, but I figured she'd come on hard times or she wouldn't be answering an advertisement for a bride."

Mr. Doyle scowled at him. "That doesn't make sense. Why would my daughter keep her money a secret from someone she claims to love?"

Ben removed his hat and scratched his head. "I'm not sure, but I think she was afraid. After I'd shared snippets of my hurtful experience at Harvard, she avoided any discussion about her past. I'd won a full academic scholarship and didn't quite fit in with the students from wealthy parents. Looking back, I regret I didn't try harder to make friends. Instead of dismissing them as spoiled rich kids, I should have gotten to know them as individuals."

Ben looked up at the clouds and winced. "I wasn't very nice to your daughter when she first arrived. She reminded me of the woman who broke my heart, and I judged her unfairly based on past experience. Fortunately for me,

Cathleen wouldn't let me get away with such behavior. She moved in and took over my children, my house, and my heart."

Mr. Doyle chuckled. "Cathleen's very much like me. We're both stubborn and controlling but resist anyone who might challenge our way of thinking. That's why she ran away. My plans and hers didn't quite agree, and she didn't yield to my demands. I can't believe how blinded I was to the character of that young man I'd picked for her to marry. She had to run away before I could see the truth. I found out almost too late that he and his family were only interested in our fortune."

"Your daughter does seem to have an unusual ability to judge character. I'm glad she looked beyond my pitiful situation and gave me a chance."

Mr. Doyle shook his head as if questioning the turn of events. "My daughter did always love a good challenge. Not long after she visited the bank in Laramie, her accountant informed me of her whereabouts. The private investigator I'd hired had reached a dead end when she disembarked the train here instead of California. By the time I knew where she'd settled, my wife and I were both torn to shreds emotionally and physically. After my detective made sure she wasn't in danger, weeks passed before I felt well enough to make the trip."

"I'm sorry you and Mrs. Doyle were so upset, but I can't object to your delay. If you'd arrived soon after she came, I might have let you have her." The men chuckled as they each considered the unique young woman who'd impacted them both.

The two men continued exchanging knowledge and ideas. Their love for Cathleen seemed more than enough to allow them to engage in pleasant conversation accompanied by mutual understanding.

Annie babbled from her leather seat on her father's back, and Sammy ran ahead excited with his usual discoveries. As they neared the spot where the bear had attacked his wife, Ben thought about how close he came to losing his entire family. He released a pent-up breath when the boy ran past without telling his grandfather an embellished version of the story.

"Sammy, come back, son. You have to hold Grandfather's hand when we're near the water." The child came running to them with a bouquet of flowers.

"For Mama."

"They're beautiful. What a good boy to think of your mother. She'll be so happy with your gift. Here, give me your free hand. I see the creek ahead."

Ben thanked God when he saw how readily Cathleen's father had accepted his children. Even Annie seemed comfortable around the man. When they came close to the stream, he saw Myriam wading in the shallow creek. The tail of her dress was drenched from bending over. Before she noticed them, she made another scoop through the water and came up with a nice sized fish.

"I know what Jim's having for supper." Ben laughed as the woman almost dropped the fish before throwing it on the bank. She gave a shy smile while tossing her braids across her shoulder. Looking down at her drenched dress, she groaned in embarrassment.

"Ben Sorenson, are you trying to bring on a heart attack? How's Cathleen."

"Gradually feeling better. Your salve worked wonders on the congestion."

Ben turned his attention toward his father-in-law. "Myriam, I'd like you to meet Cathleen's father, Mr. William Doyle, from Boston. Sir, this is Myriam Henson. She and her husband, Jim, are our closest neighbors."

"How do you do, sir? I'm so happy to know that Cathleen has a family. Your daughter managed to steal our hearts without revealing the first thing about her past. Regardless, she's a jewel, and we've become the best of friends."

"I'm pleased to meet you, Mrs. Henson. Are you Indian?"

Myriam brushed at her wet dress before continuing. "Yes, my family lives on the Cherokee reservation in Oklahoma. I must say you reacted better than your daughter. At our first meeting, she feared my husband and I would scalp her."

After they laughed, Mr. Doyle continued his questioning. "Is your husband also of the Cherokee tribe?"

"No, he's a retired Army officer. You'll have to meet my Jim. He's a fine man."

"I'd love to meet him. I notice you handle the English language well. I assume it's your second language."

"Yes, English came easy for me. While I was a child, a wonderful missionary couple came to the reservation. They taught us about God and set up a school for the children. Some of the young men resented the intrusion, but I believe God sent them our way."

"You seem content with your life, Myriam. Thank you for befriending my Cathleen. I'm certain you helped her adjust to the western culture."

Ben interrupted the conversation. "I wanted to tell you, Myriam, that Cathleen and the children will be returning home with her father for a few weeks. Not only does she need time to recover, but she has some unfinished business back east. Please pray for them as they leave on tomorrow's train."

"You're the one who will need prayer, Ben Sorenson. How will you get by without your family?"

"I'll miss them, for sure, but the trip will be good for Cathleen. I want her well and strong again, like the day she arrived.

"Also, I don't want her out here alone during the roundup. We'll need every able-bodied man to bring in the cattle. My only other option would be to have her stay in town with my parents."

"I understand. The trip will be good for her. I always suspected she left a few issues behind when she boarded the train west."

Myriam turned her attention back to Ben's guests. "I know you will enjoy your visit with your daughter and your new grandchildren, Mr. Doyle. Your daughter's interaction with those two little ones will bring you hours of pleasure. It was nice meeting you, sir. I hope you'll bring your wife along on your next trip."

"We don't seem to have a choice. Our daughter is determined to live in the wilderness, and I'm beginning to understand why."

Myriam climbed the hill with her string of fish. Mr. Doyle continued quizzing his son-in-law.

"Back at the house, you mentioned your parents also live in the area?"

"Yes, my father is the one who placed the advertisement for a mail-order bride."

"Your father?"

"Similar to another father I've recently met, he also has an interfering streak. I didn't appreciate his actions when he first sprung Cathleen on me. Now, I am most thankful." Ben chuckled lest his opinion offend his father-in-law.

"How so?"

"After my wife died giving birth to Annie, I turned inward and couldn't come to terms with the heavy sorrow and loss. Feeling abandoned and helpless in the face of dire circumstances, I couldn't even manage the ranch, much less care for two small children.

"My parents came out often to assist with the children and housework while my foreman kept the ranch running. In desperation, I hired a couple of teenagers on the days my parents weren't available. Two giggly young girls turned into a disaster. The last thing I needed was a couple of husband-hunting maidens vying for my attention instead of taking care of my children. They had about convinced the whole town that I'd soon be meeting one of them at the altar. What a mess!"

Mr. Doyle chuckled under his breath as if enjoying Ben's predicament.

"As he is the minister of one of the churches in town, my father didn't think either one of us needed the gossip and speculation. It's not that Papa didn't consider marriage the answer—he'd already suggested every available woman from miles around. But he wanted the best for his grandchildren, and he felt confident if a potential wife arrived from back east, I wouldn't refuse."

"And you accepted that?"

"Not at first. I knew nothing of my father's advertisement before the day Cathleen arrived. I was angry and wanted Father to send her packing until I walked into the kitchen late that afternoon. When I saw your daughter with my children, that's all I needed to convince me. I didn't care what she looked like or if we were even compatible. I would marry a perfect stranger if she would love and care for my children."

"That's an amazing story, but I'm surprised my daughter agreed. When I tried to arrange a marriage for her, she insisted she wanted to find someone who'd love her for who she was. Besides, she knows nothing of caring for children or a house."

"Cathleen knows how to love, and my babies needed the love of a mother. My love for her didn't happen overnight, but now I'm crazy about your daughter. I'm not sure how long I'll survive without her."

Ben stopped his story before he let slip that the marriage had yet to be consummated. Now he understood Cathleen's attempts to woo him into their bed. What a fool he'd been! His lover would leave on the train without their becoming one. Unless …

The conversation came to a standstill when both men looked off in the distance, absorbed in their thoughts. Finally, Ben suggested they go back to the house. Mr. Doyle smiled as if he understood. He found his driver in the cookhouse and arranged to leave for the hotel in town.

"Give Cathleen my love. I'll be expecting you to join me for lunch at the hotel before we leave on the afternoon train."

"Do you mind if I invite my parents? I know they'll want to see Cathleen and the children before they leave town for so long. I'll send them word if you agree."

"Of course, I'd love to meet them. I have a bone to pick with your father for luring my daughter away from me."

Mr. Doyle laughed while Ben worried about how his parents would react to Cathleen's departure. Ben didn't doubt that the family meeting would be colorful, probably the talk of the town.

When Ben went into the bedroom to put the sleepy children down, the room looked like a prairie wind had blown through. Clothes were stacked across the bed and protruded from an overstuffed portmanteau. A few items had made their way into one of the trunks.

"Cathleen, I thought I asked you to rest. I planned to help you pack when I returned."

"I couldn't sleep for worrying about this trip. I wish you'd been here. This is the hardest thing I've ever done. I don't want to leave you, Ben."

Cathleen moved into his arms and snuggled against his chest. His shirt soon felt damp from her tears. "Honey, please don't cry. I hate to see you upset. You'll only be gone for a few weeks, and you know you should do this."

"I'm afraid you won't miss me like I'll miss you. Can't you come with us?"

"You know that's impossible now, but perhaps I'll come when you're ready to return. Besides, I'd like to discover more about the girl I married. I'm not sure where she came from, but I'm glad she found her way here. I love you, Cathleen, and no distance or anything will change that."

Cathleen smiled up at him. "You do, don't you?"

"Yes, I do. Plus, you have my children as assurance. We'll see each other again in no time."

After supper, Ben lingered in the barn, praying and struggling against what he had to do. His wife waited inside and here he sat on a bale of hay imagining every worst-case scenario. The usual fears such as train wrecks and illness were nothing compared to the wall of terror he'd built between them. What if this night of pleasure left his wife with child? He'd drenched himself in cold water for the past few months. Couldn't he hold out one more night? Though he acted like a reluctant bull, he couldn't put Cathleen on that train without knowing that she was bound to him forever.

When Ben slipped under the covers and pulled Cathleen toward him, she turned into his arms. "I thought you'd abandoned me on our last night together."

"Never, my love. Though I'm shaking with fear, I can't let you leave without making you mine."

"Oh, Ben."

## Chapter Fifteen

When Cathleen stretched awake the next morning, she knew she'd experienced something amazing. At first shy and insecure, her husband led her tenderly into a realm she'd never imagined. He'd slept with her every night since she'd been sick, but nothing compared to the oneness she felt as she submitted to his advances. She could board the train with the assurance annulment wasn't an option—Ben belonged to her.

As her hand searched the empty space next to her, Cathleen felt Ben's warmth and the impression his body left. Knowing her next few weeks would be spent without him, she jumped from the bed and found her most alluring robe. After that romantic evening, no pretense would remain between them.

"Cathleen, you're up early?"

"I didn't want you to leave the house before I saw you. Thank you for last night. I have never experienced such exhilaration."

Ben pulled her to him "I see you're wearing those tempting nightclothes. You know, they made me miserable many nights. I missed them when you exchanged them for less tempting attire. How do I deserve such a woman?"

"Even before I met you, I bought this for you. The salesgirl promised the outfit would please my groom. You've been slow to notice. I'm glad you like it."

Ben laughed with her as he nuzzled into her neck. "The sight of you drove me crazy the first time you waltzed into the room with that suggestive little walk."

Cathleen hit him on the shoulder, then moved in for a kiss. "You always pretended to be asleep, but I knew better. You couldn't fool me."

"After last night, I'll have a hard time letting you go."

"I should think so."

If Ben hadn't heard the children babbling, he'd have taken his wife back to bed and continued the romance of the night before. Why did he wait so long? Now he was putting her on a train with miles of track between them. Who knew when he'd be with her again?

"Am I crazy for letting you go?" Ben mumbled as he kissed her neck and allowed himself the pleasure of her curvaceous body leaning against his.

"You won't forget me?"

"How could I forget you? Write me and tell me all about your time in Boston. My life began the day you stepped from the wagon and made friends with my dog. I want to know about all the years before. Let me into your life, Cathleen."

"I'm only now coming to terms with some of the trauma, but I'll do my best. Get the children while I work on breakfast."

Cathleen wished for time to standstill as the buggy trekked over the rough road to town. Not wanting to share her family with her father and her in-laws, she begged Ben to cancel the family meal.

"That wouldn't be fair to my parents, honey. They'll want to see you and the children before you leave."

When they arrived at the hotel, Ben tied the horses to the post. Reluctantly, Cathleen handed the snuggling Annie to Ben, who then reached for Cathleen's hand. She wanted to collapse in his arms. She didn't want to pretend she was happy, but she held back the tears and forced a smile for Ben's parents.

"Cathleen, I couldn't believe my ears when Dan told us you're going away. What's going on?" Her mother-in-law hugged her, concern marring her usual pleasant features.

"Hello. I'm William Doyle, Cathleen's father, and I'm responsible for all the stir. You must be Ben's parents. High time we met."

"I'd say so, Mr. Doyle. I'm Ben's father, Benjamin Senior, and this is my wife, Margaret. I regret my deception, though I gladly take full responsibility for these two finding each other."

Cathleen's father tipped his hat at her mother-in-law before shaking hands with Ben's father. "Well, I wouldn't be so happy about your accomplishment. I'm not at all pleased with you dragging my daughter away from her mother and me."

"Down, boys." Maggie smiled as she grabbed her husband by the arm. "I regret your loss, Mr. Doyle, but Cathleen is the best thing that ever happened to my son and grandchildren. She makes him smile, and that's worth everything to us."

Ben inserted himself into the conversation and pointed the way to the dining room. "Could we discuss my happiness over dinner? The train won't wait while you draw the battle lines."

Smiling to soften the tease, Ben held his arm for Cathleen and noticed how pale and shaky she'd become. She looked too weak and vulnerable to endure so long a trip. Ben didn't want to let her go, but leaving her alone during the roundup wasn't an option.

When he pulled out Cathleen's chair in the hotel dining room, she raised her head and smiled—her first since they'd left the ranch. Ben returned the smile and patted himself on the back for discovering yet another way to please his wife. Not only did she thrive on praise, but she wanted him to play the role of a gentleman. He'd do anything to gain her approval, even resurrect his eastern manners.

The meal flew by with the conversation batted back and forth between the older generation. The two gentlemen found mutual subjects to discuss. His mother inserted her peaceful charm when a disagreement threatened to dismantle the peaceful meal.

As Cathleen rearranged the food on her plate, he recognized the look of pain. When their eyes met, he grabbed her hand under the table. Caressing her knuckles with his thumb, she smiled through eyes glistening with tears. They mouthed the words, "I love you," before returning their attention to the children.

The walk to the train more resembled a funeral dirge. He ached at the thought of his family heading off without him. Public displays of affection might not be acceptable back

East, but he couldn't resist kissing his wife and children one last time.

"You'll be okay, Cathleen. The time will fly and before long, you'll be coming back to me."

Ben knew the words couldn't be true. He felt stripped bare as he watched his family climb the steps to the private car. His sorrow was nearly as strong as the day Lana died, and that event had sent him into deep depression. By the time Cathleen came to him, he had pasted on a fake smile and learned to cope. But, in a short time, the joyful woman had given him reason to rise from bed in the morning. She brought sunshine to his dark soul, and he didn't know if he had the emotional strength to survive without her.

With the sun behind him Ben watched the train disappear into the eastern horizon. An eerie feeling came over him as the wind cleared the air of the puffs of smoke. He'd never felt so alone and abandoned as he stared at the empty tracks. Confusion and doubt attacked his thoughts. Moments before, he'd ushered his family into a private car that reeked of money and privilege. Only the wealthiest passengers could afford such luxury. He slapped his forehead. How could he have fallen for a woman he didn't even know?

Suddenly, Ben remembered her visit with the banker. Curious, he turned in the direction of the bank. He rushed to reach the establishment before it closed.

Mr. Jacobson stood when he saw him enter the double doors. "Ben, it's good to see you. I wondered how long you'd wait before coming. You've managed to avoid me until after you put your wife on the train. If I hadn't seen her leave with those two youngsters, I'd be worried. Come in and have a seat."

"It seems you know more about my wife than I do, Gil. I understand she opened an account shortly after we married."

The smug bank official began removing papers from a folder on his desk. "I had my secretary pull your folder in anticipation of your visit." He slid the folder across the desk.

Ben raised his eyebrows. He studied the documents and assessed the numbers. "This can't be right." Ben frowned at the banker's knowing smile. "Nobody has this much money."

"It appears your wife does, and I'm pleased to say she's chosen our bank as its resting place. Every month additional funds arrive to sweeten the coffers. Instead of allowing anger to get the best of you, I suggest you put your mind at ease and enjoy your good fortune."

"This is my wife's money, and I refuse to touch the first cent. Forget I ever saw this." Ben stood so fast the chair teetered for a moment before righting itself.

"Sit back down, Ben. Did you see the other accounts? Cathleen set aside money for each of the children's education, and her first expenditure was to pay off your bank loan. Does that sound like a woman who doesn't wish to share with her family? She wants what's best for you. How can you be so stubborn?"

Ben didn't bother to answer the banker who followed him to the door. The stranger he'd allowed into his home had deceived him. How could he be so naïve? Not only had he married her, but he'd permitted her to drag his children off to a world he despised. She'd swooped into his life, pulled him out of misery, and released him from his fears. Now, he doubted he could ever trust her again. She couldn't have hurt him more if she'd shot him with the gun he'd given her. He kicked the first rock he found on the wooden sidewalk and muttered a bitter curse word when the stubborn rock refused to dislodge from the crack between the boards. Would Cathleen ever need him and his sparse bank account? He didn't even have enough money to pay for her frivolous spending at the mercantile.

Unable to face his parents, Ben climbed in the buggy and stewed all the way home. Why did he agree to let Cathleen take the children away? He wanted to ring her pretty little neck. The unscrupulous woman lied to him when she waltzed into town and pretended to need him. She could take her deceiving ways along with her money and stay in Boston, but he wanted his children back where they belonged.

Ben's life spiraled into self-pity and loneliness. His parents and men presumed he missed his family. Mulling the motives of his wealthy wife, he avoided town, the neighbors, and even his foreman. The work piled up. He couldn't focus enough to complete even one item on the long list of chores. His horse and dog became his companions. They didn't grill him with questions or offer polite platitudes. Long rides through the pastures provided a means of escape.

When the first letter arrived with a Boston postmark, Ben carried it around for days. His curiosity and longing to hear about the children finally forced him tear open the envelope.

Dear Ben,

> You can't know how much I miss you. I dream of lying on our lumpy mattress in our little ranch house and feeling the warmth of your body against mine. When I awaken, my first thoughts are of you and the love we shared that last night together. I felt alive for the first time. Don't ever let me go away again without you.

The train ride was difficult even though Father had secured a private car. Sammy seemed confused after a few hours when you didn't appear. I hadn't realized how much a little boy could miss his father until I reassured him numerous times that we'd be seeing his papa again, soon. Since this is your first time away from him, I understand how you must feel as well.

These first few days have been spent resting from the journey and avoiding my mother as much as possible. I'll save my confrontation with her for another letter.

I love you and never want us to be apart again.

Yours forever and ever,

Cathleen

The letter sounded like the Cathleen he loved and wanted, not the deceitful person introduced to him by the bank president. In his mind, they were two different people. When he could no longer bear the confusion and anguish, he rode into town on a Sunday afternoon. He'd avoided the worship service the past few weeks—pretending wasn't in his nature. Yet, he would burst if he didn't bare his soul to someone. Since his father got him into this mess, perhaps he could help him sort it out.

Ben greeted his mother when she opened the door. "What's wrong, Ben? You look awful. We've missed you at church and according to your friends, you've made yourself scarce. Everyone's been asking about you."

"Thanks, Mama. It's good to see you too. Where's Father? I need to speak with him."

"He's over at the church. He wanted time alone to pray, but I'm certain he'll be glad to see you. You want something to eat before you go?"

"Not now. I'll see you later."

Ben found his father on his knees before the altar with his Bible open on the floor. Tears of love softened the harsh words he'd rehearsed on the trip into town.

"Father, Mama said I'd find you here. Do you mind?"

"Not at all, son. In fact, you were the main topic of my prayers. How are you holding up since your family left?"

"Not good. I'm sorry you ever brought that deceitful woman into our family." Ben tightened his fist at his side. "She lured me into her net as easily as Myriam Henson captures a fish with her bare hands. I feel like a fool. You knew I detested spoiled, rich girls with their snobbish ways, and you managed to find the worst possible kind. They have no need of anyone but themselves."

His father wrinkled his brow and stepped back as if Ben had slapped him. "Now wait a minute, Ben. Just who are you talking about? I don't know anyone like that, especially Cathleen. That wife of yours is the most selfless individual I've ever met."

"You think you know her, but you don't. Do you know she has several times more money than all the people in the town of Laramie put together? Why do you suppose she chose our little town to wreak her havoc?"

"Ben, listen to yourself. Why are you so angry? I taught you years ago not to judge a person by the color of their skin, their education, or the amount of money in the bank. At the time, I was attempting to teach you a lesson on being kind to the poor. Never did I consider that you'd have animosity toward a person with money. The principle works both ways, you know. I thought you got over that hurdle of prejudice a few months ago. What brought this on, son?"

"I went to the bank after I put my family on the train." Ben grumbled under his breath. "I can't believe I let her take the children."

"Regardless of what you discovered at the bank, Cathleen is a good woman, and she loves you and your children. She might have withheld some information, but she's far from deceitful. Have you heard from her since she arrived in Boston?"

"I received one letter which sounded like the Cathleen I thought I married, but it's too much. She even paid off my bank loan. What kind of woman has that kind of money?"

"I'd say she's a very unselfish woman who loves her family. Are you going to judge every woman from the East against one unpleasant experience? You never told us what happened in Boston."

"The pain was too great, Papa. I dismissed that time as the worst mistake of my life and came home to my childhood friend where I belonged. Lana understood and gladly forgave my few months of insanity. Now, I seem to have made an even greater mistake."

"You're not thinking clearly, son, or you wouldn't judge Cathleen based on one bad experience. Think about her character, her kindness to everyone she meets, and her love for the children. Did you ever consider she might have withheld the information because she feared your reaction? You weren't the most cooperative groom at first, but I saw the way you looked at her before she boarded the train. You're in love with her.

"Go home, Ben, and pray for your wife and family. Ask God to remind you of how you felt when you held her in your arms that last time. Remember the good that characterized her from the very beginning. Don't allow stubborn pride to rob you of love."

## Chapter Sixteen

With his father's words ringing in his head, Ben left the road and gave Prince his head to gallop across the meadow. Cathleen's bulging bank account kept interfering with any voice of reason. He saw bank notes instead of trees and piles of gold bullion instead of mountain vistas. He felt like one of Myriam's fish floundering on the bank. When the horse slowed to a walk and approached the creek, Ben slid off and took a few steps before falling to his knees at the spot he'd picnicked with Cathleen and the children. The peaceful memory pricked his heart as the damp moss saturated the knees of his pants.

The ache in his chest grew stronger. Though his father asked him to pray, only words of anger, doubt, and despair poured from his mouth. *O God, how could you let this happen? I've been deceived again by a spoiled society woman. She's stolen my children and my heart. I can't live like this, help me.*

His anger exhausted, Ben cradled his head on his arms and waited. Even sounds of the creek seemed to disappear as his thoughts turned to Cathleen. The oneness he experienced on their last night together started a fire deep in his belly. His body shook under the force of raw passion, and he collapsed onto the cool bed of moss. Neither his college girlfriend nor Lana ever made him feel this way. But was love enough?

When Ben regained control of his emotions, he did as his father suggested and prayed for his family. He asked God to forgive him for jumping to conclusions. If he loved his wife, he'd patiently wait to hear her reason for withholding such vital information. Though her money built a wall between them, he asked God to fill him with the kind of love that overcomes fear and suspicion. Toward the end of his prayer, an unfamiliar thought popped into his mind:—could God have possibly chosen him for Cathleen?

At the sound of splashing water, he stood and wiped a few twigs from his trousers. The pleasant sound reminded him of a recent afternoon with his wife and children. They'd taken a picnic supper to the creek to cool off. Cathleen held Annie and let the cold water tickle her toes. Their giggles spread to his son who wanted the same from him. Not once did he consider her unworthy of his love and affection. How could he allow such a stumbling block to come between them?

"Hey, Ben, you missing your family?"

As Jim and Myriam came downstream, Ben noticed the older couple's undaunted affection. His friend guided his wife gently through the rapids created by the fast-moving water. "Yes, I am. Are you enjoying your lazy Sunday afternoon?"

"We missed you at church the last couple of weeks. Are you ready for the roundup?"

"I think so. I plan to go over the list one more time with Dan this evening. We'll be ready to head out first thing tomorrow. How about you?"

"We're ready. I'm glad ole grizzly can't give us any more problems." Ben's heart leaped when he remembered that frightening day. If not for Cathleen ... *Oh, God.*

Ben turned back to Jim and Myriam. "You have no idea how thankful I am. I trust you and the men enjoyed the feast."

"We did. How about you? Had Cathleen eaten bear before?"

Ben laughed and shook his head. "My squeamish wife would have none of it. Dan brought a couple of steaks over from the bunk house. They were cooked to perfection, but the memories of the experience upset Cathleen so much, she asked him to take them away. My mouth watered as the wild aromas drifted past me and out the door."

Jim threw his head back with peals of laughter. "My sympathies, friend. The sacrifices we make for our wives and children."

Ben remounted Prince and touched the edge of his hat in farewell. Remembering the bear, he realized again how close he'd come to losing his family—not just a train ride away but forever. Cathleen would have died before she allowed that beast near the children. His head dropped in shame at the anger and bitterness he'd harbored against her. How easily he'd forgotten his wife's sacrificial heart and slipped back into self-preservation. A few morsels of bear meat in no way compared to the sacrifices Cathleen had made for his family.

Back at the barn Dan, Pedro, and Walt were deep in conversation. "What's going on?"

"I'm not sure you'll be happy with the situation, but you need to see what arrived this afternoon."

Dan directed him out the door and toward the back of the barn. A group of Mexicans were assembling a tent and making themselves at home. "Pedro, do you know these people?"

Pedro shifted restlessly as he studied his cowboy boots. "My family, sir," he answered in broken English. "This my wife, Maria, my sons, Alejandro and Mateo and my daughter, Mariana. The other woman is my wife's sister. They come without me knowing, and I not know Isabella come with them."

"I wish they had waited until we could build the new ranch house and expand the cabin. With us heading out tomorrow, this is the worst possible time for them to show up."

Pedro shrugged his shoulders and looked down, waiting for a verdict. Ben took off his hat and wiped the sweat with his shirt sleeve. "Guess there's nothing to be done. Since Cathleen's away, you might as well move your family into the cabin. Maria can pack up our personal items, and we'll store them in one of the empty stalls until we have the other house built. I'll clean out anything that belongs to me and move my clothes into the bunkhouse."

Memories overwhelmed Ben when he entered the cabin and looked around. The smell of lilac smarted his eyes and reminded him of the mysterious woman he'd married. Though she came unwanted, she brought with her the healing balm that he needed. Everywhere he turned, he found evidence of her touch. Using the stack of clothes from the dresser, he wiped the moisture from his eyes. Even the laundry reminded him of her unselfishness. How could he have judged her with such harshness when she brought nothing but love and kindness into his home? Ben shook his head at his irrational behavior. He'd have to let Maria deal with the rest—he couldn't turn to mush in front of his men or the new arrivals.

Leaving the cabin, he heard Pedro translating the plan to his family. The only thing he understood were the excited gestures as his ranch hand pointed toward Ben's former residence. If he hadn't misinterpreted the signals, the visitors were excited about their new home. "Gracias" he understood, as they smiled, bowed and repeated the word over and over.

Ben reprimanded himself for not learning their language—most of his men struggled to understand and follow his orders. When he hired Dan to oversee the ranch, he felt blessed that the man spoke fluent Spanish. But Dan wasn't always around. Now he had a houseful of Mexicans who'd also look at him with blank stares. Poor Cathleen. How would she ever communicate with Maria?

With fewer memories to haunt him, Ben considered the bunkhouse a blessing until he tried to find a comfortable spot on the too-short cot. He thought back to the first night after he'd married Cathleen. The knock on the door and those revealing nightclothes robbed him of sleep. After a few more tosses and turns, he went outside to the pump and doused his head with cool water. Looking up, Ben watched a star shoot across the sky. He wondered if Cathleen had this kind of view in Boston. What a fool he'd been to let her go. *Pull yourself together, cowboy. You've got a roundup in a few hours. No time for crying over losses.*

At four the next morning Ben awakened to the clang of the bell and the smell of coffee coming from the dining hall. Strong and pungent—just the way he liked his brew. As he pulled on his jeans and let his eyes adjust to the trickle of light coming through the door, he looked back at the rumpled sheet and remembered his sleepless night. How would he survive the long day?

"Hey, boss man. You ready to round up some cattle?" The energetic Dan stuck his head in the door grinning at Ben's unenthusiastic response. "I know. You'd rather be in Boston with your pretty wife"

"I'd rather be anywhere than that narrow cot. Don't we have a larger version somewhere?"

"Clint nabbed the only extra-long-sized cot for the chuckwagon. He said his rheumatism wouldn't take another year of sleeping on the ground."

"Fair enough. I'd rather not inconvenience my cookie." Ben knew the inadequate cot hadn't kept him awake, but he couldn't tell Dan how much he needed to hold his wife and kiss his babies one more time. His men would think him a sissy, and he was inclined to agree. He shook himself and stepped out into an early morning mist. After a visit to the outhouse, he stopped by the pump and splashed more cold water on his face—this time to clear his mind for the busy day ahead. Not only would he need his own wits about him but those of every available vaquero. The next two weeks would be taxing enough without him acting like a love-sick puppy.

The chow bell rang, and Ben headed to the dining hall. With his breakfast in hand, he found Dan sitting alone reading his Bible. The young man kept his priorities straighter than his boss ever did. Though he hated to disturb Dan's reading, he had no choice.

"What's the deal with Pedro's family? Did they get settled in the cabin?"

"As far as I can tell. According to Pedro, they were forced to leave Mexico when the oldest son found himself in trouble with the law. Alejandro fought against three gringos who were attacking Maria's sister. And yes, they seem happy with a roof over their heads, after sleeping for weeks out in the open."

"Please tell me you don't mean the aunt they brought along?"

Dan pinched his eyebrows together. "The one and the same. I had never felt happier to see someone as I did you when you rode in yesterday. I thought I'd entered the Spanish/American war at the heat of battle. Pedro's bristles were raised pretty good after hearing his family's explanation for coming without his consent. He couldn't decide whose neck to ring first. Your calm reaction to the situation helped settle him down."

"I wasn't too happy with their arrival in the middle of preparations for the roundup, but what's done is done. You don't think the sister-in-law will be a problem, do you?"

"She's trouble. You can tell by looking at her."

"Now, Dan, hasn't that book you've been reading taught you anything? We don't judge people by their outward appearance. She can't help that she's pretty and probably attracts more attention than is good for any woman. I just hope Pedro can keep her in line."

"I hope so too. Speaking of his family, I'd like to take Pedro's boys with us. He says they're good drovers, and we could use a couple more hands. Are you still leaving Walt behind?"

"That was the plan when Cathleen and the children were here. I'm sure Pedro's women can care for the farm animals and the garden, but I hesitate to leave them without the protection of at least one man. Since Toby seems upset by the intrusion of the strangers, I'll probably take him with us. What are your thoughts?"

"I agree. I'd feel better if we left Walt here. Like Clint, he's getting a little old to sleep on the ground."

With the personnel questions settled, Ben finished his breakfast and gulped down a second cup of the dark coffee. He rose when he heard the familiar order from Dan, "Monten, buckaroos. Es hors de montar." He repeated the words in English, "Mount up, buckaroos. Time to ride."

As Ben threw his bedroll to Clint at the back of the chuckwagon, he noticed Pedro bestowing passionate kisses on his wife. Each time the cowboy tried to leave, she pulled him back for more. It didn't take much imagination to guess what kind of night that man had. Nothing similar to his own—that's for sure.

Not wishing to intrude on their romantic farewell, Ben turned his attention toward the Spanish beauty standing near the pump. One hand on her hip and a frown on her face contrasted to the other hand spread across her chest. Her index finger massaged her throat as her big brown eyes glistened with tears.

When Ben searched for the object of her attention, he noticed José adjusting his saddle and staring, wide-eyed over his horse at Isabella. Too bad, Ben thought as he followed the young woman's eyes toward Dan. His foreman sat straight-backed on his mount and returned the woman's glare with one of angry defiance. Poor José—stricken with unrequited love. As for Dan, better him than his boss.

Ben continued to watch the threesome as Dan huffed and turned away in frustration. Jerking the reins with a stronger force than necessary, he moved the horse forward and signaled for the caravan to follow. José mounted his horse with one last look at the beauty that had captured his attention.

Mounting his own horse, Ben rushed to pull Prince in line with Dan's horse. "Did you have words with Isabella? She doesn't look too happy."

"Let's just say I put her in her place when she rolled those sexy browns at me. With all the good-looking vaqueros here, why would she want to sink her fangs into a gringo like me?"

"Really? What did you say to discourage her?"

"I'm not in grade school, Ben. Let it be."

Ben snorted and turned back to check on Clint. He had enough women problems of his own without taking on Dan's. His cookie had Mateo, Pedro's youngest son, riding on the wagon bench with him. At least somebody was in a good mood. Spanish flew from Clint's mouth as if it were his native tongue. Whatever they discussed, the older man had the boy's undivided attention. How could the owner be the last person on the ranch to learn the language of his cowhands?

# Chapter Seventeen

Ben and Dan had made plans for the roundup along with Jim Henson and his foreman. In a central location, they'd built two massive holding pens to serve as headquarters for the next few weeks. Chuck wagons from each ranch made camp between the enclosed areas. Four teams were sent in different directions. A rancher or foreman headed each team. The first team back would begin separating and tagging the cattle for market.

After a few days out on the range, Pedro's oldest son, Alejandro, took over as wrangler to care for the horses. His younger brother helped Clint with the meals when he wasn't needed elsewhere. Ben was impressed with the boys' behavior and work ethic. The timing of their arrival might have been a surprise, but in the long run, he appreciated the extra hands.

By the beginning of week two, Ben could tell from counting the herds they would have a profitable year. The steers culled out to sell never looked better while the cows and calves left behind were healthy and virile. The challenge would be to ship the steers to Chicago before the market became glutted. With the ranch situated so close to the railhead, the last leg of the journey would be easy on everyone, including the cattle.

The winters were hard on livestock out West where snow often drifted higher than a man's head, but Ben's cattle had the stamina to survive. They were crossbred with Longhorns for that very reason. The European breeds with their tender steaks wouldn't survive without the mix of those hardy bloodlines. Things were looking up, and he felt grateful.

Pedro had the fire going and the iron sat ready, glowing white with heat. Ben couldn't get away fast enough. Branding the young cows and steers left a bad taste in his mouth. He used the excuse of driving a few cows over to his neighbor's lot, but he suspected the men knew how he felt. They grinned at each other when his careful search resulted in only a few strays belonging to Jim.

The cows weren't interested in leaving their feast of hay, but Ben threatened them with his cattle probe. The calves bawled, rushing to catch up with their mothers. The noxious smell of burning flesh followed him across the field and made him shiver. He found nothing gratifying about the procedure except that when the herd returned to the range, they'd carry the mark of the slanted "S" with them. He'd only gone a short distance, when he got a whiff of the Henson brand burning into their own calves. Ben cringed and longed for a breath of fresh air.

After more than three weeks of searching gullies, hills, and plains, the last of the vaqueros rode into camp driving a few strays. Ben knew the time had come to discontinue the search. He'd already helped Jim butcher a fat steer for their celebration supper. Now that was the kind of burning flesh he loved to smell—tender steaks sizzling over the open pit. Their men would eat well tonight before moving the first herd of cattle into Laramie the next morning.

Following the meal of huge steaks and baked potatoes, the men groaned with pleasure at the sight of Clint's apple pies. His cookie knew how to cook regardless of the circumstances.

And that wasn't all he could do. The older cowpoke pulled out his fiddle, and the camp came alive with music. He started with his favorites, "Home on the Range" and "Get Along Little Doggies." The men settled into peaceful contentment.

But the vaqueros had their own brand of music. Pedro disappeared briefly and returned carrying a *requinto*. He tapped his foot and counted in Spanish to pick up the beat. Clint's head went back in a hearty laugh, and his strings sizzled as they caught the new tempo.

Ben chuckled when some of the younger men left their seats clapping in time with the music. They formed a circle around the campfire and let their feet do the talking. One of the dancers kept the beat with the clicking rattle of castanets. The boys laughed, pushed, and teased when a tenderfoot gringo tried to mimic the fast-paced steps.

Pedro's boys acted quiet and shy around Ben, but from the moment their father made the first strum of his instrument, they jumped to their feet with the other vaqueros. A sparkle of pride danced in Pedro's eyes as he watched the boys enter the fray. Enthusiasm and energy popped along with the dry branches burning on the fire. Even Jim's boys danced with their new Mexican friends. While Ben felt ready to hit the sack, the boys looked as if they could dance all night.

When Dan stood and stretched, Clint and Pedro nodded to each other. The lively tunes faded into the melancholy sounds of Clint's rich baritone. "Swing Low, Sweet Chariot" filled the night air. The dancers arched their backs and slowly moved to their bedrolls. Those assigned night watch dispersed to their posts as the last vibration from Clint's fiddle faded. Contrasting sounds took the place of the music—a lone coyote in the distance and frogs in the creek competed with the bray of cattle and the occasional neigh of a horse.

Ben settled his bedroll on the trampled grass and watched the sparks fly from the fire. Toby arrived from his nightly hunt, panting, nudging Ben's arm and seeking approval.

"Good boy. You worked hard today, my friend." Ben gave the dog a hearty rubdown before he snapped his fingers and pointed to the ground. The dog twisted and turned several times before Ben felt warmth against his back. He reached behind him and gave Toby an affectionate pat before shifting his own position. The dog moved with him, and soon, Ben heard soft snores behind him. He pinched his nose and breathed through his mouth to dispel the pungent, wet-dog odor coming from his bedfellow. What he wouldn't give for a whiff of his wife's perfume.

*Cathleen.* Thoughts of his beautiful wife assaulted his whole body with tremors. He didn't care how much money she had. That last night together bonded them in such a way he felt lost without her. Ben pulled his knees tight against his chest to ease the pain. With no relief, he turned over and moaned when a rock pierced his thigh. He removed the sharp object and tossed it aside.

Toby whined in protest. A sudden chill hit his back. Ben lifted his head, curious to see where the dog had gone. He watched Toby turn his head and sniff the air. Finding his target, he took one last look at Ben and made himself comfortable next to Dan. Even his dog had abandoned him. Longing for his wife's slinky nightgown had robbed him of his companion and the satisfaction he should feel over a successful roundup.

Sleep came and went throughout the night, but his thoughts of Cathleen made their way into his dreams and continued to torment him. Was she thinking of him? Did she miss him as much as he missed her? How could one woman wreak havoc from miles away.

The ranchers arranged with the train officials to move the cattle by smaller herds to the holding pens at the railhead. Only a few hundred could be transported with each shipment. Jim and some of his wranglers had left early with the first herd. Ben and his men hauled bales of hay from the barn to fatten up the remaining steers. When the last of his neighbor's cattle had been loaded, Jim would travel to Chicago to coordinate with the buyers while Ben supervised the transport of his own herd.

After the last steers were loaded, some of the temporary hands would hang out in Laramie until their bosses returned with the long-awaited payment. Their pockets itched with the promise of a hefty bonus if the beef brought the expected price. The saloon owner would entertain several while the regulars would stop by the general store and then return to the ranch.

As the train pulled out of the station a few days later, Ben hopped on board. He'd stopped by the creek to wash away the weeks of grime before donning his best suit and trailing the last of the steers into town. If he hadn't given his house to Pedro's family, he'd catch the next train to Boston. The idea of Cathleen's return without a place to live demanded he waste no time building their new home.

After Dan, Clint, and Pedro packed away the roundup gear, he'd asked them to clear the area designated for the house. The building supplies unavailable in Laramie would be purchased before Ben left Chicago. Topping his list was a modern cookstove he found advertised in one of Harvey's catalogs. Maria would eventually do most of the cooking, but Cathleen would want something better than the unreliable stove she'd grappled with the past few months. He chuckled thinking of his wife's complaints against the beast she called, "Sassy Sally."

Ben fumbled inside his coat pocket for his kerchief as he searched the Chicago stockyard for his friend. He could almost see the foul-smelling fumes rising above the thousands of bawling cattle. He wiped the sweat from his brow, sniffed for a slight breeze and found Jim half-way down the walkway.

"Looks like we arrived before the onslaught." Jim greeted him with a satisfactory smile. They shook hands and gave each other a hearty pat on the back.

"More cattle are arriving every day, but the market isn't nearly as crowded as last fall. We're fortunate too by how well our herd made the trip. I feel blessed we live close to the railhead. I've seen a few envious looks from the ranchers whose herds had to endure long drives. Look how healthy our steers are compared to those over there." Jim pointed to a neighboring pen where the occupants resembled cowhide stretched over bones.

"They'll need a couple of weeks of frenzied feeding to regain the body weight lost in transport. We should do well, my friend."

"Yes. I see the difference, and I agree that Laramie is perfect for cattle ranching. Though I wouldn't object to a few milder winters, I'm thankful my father answered the call to bring his new bride to Laramie long before the railroad made its way west. Not only is the area convenient, but the scenery makes the hours out on the range pleasant and peaceful."

"Yep. We are truly blessed. Did you hear from Cathleen before you boarded the train?"

Ben patted the pocket that bulged with the letter he'd read at least a dozen times. Any fears of his wife returning to a life in Boston flew out the window along with the feelings he harbored when she first left. Her words sounded similar to his own longing.

> What have you done to me, Ben Sorenson? Though the children have adjusted well, I'm miserable without you.

"The postmaster had the mail waiting for me as I dashed by on my way to the station. Mr. Dunkin is more of a romantic than he lets on. When I didn't give him a return letter for Cathleen, you should have heard the ruckus. He said if he had a pretty wife like her, he wouldn't let her out of his sight."

The men laughed at the confirmed bachelor's involvement in the love interest of his patrons. The jovial mood did much to cover the stench of the cattle as they made their way to the Exposition Center. Their herds were some of the first scheduled for auction.

After their stock went to the highest bidders, Ben left Jim at the hotel and visited a large general store in search of his wife's new cookstove. He longed for his family, and the temptation to trade his return ticket for passage to Boston gnawed in his gut. But remembering that his former home had been turned into a Spanish casita was reason enough to resist the temptation. Despite the eastward pull, he'd be on the morning train to Laramie.

# Chapter Eighteen

Six long weeks away from her husband, and Cathleen ached for his arms. Only her dread of the tortuous train ride kept her from buying a return ticket. A few hours into the trip, her flu symptoms had returned, and she felt too sick to enjoy the benefits of the private car. The frequent stops jerked and pulled her until her head ached and her stomach quivered. She could barely hold her head up to feed herself much less take care of the children. She kept to her bed for most of the trip.

Every waking moment, Sammy rushed from one window to the next afraid he'd miss something. While the rocking of the car made Cathleen dizzy, the steady rhythm had the opposite effect on Annie. She napped longer and rarely woke during the night. When she did, Cathleen's father took care of her. His soothing voice and soft hum calmed the baby while they waited for the porter to bring a bottle of warm milk. Annie didn't seem to mind as long as she could see her mama reclining on the opposite side of the car. The child lifted her head and stretched her neck until their eyes met. Then she'd go back to the bottle. If not for their grandfather, the children would have been neglected.

Even after the train came to a halt, Cathleen's body continued to sway, mimicking the constant motion. She stepped off the train in Boston on weak, wobbly legs. Scanning the crowds, she longed to see her husband's face— the kind man she'd left behind in Laramie.

Despite the telegram her father had sent, her stubborn mother chose not to meet them at the station. Since she'd not been told about the children or her daughter's illness, Cathleen wondered if that would have made a difference. When they arrived at the house, Cathleen lingered in the motor car with Annie, dreading what awaited inside.

While she gathered some of her belongings, her father bounced up the front steps with Sammy. Winston opened the car door and waited to assist Cathleen. Looking past the chauffeur, she watched her father and Jenson greet one another at the top of the stairs. The butler stood with one hand on the open door and reached for her father's portmanteau with the other. Their discussion would have been comical if not for the sinking feeling in the pit of her stomach.

"Why don't you take the baby from Cathleen while Winston helps her out of the car?"

The proud butler recoiled as if he'd been asked to handle a poisonous snake. "I beg your pardon?"

"Annie won't bite, Jenson. She's just a baby, and she'll be more afraid of you than you are of her." Jenson wrinkled his face and looked toward the car.

Reluctantly the butler went down the steps and scowled at Cathleen. He picked up Annie and held her at arm's length. Cathleen couldn't fault the man. His reaction matched her own first encounter with the child.

Sensing his unease, Annie kicked and screamed and reached flailing arms toward her mother. Jenson, acting as if someone set a fire under him, hurried up the steps and practically threw the baby at her grandfather. With upturned nose, the butler sniffed, straightened his clothes, and stepped as far away from the children as possible. Cathleen relaxed when Annie stopped crying and snuggled against her affectionate father. No need to worry over Jenson. She'd learned to tolerate his irksome personality years ago. The person she dreaded more waited in the parlor.

Winston chuckled and stared after Jenson in disbelief. "Never saw the fuddy-duddy so rattled."

"Be nice, Winston."

"Miss Cathleen,"—the chauffeur turned back to her—"please leave everything behind. I'll bring your belongings in with the luggage. I'm sorry you've been sick, but what a pleasure to have you home."

"Thank you, Winston. I trust you and your parents are well?"

"They are, and they're looking forward to seeing you, miss … er … ma'am."

Winston offered his arm and helped her up the steps. The man was both handsome and a charmer. If he'd been born into an affluent family, anxious mothers would be begging him to marry their daughters. Cathleen sighed at the injustice.

At the landing, Winston withdrew and returned to the car while Cathleen took Annie and followed her father into the drawing room. The baby smothered her face against Cathleen's neck once they approached her mother.

"Cathleen, I'm so glad you finally came to your sens—" Her mother's mouth dropped open when she realized her daughter hadn't arrived alone. "What have you done? Who are these children?" her mother shrieked.

The tension in Cathleen's shoulders subsided as her father took over the introductions. "Eugenia, I'd like you to meet Cathleen's stepchildren. This handsome young man is Sammy. Can you shake hands with your grandmother, Sammy?"

Her mother's wrinkled frown deepened at the word *grandmother*. The blood drained from her face, and she looked as though she might faint. She eyed Sammy with disgust and ignored his outstretched hand.

"What is the meaning of this, Cathleen? How could you do this to me? I am not a grandmother, and I will not accept someone else's children in my home. Get rid of them immediately."

Cathleen could see her father's Irish temper rising along with her own. His faced turned red, and he held his hand in front of Sammy as if protecting him from assault. "Eugenia, you will not say such things before our daughter and her children. She's been unwell for several weeks and has come a long way to see you."

Her father turned back to Jenson, who listened at the door with his mouth agape. "Jenson, would you ask Mrs. Murphy to take Cathleen and the children upstairs. The children, of course, will be in the nursery, and the room across the hall should be made up for Cathleen."

"Cathleen will stay in her old room where she belongs."

A cloud formed around Cathleen's head and she closed her ears to the argument. Her head swirled and her vision blurred like she'd boarded a fast-moving merry-go-round. The angry voices faded into oblivion. The last thing she remembered was the sensation of falling with Annie still clutching her clothes.

"Miss Cathleen, wake up, honey!"

Cathleen coughed and turned her head away from the bottle of smelling salts. Mrs. Murphy stood over her wearing her perpetual frown. *Wasn't anyone happy in this household?* Cathleen heard Annie crying. When she pushed the housekeeper away and tried to stand, dizziness forced her to retake her seat on the sofa.

"Where are the children?" Cathleen held her head and made another attempt to stand. Rising in slow motion, she stood and reached for her father's arm.

"They'll be fine as soon as they see you. One of the maids took them into the kitchen. I'll ask Nella to bring them back when you feel like dealing with them."

The worried look on her father's face contrasted with the angry glare coming from her mother. When the woman tried to speak, Father stopped her. "We can talk about this later, dear. I know you were expecting something different, but trust me for once. Our lives are about to get better."

Her father ignored the angry scowl on his wife's face and turned his attention to his daughter. "Are you feeling better now, Cathleen?"

"Yes. I'm fine, Father. I'll get the children and take them upstairs. Thank you for your hospitality, Mother. If we're too much of an inconvenience, the children and I can always stay at Grandmother's house."

"Of course, you'll stay here. It seems I've been overruled." Her mother sniffed into her handkerchief. Father must have stood up for her while she was unconscious. Could she have fainted on purpose to avoid the conflict?

The minute she opened the swinging doors into the kitchen, Sammy came running. He captured her legs with a tight hug. "Sammy make Mama better."

"That's right, little man. I can't do without your hugs and kisses. We'll all feel better with a little rest. Looks as though your sister has cried herself to sleep."

Cathleen tried to take Annie from Nella, but her father intervened. "Let Nella take her upstairs for you. Give me your hand, Sammy, and we'll climb the stairs together."

The unbelievable change she'd seen in her father brought tears to her eyes. For years, she had longed for such attention.

Her mother, on the other hand, made her want to return to Wyoming—a place where she'd been welcomed with open arms. In her new hometown, she was accepted without fault or unreasonable expectations. There her family and friends loved her and went to great efforts to make her life easier.

Cathleen struggled against exhaustion. Her breathing came in short gasps before she reached the top of the stairs. She had to hold on to the banister to regain her strength before walking down the hall toward the nursery. Feeling a chill, she pulled the collar of her blouse tighter around her neck. The large mansion felt cold and unwelcoming as she went to find the housekeeper.

"The upstairs maid hasn't had time to prepare your room, Miss Cathleen, but the nursery is ready for the children."

Cathleen ignored Mrs. Murphy's reference to her as a "miss," and entered the room where she'd spent many hours before her sixth birthday. Nella put Annie in the crib, and Cathleen snuggled with Sammy on the small bed across the room. Her father gave them each a kiss and held the door for the maid to leave ahead of him.

"We'll be downstairs if you need us. Meanwhile I have a few feathers to smooth over with your mother." Father winked as he closed the door.

# Chapter Nineteen

Despite missing Ben, Cathleen's health gradually improved, and she established a routine with the children. The relationship with her mother took considerably longer. Eugenia Doyle wanted her daughter home on her terms—no children and no husband. Since the two women were at an impasse, Cathleen ignored her mother and tried to make the best of her time away from her husband.

Unable to sleep past dawn, Cathleen often dressed early and walked in the garden. Despite the efficient gardener, she couldn't help but pull a stray weed or pinch off a few dried blossoms. With little to do, she felt bored and unsettled.

"Look what I found." Winston came around the corner of the house pushing a baby carriage.

"Now that you're feeling better, I thought you might want to take the children to the park."

The carriage had been cleaned and polished until the chrome reflected the morning sun. "The carriage must have been mine, but I have no recollection. It's in great shape. Where did you find it?"

"Above the stable … er … garage. Even though your father got rid of the horses, to me it's still the stable where we played with the cats."

Cathleen laughed at her friend's memory. "Thank you for finding the carriage. Yes, I've been wanting to take the children to the park."

During an early morning stroll with the children, she heard whimpering that sounded foreign against the peaceful setting. Cathleen stopped the squeak of the carriage wheels and listened. Even the songbirds had hushed their singing. Easing further down the path, she came upon a young woman wearing a maid's uniform. Slumped over on one of the park benches, the distraught girl hid her face and cried into her apron.

"I'm sorry to disturb you, miss. Is there something I can do for you?"

Fearful eyes, wet with tears met Cathleen's gaze. "No, please forgive me. I must go."

Sniffling, she stood to leave, but Sammy's squeals of laughter caught her attention. He had discovered a massive pile of leaves near the path. The wind had drifted the red maple fronds against a low rock wall. He grew even more excited when he threw a handful into the air and watched them float down around him. "Snow, Mama. I play in the snow."

"Yes, Sammy, the leaves do remind us of falling snow. When we return to Wyoming, you can help me build a snowman with real snow. Would you like that?"

"Me build a big snowman."

Cathleen laughed as she watched the girl look with longing toward her son. Whatever troubled her seemed to diminish as she observed the joy on a little boy's face. "I used to love playing with my younger brother in the leaves. Your little boy reminds me of him."

"Where is your brother now?" Cathleen touched the girl's arm and urged her to sit beside her.

A sadness came over the distraught young woman, and she shook her head. "It seems so long ago. It hardly matters now."

"Everything matters when it comes to family. My name is Cathleen Sorenson. Perhaps I might help."

The girl peered intently at Cathleen before answering. "I don't know why someone like you would even talk to me. You obviously have money, and I just walked out on my only means of support. Unless you have a job for me, we have nothing in common."

Cathleen rubbed her chin while studying the girl. She was young, probably not more than sixteen, but Cathleen saw intelligence and kindness in her keen, blue eyes. "Your accent betrays you, my dear. You are not the normal servant girl. What is your name?"

The girl shifted nervously and frowned. "Don't be afraid. Whoever hurt you is no friend of mine. Please, I won't betray you. I want to help."

The maid cast a suspicious look at Cathleen, then flashed an appreciative smile at Sammy. He'd built a wall of leaves around him.

"Mama, I build a house."

"Yes, and it's a fine house too. What a creative boy you are!"

"My name is Bridget, Bridget Fulcher."

Bridget turned away. After a long pause, she glanced back at Cathleen as if begging for her to understand. "I don't know why I'm telling you this, but my parents died a few months ago and left my brother and me homeless and penniless. Because I'd turned sixteen the month before, I was put out on the street. Our house was sold to cover my father's debt, and my brother was sent to an orphanage.

"When I found a job as a maid in a nice home, I felt blessed to have a roof over my head. The housekeeper showed me kindness, and everything seemed fine. That is, until my employer's son arrived home from the university. The looks he gave me made me uncomfortable. If I came upon him in a room alone, I excused myself and worked in another area until I saw him leave.

"Once, he caught me as I entered the library. His hands were all over me before I could get away. He laughed and called after me, 'You escaped this time, little wench, but one day I will have you.'"

Cathleen reached over and patted her hand. "I couldn't sleep at night without barricading the keyless door with my trunk. I'd managed to escape his attention until last night when he caught me on the last step of the servants' stairway. The moment I started to scream, he put his hand over my mouth and slammed me against the wall. I knew I'd be ruined if I didn't do something. Using every ounce of strength, I pushed my body away far enough to knee him in the groin."

The girl stared into the distance. "When the beast turned me loose and doubled over in agony, I escaped and fled the house through the kitchen. I could hear him cursing and kicking the wall as I slammed the door behind me. I can't go back, not even to collect my belongings or the money I'm owed."

Cathleen put her arm around the weeping girl and remembered the brutality she'd received from filthy-minded men. "I'm sorry that happened to you. I don't understand why men have to be such beasts."

Cathleen shivered and pondered how much to share. "We have more in common than you realize."

The girl looked at her in disbelief while Cathleen briefly described her own experiences. "Escaping that terrible man my parents wanted me to marry was the best thing that ever happened to me. With a lot of patience and much prayer, God blessed me with a loving husband and these two beautiful children. I now live on a ranch in Laramie, Wyoming. I'm only visiting here for a couple more weeks, but I'm looking for a nanny who'd be willing to return with me. Would you consider working for me?"

Bridget's eyes grew round as if she couldn't believe her good fortune. Her face glowed and her eyes danced with hopeful possibilities. Cathleen reached over to hug her. "Does that mean you're willing to move out West with me?"

The girl slumped in her arms and gave a loud cry of anguish.

"What's the matter? You look the adventurous type; I thought you'd jump at the chance to leave Boston. Believe me, you won't have to worry about spoiled, unscrupulous men where we live. My husband would fire any of his men he suspected of mistreating a lady."

"It's my little brother, Miss Cathleen. He's only five years old. I can't leave Boston until I make enough money to support him and get him out of that orphanage. They refuse to allow me to visit him, because they claim I upset Joey and give him false hope. We belong together, but how will I ever make enough money to support us when I can't find work around here? Thank you for the generous offer, but I'll have to keep looking."

"You know you probably won't get a good reference from the family you left. The son is never wrong, you know. They will accuse you of leading him astray."

"You're probably right, but I could never desert Joey."

Cathleen stood and walked back and forth, worrying over Bridget's problem. The thought of a little boy separated from the one person who loved him motivated her to find a solution. She'd almost given up when a brilliant idea popped into her head. She ran back to Bridget and pulled her to her feet. "I don't know why this took so long to figure out. Let's go to the orphanage and get your brother."

Bridget shook her head. "What? I know you want to help, but didn't you hear what I said? They won't let me have him until I'm at least eighteen and have a paying job."

"But, don't you see, Bridget? I'm old enough to be Sammy's guardian, and I have money to support him."

The girl stood glued to the spot as though she were one of the statues scattered throughout the park. Cathleen took her by the hand. "Let me tell you a secret, Bridget. Money changes things every time, and I have money, lots of money. Believe me, Joey will not remain in that orphanage another night.

"Sammy, come hold Mama's hand. Annie's asleep so you'll have to walk."

Turning back to Bridget, "Now, just where is that place that's housing a little boy who favors Sammy? I'm about to find my son a playmate."

"Are you sure about this? Don't you have to talk to your husband?"

"I'm not adopting him, Bridget, just taking on the responsibility for his welfare until you're old enough to be his guardian. He's your family, and he should be with his big sister. The only immediate problem will be getting the two of you into my mother's house. She still has trouble accepting my own two children. I'm not sure how she'll feel about a couple more."

Cathleen waved her hand as if to dismiss the concern. "If mother has a problem, we'll just move into Grandmother's house. Before I leave town, I should hire a housekeeper and a gardener anyway. That's what we'll do." At the moment, she wasn't sure who she was addressing—herself or her newly acquired employee.

When she realized the distance to the orphanage, they returned to her parent's house and asked Winston to drive them. Cathleen smiled at the driver's reaction to Bridget. From the moment she introduced them, the young man acted like a different person. Unlike his usual friendly chatter, he didn't make a sound except for the nervous drumming of his fingers on the steering wheel. Bridget sat on the front seat beside him, studying her hands, acting shy and awkward while Winston had trouble keeping his eyes on the road. Too bad they were heading west in a few weeks.

When Cathleen presented her proposal to the orphanage director, he jumped at the idea of one less mouth to feed. The generous check placed in the middle of his desk didn't hurt either. The look on that little boy's face was worth every penny when he saw his sister and realized they'd be leaving the orphanage together.

On the return trip, the little boy sitting between Winston and Bridget broke the awkward silence. Joey even turned around to make friends with Sammy and to tickle Annie's bare toes. The child refused to keep shoes on her feet.

Winston dropped Cathleen and her children at the front of the house. Not wanting to upset her mother more than necessary, she instructed him to drive Bridget and Joey around to the servants' entrance. Her mother's rules were a nuisance now that she'd experienced the casual behavior on the ranch.

After she asked Nella to watch the little ones, she met Bridget and Joey in the kitchen and introduced them to the housekeeper. "Mrs. Murphy, could you have someone take Bridget's bag to the room I've been using across from the nursery."

The housekeeper looked around for the luggage as the color drained from Bridget's face. Cathleen chastised herself for her embarrassing mistake—the girl had no belongings. Joey clutched only a brown paper sack to his chest. "I'm sorry, Bridget. I forgot that we still have to pick up your things."

Turning back to the housekeeper, "Regardless, please have someone prepare her room. I've hired her to take over the care of the children. Her little brother can share the room with her or stay in the nursery, whichever Bridget prefers. I'll move back into my old room."

Mrs. Murphy hesitated. "Have you talked to Mrs. Doyle about this?"

"Not yet, but I'm on my way to see her now. Is she in the dayroom?"

The housekeeper ordered Bridget and Joey to remain in the kitchen, stuck out her chin, straightened her back, and vacated the room with a haughty huff. She left no doubt in Cathleen's mind where she was heading.

"Don't worry about your things, Bridget. We'll go out tomorrow and replace them. Looks as if Joey could also use a few items."

Bridget smiled through the tears puddling her eyes. "I don't know how to thank you."

Cathleen gave the girl a tender hug and patted the little boy on the head before turning her attention toward the matter at hand.

Taking her time, Cathleen arrived just as Mrs. Murphy finished her extensive list of grievances. Her mother's facial wrinkles had deepened into a severe frown. Once again,

Cathleen had upset her mother and wondered if she would ever learn to please her.

"It will be fine, Mother. I can't expect you to house my employee and her brother while we're guests here. I'll open Grandmother's house and move over there. Besides, I need to hire someone to manage the house before I return home."

Her mother wrung her hands and gazed about the room as if searching for the right response. "This is your home, Cathleen. You don't have to move. Perhaps the nanny can take the children to the other house with her. That would be more comfortable for everyone."

"You mean more comfortable for you? I know my marriage is hard for you to accept, but I love my new family. My children will either stay here with me or we will be together at Grandmother's house. I will not be separated from them."

Her mother turned her back on her. Wishing to find common ground, Cathleen changed the subject. "Have you heard of a housekeeper or gardener who might need work?"

Looking back at Cathleen, her mother snorted. "If there was someone available, they wouldn't be qualified. Anyone worth having gets snapped up the minute they become available." Mother rolled her eyes and turned her head as if her daughter expected the impossible.

"I'm going to pray about finding someone. God sent me Bridget without the least effort on my part. If I trust him, he will do the same with this other situation."

A curious expression swept over her mother's face, and Cathleen saw interest for the first time. "I used to despise your grandmother for giving all the credit to God. Now you and your father sound just like her." Tears glistened her mother's eyes. She turned away and pulled her handkerchief from her sleeve.

"You should try prayer for yourself, Mother. I never felt real peace until I learned to trust God. Sometimes he answers before I even ask. I'd only thought about needing someone for the children. Ben plans to bring a family from Mexico to cook and clean, but I doubt they speak English. I prefer an educated person like Bridget to care for my children and assist with their education. Her little brother can learn along with them."

Cathleen saw her mother stiffen at the mention of another child in her home. Or, perhaps she resented her reference to Ben's children. She had yet to accept them as her grandchildren. "Mother, is something wrong?"

"You aren't going to annul your marriage or give those children back to their father, are you?"

"No, Mother. I can't imagine life without Ben or the children. God sent me to them at a time when they needed me, and I needed them. For the sake of our relationship, please try to accept my family."

"I'll try, Cathleen, but it won't be easy. I had such great plans for you here in Boston where we could shop and enjoy a social life together. Introducing you at soirees and balls gave me a sense of worth and importance. I was proud to have such a beautiful daughter." Her mother sniffed and dropped her shoulders in resignation. "But I see that isn't what you want. We don't have anything in common. Looking back, I'm not sure we ever did."

"I'm sorry, Mother. Forgive me for not being the daughter you wanted, but I can't change who I am. Perhaps if we worked at listening to one another, we could find mutual interests and build a relationship from there."

Cathleen hugged her mother before leaving the room. A sadness crept over her when she considered the impossibility of ever meeting her mother's expectations.

Bridget turned out to be a well-qualified nanny. Growing up with a younger brother, she had experience caring for children. With little effort, Annie and Sammy warmed to the young woman, while Cathleen moped around at the opposite end of the house, bored and without purpose. Relinquishing the care of the children hadn't been her original plan.

While the arrangement made her mother happy, being that far removed from the nursery kept Cathleen in a constant state of worry. What if Annie needed her in the middle of the night and no one heard her cries? To alleviate Cathleen's fears, Bridget had the baby's crib moved into her own room. Though the girl used the excuse the move would keep Annie from disturbing the boys, Cathleen recognized the concern and sensitivity of her young friend. She had to reprimand herself for feeling jealous of the bond she saw forming between the children and their nanny.

When the boredom became too great, Cathleen made her way to the nursery. Bridget seemed relieved with a little adult conversation while Cathleen wanted nothing more than to engage the young minds of her children. Though she knew she'd done the right thing by offering the young woman a job, she couldn't release the responsibility.

Finding a caretaker for her grandmother's house proved more difficult than securing a nanny. Her mother had been right. Every person she'd interviewed presented either poor or no references at all. She couldn't return to her husband until she found someone responsible. Her grandmother's will had designated retirement trusts for the few remaining servants who vacated the house soon after the funeral. Though she knew they'd earned their reward, Cathleen couldn't allow the beloved home to depreciate for lack of care. Just when she'd about given up hope and considered bringing some of her grandmother's staff out of retirement, Bridget knocked at her bedroom door.

"May I talk with you about something?"

"Of course. How can I help?"

"When my parents passed away, Joey and I were not the only victims. My father and his brother had shared ownership of a business importing fabrics. The business was heavily indebted. As a result, my uncle also lost his home and means of support. Uncle Sean took a job in a fabric mill. He and Aunt Alice have five children but can only afford the rent of a small apartment. That's why they couldn't take in my brother and me when we lost our parents.

"At first, I resented him for turning us away, but when I saw the way they lived, I understood. They lost a lovely, spacious home in a good neighborhood. They now live in squalor, close to poverty. My uncle said that rejecting us was the hardest decision he'd ever made."

Tears glistened in the girl's eyes as she remembered her family in better circumstances. "Would you consider hiring my aunt and uncle to take care of your grandmother's house? I know they'd do a good job, and you'd never have to worry about the place with my uncle in charge."

For the first time since she'd decided to keep the house, Cathleen dared to hope she might have found a solution. But what would five young children do to that beautiful old home? Would her worry over the wear and tear on the house overshadow her relief in securing a caretaker? Bridget patted her hand and gave her an understanding look.

"I know you're concerned about that many children in such a fine house. The youngest just turned eight and the oldest is almost sixteen. Believe me, they're bright, well-behaved children. Please, at least consider the possibility and talk to my uncle."

"Are you a mind reader in addition to your other qualifications? That's exactly why I hesitated. I imagined my grandmother's beautiful home being damaged. Are you sure about this?"

As she reached for Cathleen's hand, the girl seemed far older than sixteen. "You will not be disappointed and neither will my uncle's family. You could be the answer to another prayer."

"If you're sure, I should meet with them and see the situation for myself."

The next day, Cathleen left the children in the care of her father and asked Winston to drive her and Bridget to the shabbiest neighborhood she'd ever seen. After he saw the address, he almost refused to take them. The evidence of poverty hung out on every street corner. Rodents sifted through the rot and decay. The wind blew loose trash into the street. How did anyone stay healthy in such an environment?

Cathleen almost reneged when Winston stopped in front of the tenement building where Bridget's family lived. The stench in the hallway brought back memories of her first trip to the outhouse at the ranch. Coupled with the smell of boiling cabbage, she wanted to gag. She pulled her handkerchief over her nose and knocked on the filthy door. The door opened with a creak. Clean, smiling faces welcomed them into another world—one that belonged in a better neighborhood.

Although the furniture was well-used, the small room appeared clean and orderly. The fragrance of baking bread overpowered the noxious odors from the street. An older woman wiped her hands on her apron as she invited them into the room. A huge smile brightened her face when she recognized her niece.

Once inside the apartment, the outside noise disappeared into a haven of peace and quiet. Children looked up from their books and ran to greet Bridget. An older man took his time lifting himself from a comfortable chair and placing his glasses on the newspaper he'd been reading. He seemed hesitant to join the fray.

"Bridget, how good of you to visit. Are you still enjoying your job?"

Bridget's countenance fell and a look of guilt took the place of her momentary happiness. Cathleen suspected the girl hadn't seen her family since she changed jobs. "I apologize, Aunt Alice, but much has happened since I last visited. I have a new job."

The young girl turned toward Cathleen and took her hand. "Aunt Alice and Uncle Sean, I'd like you to meet my employer and friend, Cathleen Sorenson. She rescued Joey and me when I was almost at the end of my rope. I brought her here to share an opportunity that might interest you."

The uncle frowned, while the aunt gave them a welcoming smile. The plump woman turned around a couple of straight-backed chairs from the table. "Please, take a seat. We're honored to have you in our home."

The suspicious uncle kept staring as he backed into his seat near the fireplace. Bridget squeezed Cathleen's hand, encouraging her to pick up the conservation.

"It's so nice to finally meet Bridget's family. She's spoken highly of you." The aunt beamed at her niece.

"We're proud of our girl. Have you seen Joey recently? We were so concerned when they wouldn't allow us to visit."

"Your nephew is now content and happy with his sister. Bridget can tell you all about it on her next visit." The aunt smiled, then jumped to her feet.

"Forgive me, Mrs. Sorenson, but would you like a cup of tea?"

"No, thank you. I left my children with my father, and I can't be away long." The aunt again took her seat but fidgeted anxiously.

"What's this about, Bridget?" With raised eyebrows and a worried frown, the uncle brought them back to the matter at hand. Cathleen felt at ease with everyone in the room, except the one person she needed to convince. The humiliation of losing his financial status wouldn't be easy to overcome.

"Mr. Fulcher, Bridget told me about the loss of your home and livelihood. I'm sorry about your brother and his wife, along with your monetary losses. That must have been a terrible time for your family."

The man stiffened and studied his hands. He mumbled a thank you before turning an accusing gaze toward Cathleen, causing her to shift uneasily on the hard chair. Why did she let the man intimidate her? Did he blame her for his tragedy? She straightened her back and cleared her throat to speak.

"My grandmother passed away over a year ago and left me her home here in Boston. When I moved to Laramie, Wyoming, a few months later, I'd planned to sell the house. Now, I can't bring myself to part with a place that holds such fond memories. My grandmother's beloved home will deteriorate if I don't soon find a caretaker. In addition to maintaining the house and grounds in my absence, I would require your family's services when we return for visits."

When Bridget's uncle didn't respond, Cathleen continued. "The servants' quarters on the upper level have several rooms, probably twice as large as your current situation. I should think the space would work well for your family. I realize being in service isn't your desired occupation, but I feel I should offer you the job. Do you think this might be something that would interest you?"

By his surprised look and wrinkled brow, Cathleen knew Mr. Fulcher didn't have a ready answer, and she preferred not to linger while he made up his mind. "Perhaps you'd like to pray about this with your wife and children. God knows where he wants you, and if you ask, he'll make it clear to you as well."

The man continued to stare at her. She couldn't decide if his reaction indicated anger or disbelief. Regardless, she needed to take her leave. "It has been a pleasure meeting you. Here is the address where we are staying until I find someone to open the house. Why don't you let me know what you decide?"

Cathleen couldn't get out of the neighborhood fast enough and didn't understand why the uncle wasn't right behind her. He had to be appalled at the living conditions fate had thrust upon his family. They were good people who'd fallen on hard times, and she wanted to help them. Well, she'd offered. Now, the decision would be Mr. Fulcher's. Longing to return to her husband, she prayed the man wouldn't take forever.

When they arrived back at the house, Jenson handed her a letter from Ben. She clutched the envelope to her chest and rushed upstairs. In the quietness of her bedroom she savored every word.

Dear Cathleen,

I'm sorry you took so long to recover from your illness. The trip had to be difficult under the circumstances. You can't imagine how much I wanted to head east after we finalized the cattle sale in Chicago. How I long to hold you and the children and never let you go.

Unfortunately, circumstances prevented me from doing so. The evening before the roundup, Pedro's family arrived without warning and set up camp behind the barn. The only solution was to move out of our cabin and turn it over to the family—two boys, a girl, and Pedro's sister-in-law, who came along uninvited. Dan thinks the young woman is trouble, but I'm convinced he's just uncomfortable with the unwanted attention.

Now, I can't bring my family home until I have the new ranch house built. Do you understand the urgency I felt to rush home and brush up on my carpentry skills? I would have preferred we work together on the plans, but I guess you'll have to trust me. If you really don't like the final product, we could always give the house to Dan and build another more suited to your taste.

When I finally overcame the anger associated with being married to a wealthy woman, I prayed about how we might share your fortune with others. Have you considered that God entrusts people with wealth because he wants them to bless others? Could we pray about this together?

I love you, darling, and am so relieved you're feeling better. Write me soon and tell me all that's happening. Have you found someone to act as caretaker of your grandmother's house? I know that is a concern, and I've been praying for God's provision.

Kiss the children for me and don't forget the man who tosses and tumbles each night wishing he could go to sleep in the arms of his passionate wife.

Love,

Ben

Cathleen and Bridget took the children to the park the next afternoon. Weary after a sleepless night worrying about securing a caretaker, Cathleen couldn't stop thinking about the Fulcher's dreadful living conditions. How many other families found themselves in similar situations? Perhaps God had a hand in her visit to that deprived neighborhood. As for Bridget's uncle, she prayed he would put aside his stubborn pride and allow her to help his family. She needed them and they needed her.

Back at home, while the children napped, Cathleen retired to the library to read. She had decided on Louisa May Alcott's, *Little Women,* when she heard a knock on the front door. A short time later, Jenson stuck his head in the open library door.

"There is a gentleman to see you—a Mr. Fulcher." The inquisitive butler prided himself on knowing most of the people who visited her parents. Cathleen recognized the familiar look of disapproval, but he'd be further annoyed if he knew Mr. Fulcher's reason for coming. Without delay, the visitor would be directed to the servant's entrance.

"Show him into the parlor, Jenson. I'll be right there."

Hoping Mr. Fulcher had the answer she needed, Cathleen tucked the book under her arm and rushed down the hall. Bridget's uncle stood when she entered the room. Though his shirt was worn around the cuffs, he wore a clean suit and carried a stylish cane. From his appearance, anyone would think him a gentleman of some means. Cathleen rested her book on a nearby table and reached for the man's hand.

"Mr. Fulcher, how kind of you to come. Please, have a seat. I hope you have decided to accept my offer."

"This isn't easy for me, Mrs. Sorenson. Dealing with the loss of one's livelihood leaves a man stripped of everything he thought important. My family has been the only thing that held my self-destructive thoughts at bay."

"You do have a lovely family, sir. I'm so thankful that your niece introduced us."

"After hours of discussion with my wife, I feel we should accept your generous offer. Before my misfortune, my wife managed a house full of servants and groundskeepers. Yet, she has willingly adjusted to our change in circumstances and expresses excitement about this new opportunity. Unlike my wife, I will have to swallow my pride and learn to cope with the new situation."

Cathleen sympathized with the proud man and thanked him repeatedly for accepting her offer. Together, they worked out the details, and Mr. Fulcher agreed to move his family into the house as soon as possible.

Before he turned to go, she handed him a bank draft. Mr. Fulcher frowned at the amount. "I can't accept this, Mrs. Sorenson. I have vowed to never accept charity."

Cathleen stopped the man when he pushed the check back toward her. "Mr. Doyle, you will need money to cover the moving expenses. Shall we consider the gift an advance?

The man swiped his hand across his face. He took another look at the check and eased it into his coat pocket. He bowed politely and shook her hand before turning to leave. Cathleen followed him to the front door.

"Men and their pride," she grumbled as she watched him walk down the sidewalk. After he disappeared around the corner, she rushed up the stairs to share her news with Bridget.

# Chapter Twenty

Ben rode into Laramie on Tuesday looking for more carpenters to work on the house. They'd made good progress so far, but the cold mornings prompted him to finish before winter. He cringed at the possibility of spending a lengthy blizzard in a bunkhouse with ornery, smelly cowboys. Longing for his family brought peaceful visions of sitting around the fireplace, playing with the children and snuggling with Cathleen.

Thinking of his wife, he guided his horse toward the middle of town and walked into the post office. Sure enough, there was a piece of mail with her signature scent. He passed the letter under his nose, slid his index finger beneath the flap and had the envelope open before he left the building. He mindlessly walked outside and relaxed on a bench near the entrance.

Dearest Ben,

The days are long and weary in Boston without you, but you were right when you insisted I return. My father seems pleased to have us around, and I'm seeing a gradual change in Mother. At first, she ignored the children and became so controlling, I wanted to move into Grandmother's house. Father kept working on her and, at the same time, encouraging me to be patient. Now, I'm glad I did. She has finally accepted the children and my choice in husbands. Don't you feel pleased?

Ben imagined his wife's teasing grin as he stopped a moment to relish her endearing personality. He returned to the letter and smiled at his wife's compassionate nature. His sweet lady collected strays like the ranch had since she left. With the provision of the caretakers for her grandmother's house, Cathleen would be free to return as soon as he completed the new house. He hoped she would be pleased with her new home and the help he'd acquired for her.

Pedro's boys were some of the best cowhands he'd ever hired, and no one could fault Maria's cooking skills. The few times he'd been invited to share a meal with their family, he'd been impressed with the cooking and the way they maintained the small cabin.

Dan still complained about Isabella, but the young woman helped Maria with the chores and mostly stayed to herself. That is, until someone mentioned a trip into town. Then, she dropped everything and insisted on tagging along. Ben didn't know what motivated her, and he didn't care to find out. When he had business in Laramie, he sneaked away without her knowledge. He didn't need another reason for folks to gossip, especially with Cathleen on the other side of the country.

Ben finished the letter and read it again before renewing his search for someone in need of work. He'd only taken a few steps in the direction of the saloon when he ran into a dirt farmer who attended his father's church. Ben tipped his hat and greeted the man.

"Frank Collins. It's good to see you. How did your corn crop turn out?"

"Not too good, Ben. I'm heading for the bank now, hoping Mr. Jacobson will renew my note. As you recall, we had a dry spell during the summer that purdy near wiped me out. The corn didn't mature without the rain. Unlike you, I don't have the benefit of a creek running along my property."

Ben understood the man's concerns. He'd had a few dry years himself. "You wouldn't happen to be gifted in using a saw and hammer, would you?"

"What do you mean? I was a carpenter before I tried my hand at farming. Sometimes, I think I should return to my former trade. Do you need some help with that house I heard you were building?"

"I sure do. My wife is in Boston and needs to come home before winter sets in." Ben went on to describe his situation. "Do you think you could help me out? I'll pay you good money and even loan you the money for your bank payment if you prefer dealing with me. What do you say?"

The man's deep frowns lifted when he heard the offer. "My son is also purdy handy with the hammer if you need another hand."

"Well, I came to town to hire two carpenters. Looks as if the good Lord provided just what I needed. Could you start early tomorrow morning?"

The pounding of hammers and the scrape of trowels against the brick could be heard in the background as Ben unrolled the house plans and spread them out on the rough table. The factory outside of Laramie made brick more accessible than lumber and the skilled masons he'd hired were specialists in the trade. His family would have a solid home to shield them from the wintry blizzards sweeping down from the north. Ben worried about how Cathleen would handle the endless weeks of confinement. The idea of snuggling with her behind the walls of a sturdy home wouldn't bother him at all.

With the addition of Frank Collins and his son, Luther, he now had a good crew of carpenters. None of his cowboys were skilled in the building trade except Walt, who handled a saw and hammer like a pro. A few additional men were recruited from nearby ranches. Dan had freed Ben so he could devote every daylight hour to the house.

Studying the drawing, he wondered how he could expand the house to make room for his wife's hired nanny. He didn't want strangers sharing his home, but Cathleen seemed to have other ideas. Knowing how she felt about the children, he wondered why she even hired someone. Ben massaged his neck and took the pencil from behind his ear. If he moved a wall a few feet on one side, there should be enough room for a downstairs bedroom on the lower level.

Dan galloped up as Ben finalized the changes before the workers advanced too far in the construction. His foreman dismounted even before the over-heated animal came to a complete stop. Bending over with his hands on his knees, Dan caught his breath before speaking.

"What in the world, Dan? Is the barn on fire? Is someone hurt?" Ben sniffed the breeze in the general direction of the barn and turned a worried look on Dan.

"Nothing like that." Dan twisted the bridle reins in his hands as if searching for the right words. "It's Isabella. I told you she'd be trouble from the very beginning. Now I don't know what else to do but marry her."

"What?"

"She's pregnant, Ben. Those men who raped her in Mexico left their seed behind."

"If someone raped her, being with child is not her fault, Dan. This isn't your problem unless you're the father. You aren't, are you?"

Dan's nostrils flared. "You know better than that, and I refuse to answer such a ridiculous accusation."

Ben swiped his hand across his mouth to hide his amusement. "Well, there must be a reason for wanting to take on such a responsibility. What they did to her was detestable, but she doesn't have to get married. No one will ridicule her here. You know we'll help her every way we can."

"You don't understand. She'll be humiliated by her family and anyone who shares her faith. They won't believe her. They will just assume she brought the problem on herself."

"Do you suppose the rape was her fault? You did accuse her of being a flirt."

"I did until I understood her problem. The men were gringo drifters who attacked her on her way home. She thought she had to find a white husband to make her story believable. That's why she insisted on going into town. After I rejected her, the possibility of finding a white father on the ranch proved slim."

Ben rubbed the back of his neck and searched the cloud formations overhead for a logical solution. "Do you love the woman, Dan?"

"What does love have to do with anything? I feel responsible even though I was hundreds of miles away when the woman got herself into this mess. What are you getting at?"

"Love has everything to do with marriage. Not sure why I remember this, but when Isabella first arrived, I noticed one of our Spanish cowboys leaning against his horse and staring at her from a distance. The painful look he gave her resembled a man suffering from unrequited love. If I'm not mistaken, that wasn't the first time José laid eyes on the young woman. Find him and tell him what's happened. I'd be interested in his reaction. If he receives the news the way I hope, you'll need to talk Isabella out of a gringo husband."

"I don't know." Dan removed his dusty hat and scratched his head. "It's possible they knew each other. I believe he's from the same area and arrived here with Pedro. But he's not what she's looking for, and I pretty much committed to her when she turned those big brown eyes on me and confessed her sad story. My shirt's still moist from her tears." Dan glanced at his shoulder and seemed surprised to discover the whole shirt soaked in perspiration. He pulled the wet fabric away from his body and shrugged.

"Do you really want to crush José's heart by trying to fix things? I appreciate you playing the role of martyr to rescue a lady in distress, but marriage needs to be based on more than feeling sorry for someone."

"Look who's talking. I don't remember you being madly in love with Cathleen when you tied the knot. You couldn't get away from her fast enough."

Ben smiled at his friend's honest evaluation of his own marriage. "I know, but there wasn't a love-sick suitor waiting in the wings. And thank God there wasn't, because with my attitude at the time, I would've let him have her."

The two men laughed while Dan mounted his horse. "I'll talk to José and see what's going on, but I won't back down from my commitment unless she's happy with him."

Ben shook his head as he watched Dan trot off. The man's heart was in the right place, but Ben wondered what God had in mind. He bowed his head and prayed for God's will in the situation.

By the following evening, Maria rushed about the ranch planning a wedding for her only sister. Pedro had been dispatched to Fort Sanders in search of the Catholic priest who made regular visits to the ranch. When Dan talked to José he had insisted on appealing to Isabella in private. No one heard his side of the conversation, but they got an earful of hers. She fussed and fumed while the soft-spoken young vaquero convinced her of his feelings.

After about an hour, they emerged from the meeting with joy dancing in their tear-filled eyes. With one arm around Isabella, José looked like the happiest man in the world. Ben was glad he'd deserted the house plans in time to observe the outcome.

The wedding turned into a celebration with neighbors and a few friends from town. Ben had been right about a past relationship between the two. The two had dated back in Mexico, but Isabella broke off their engagement when he insisted on accompanying Pedro to Wyoming. She never wanted to see him again and even blamed him for what happened to her. Begging her forgiveness, José groveled considerably before convincing her of his love.

For a wedding gift, José presented Isabella with his mother's rosary. When she lifted the precious gift to her lips, the beads sparkled in the light shining from the campfire. Tears of gratitude glistened in the bride's eyes as she faced her anxious groom. Lonely and feeling abandoned by his own love, Ben turned away and headed toward the barn. He couldn't keep pretending when he ached to share such moments with Cathleen.

Soon Ben heard the musicians tuning their instruments. Knowing he would be missed, he left the confines of his office and moved to the edge of the crowd. Even the shy Henson boys were pulled into the wedding dance as most of the guests joined the march. The line of happy dancers zigzagged around the cabin and barn and into the pasture.

Ben declined every invitation. He couldn't bring himself to join the fun without Cathleen.

Walking near the barn, Ben noticed Dan also standing on the sidelines. The man's eyes were glazed over as he stared at the happy bride. "Surely you aren't longing for that Spanish beauty. I thought you were relieved when she accepted someone who would love and care for her and the baby? Tell me you aren't jealous of José."

"You can't blame me for wanting a wife and family. I guess I am a bit jealous. José is one blessed man. Did you ever see a more beautiful woman?"

"Seems to me you said the same thing about my wife a few months ago. I agree with your first assessment. No one is more beautiful than my Cathleen, and I miss her like crazy." The two men laughed and slapped each other on the back. As they left the celebration, Ben thanked God for the look of love he had recognized on José's face that day when he caught him staring at Isabella. He shook his head in wonder at how God worked in their lives to bring them back together.

The young couple would live in the cabin across the creek which had been Jim and Myriam Henson's first home. Myriam kept the place clean and tidy in case a family needed emergency housing. Though Ben offered to buy the small piece of land, they insisted the house would be a wedding gift to the young couple. Not knowing what would help them most, Ben gave José an extra bonus. Cathleen would probably want to do more when she returned.

Thus far, pride had kept Ben from delving into his wife's bank account, but if they were to have more than a sparsely furnished home, her money would be needed. He'd nearly choked when Harvey gave him the huge mercantile bill. Embarrassed, the man avoided eye contact and looked everywhere in the store but directly at him. *God, help me come to terms with this wealthy wife you've given me.*

The workers had the house under roof, and despite the early snow, work continued inside. Ben wrote Cathleen a letter with a progress report and asked her to shop for furniture in the Boston area. As Christmas drew near, Ben worried about the separation from his family. But with the house still unfinished, he had no choice. Months had passed since he had held them in his arms, and every day, he despised himself more for letting them leave.

As Ben entered the bunkhouse that evening, he hung his jacket and hat over the row of pegs near the door. Turning around to shut out the cold wind, he noticed a rider dismounting near the corral. Walt met the visitor and walked with him to the porch. Ben recognized the young man from town.

"Hey, Lucas. What brings you out here on this brisk evening?"

"Got a telegram for you, Ben, from Boston."

Ben's heart leaped in his throat as he took the missile from Lucas and reached for his wallet. The tip in no way reflected the fear that overtook him. He thanked the messenger and returned to the bunkhouse in search of a lantern.

Come as soon as you can. Your wife needs you.

The words jumped off the thin paper and clawed his insides. He should have never let her out of his sight. Something terrible must've happened for Cathleen's father to send that urgent a telegram.

Ben tossed clothes into a beat-up suitcase while making a mental list of things to do and instructions for Dan.

Unfortunately, the next train to Boston didn't come through until late the following day. How would he survive until then?

# Chapter Twenty-One

Ben searched the faces rushing about the crowded Boston station. He'd sent a wire before boarding the train and expected to see Cathleen's father waiting for him. Just as he walked outside to secure public transportation, he noticed a motor car parked along the curb. A younger man held a dog-eared piece of cardboard with words scrawled in uneven letters. He moved closer to read what looked like his name.

"Are you Mr. Sorenson?"

"Yes, I'm Ben Sorenson."

"Mr. Doyle asked me to pick you up. I'm Winston, his driver and whatever other job he has for me. Are you Miss Cathleen's husband?"

"I am. I believe she mentioned you a time or two in conversation. She gave me the impression that you are friends."

The young man ducked his head before relieving Ben of his small bag. He placed the lone suitcase on the front seat while opening the back door for his passenger. "I'm not used to this kind of service, Winston. Do you mind if I sit up front with you?"

Winston smiled as he retrieved the suitcase and stepped aside for Ben to enter the car. "I can see why Miss Cathleen married you."

"Why is that?"

The young man didn't answer until he'd cranked the engine and seated himself behind the wheel. A wide grin spread over his face. "I wanted to marry her when we were children. I thought she was the prettiest and sweetest girl I'd ever seen. She could talk me into doing most anything. Even if it meant I'd have to take the blame. She ruined a many fancy dress with her escapades, but I loved every minute of following her around."

"That still doesn't explain why you understand Cathleen's choice."

"There's something about you, Mr. Sorenson. I'm not sure what, but you suit one another."

"Thank you, Winston. I know she makes me a better person. Do you know why Mr. Doyle sent for me?"

"Not exactly, but I know your wife needs you." He paused and lowered his head. "It's not for me to say, sir."

A tear formed in the corner of Winston's eye as he checked the street ahead. Ben bowed his head and prayed for strength to face yet another trial.

The car had barely come to a stop outside the large brownstone before Ben jumped out and took the steps two at a time. Before he could raise the knocker, the door opened, and a grim-faced gentleman stood to the side.

"May I help you, sir?"

"Where's my wife?" Ben rushed past the slow-moving man and looked toward the stairs.

"Ben, I'm glad you're here. Jenson, show Mr. Sorenson to his wife's room."

When Jenson raised an eyebrow and didn't move fast enough, Ben edged around him and took the stairs on the run.

"Cathleen, where are you?"

At the top of the stairs, Ben turned toward the right and opened two doors before he found her scooting toward the edge of the bed. Her hair formed a halo of auburn curls surrounding her pale face. "Ben, you came."

Cathleen had withdrawn from everyone, including the children. Their sweet faces reminded her of what she'd lost, and she didn't want them to see her so upset. Her mother thought she should rise above the circumstances and go on with life. Her father begged her to dress and at least spend time with the children. Hundreds of miles separated her from the one person who might understand, and yet, she had been afraid to tell him.

Cathleen stirred from her slumber when she heard her name yelled and the opening and slamming of doors. The voice was Ben's. But how could that be? Ignoring the conflicting thoughts, she pushed herself upright and tried to untangle her weak limbs from the blanket. She jerked in surprise when her own bedroom door crashed open, and Ben burst into the room.

Her husband had come—the only person she longed to see. Ben rushed to the bed and pulled her into his arms. Sobs shook Cathleen as all the pent-up emotions of the recent weeks poured out. He kissed her wet face and whispered into her ear.

"Dear, sweet Cathleen. I love you. I've felt like a lonesome cowboy ever since you and the children left. Tell me what happened. Are you sick again?"

"No, not the consumption, but I'm heartsick. Ben, I've never been so upset. I lost our baby."

"You lost Annie?" Ben stared at her with the same confusion she felt as she tried to process why he thought she meant Annie.

"No, Ben, not Annie. The baby we made that last night before I left."

Ben held her at arm's length and frowned. Unsure if it was grief or anger she saw in his face, Cathleen hurried on. "When I started getting sick, I thought I had another relapse of the consumption. But when the weakness and nausea continued, my father called Dr. Landon. After he examined me and asked a few embarrassing questions, he explained I was with child." Ben inhaled sharply, and his frown softened. "You can't imagine the excitement I felt—a joy like I'd never known. I wanted to shout the news to everyone, but I couldn't because I knew how you'd feel. Writing a letter didn't seem right, knowing you'd be worried and couldn't share my joy. Despite the distance between us—in miles and in our differences—I felt your presence in the child resting near my heart."

Cathleen paused, hoping for a clearer signal from Ben. *Did he share her grief or did the demons still haunt him?* "Only a few weeks later, I started cramping and bleeding. I'd lost the most precious thing ever, and I blamed myself for being afraid to tell you. Our baby died before he had the chance to grow and feel the love of his family. The emptiness he left behind gnawed at my insides until I wanted to scream."

With no clear response from Ben, Cathleen struggled to continue. "My parents tried to console me, but I couldn't rise above the darkness. I longed for you to hold and comfort me. Though you wouldn't want me to be with child, you would understand my grief. Thank you for coming, and please forgive me for not telling you about the baby."

Ben pulled her into his embrace. "Oh, honey, losing the baby wasn't your fault. If anyone, I should be the one to blame. From the very beginning, you were forced to withhold information because you feared how I would react. Though my past hasn't been easy, I need to live in the present with you. You should never be afraid to tell me anything."

Cathleen relaxed against Ben while he rubbed her back and kissed her hair. "As for the baby, we don't understand why these things happen, but we do know that our little one is in God's hands. I'm sorry you've had to face this alone. Getting over the sorrow may take a while, but I'm here now, and we'll comfort each other. Let me hold you."

Ben removed his shoes and clothes and climbed into the high poster bed. He molded his body against her back and whispered words of encouragement while brushing her hair aside and kissing her exposed neck.

"God, please heal Cathleen's broken heart. Surround her with your love and comforting presence. Release me from my fears and give us both your peace."

Moments later Ben dropped his hand from her waist and relaxed into the feather mattress. His breathing evened, and she heard his soft snore. Cathleen silently prayed for her poor exhausted husband who'd dropped everything to come to her. She didn't want to judge him, but she wondered if he realized the wall his fears had built between them. Brushing her insecurities aside, she chose to enjoy the moment, cherishing the feel of her husband's arms and the knowledge he loved her. His affectionate words and caresses were healing oil pouring over her bruised spirit. With the tension and worry released to God, she also drifted off to sleep.

Ben awakened with a jerk. He looked around the unfamiliar bedroom and wondered how he'd landed in a life of luxury. In her sleep, Cathleen had turned toward him and snuggled close with one arm encircling his waist. He didn't want to wake her, but he needed to find the water closet. At the kiss to her lips, her eyes opened, and a slow smile slid across her face.

"Do you think my grandmother and your Lana were happy to see our baby?"

"Of course. Where did that come from?"

"I had the strangest dream. A woman resembling the one in the picture I saw of Lana at your parents' house held a baby girl in her arms. My grandmother stood over her, stroking the baby's head. They were both smiling."

Tears clouded Ben's vision, and his words caught in his throat when he realized the significance of Cathleen's dream. "I'm touched, honey. Your dream must be God's way of telling us that our little girl is safe with loved ones in heaven."

"I know. I feel so comforted and loved. Not just by you, but I feel as if we're wrapped in a cocoon of God's love. We had a little girl, Ben. Do you think we should give her a name?"

"Yes. I'd like to remember her by name. Do you have something in mind?"

"While I waited for you to wake up, I thought of the look on my grandmother's face in the dream. Could we name her Mary?

"After your grandmother?"

"Do you mind? My grandmother influenced me in so many ways. I don't think I would have had the courage to find you without her last words of wisdom. She told me that if I would trust God, he would lead me to the man I should marry."

"The name is perfect, honey."

"Yes, and that reminds me of something else Nana said. She said the person God chose would be perfect for me, and I believe she was right."

Cathleen kissed him before she rolled to her side and stood on shaky legs. "Help me get dressed. For the first time in days, I feel like leaving this room. I've neglected the children and my parents. I want to watch the look on those sweet faces when they see their papa."

"Are you sure you're well enough?" Ben hurried around the bed to help her when he saw her grab the bed post to keep from falling.

"I've stayed in bed too long. My body has healed, but my heart still aches. Seeing my family together again will be the best medicine."

Ben worried whether she had enough strength to walk down the hall much less be with the children. But at least she'd be leaving the bedroom. After he helped her dress, she rearranged a hairbrush set on her dressing table while she waited for him to change into a fresh shirt and tie.

He'd already committed the worst possible social grace when he rushed past his mother-in-law a few hours earlier. He'd heard the disdain in her voice. "What in the world, William. Tell me that isn't our daughter's husband. The man acts like an uneducated country bumpkin."

Ben had some fences to mend and looking like the man Mrs. Doyle described would only validate her first impression when he made an appearance downstairs.

Walking down the long hall together, Cathleen gained strength with each step. She left his side and walked into the nursery ahead of him. A young woman sat in a rocking chair holding Annie. Two little boys played nearby with a stack of colorful blocks. As the young lady looked from one to the other, her face broke into a wide grin.

"Miss Cathleen, how good to see you up and about. I bet I can guess what has you looking so well."

Cathleen reached behind her and pulled him forward. "Look who came to see his babies."

"Papa!" Sammy squealed as he ran into Ben's arms. After hugging his boy, he put him down and moved toward Annie. The baby didn't seem the least shy as she kicked happy feet and reached for him. Cathleen hugged his back and Sammy held onto his leg. Surrounded by those he loved made him feel like the richest man on earth.

Too soon, Cathleen turned him loose and acknowledged the other two people in the room. "Bridget, I would like to introduce you to my husband, Ben Sorenson. Ben, this is my friend and the best nanny the children could ever have. This handsome young man is Bridget's little brother, Joey. I haven't told you, but we are his legal guardians until his sister is old enough to accept the responsibility."

Ben cocked his head and raised an eyebrow. He never knew what she'd spring on him next. Clearly, Cathleen's letters had omitted a few important details. Perhaps a face-to-face conversation would answer some of the questions that dangled between the lines.

"It's nice to meet you, Bridget. Cathleen told me how you two met. I appreciate your care of the children during my wife's illness."

"The little I did was nothing, Mr. Sorenson, compared to your wife's rescue of my brother and me. We will always be grateful for her intervention in our lives."

Bridget looked at Cathleen and grinned. "This surprise visit seems to have brought about a miracle, Miss Cathleen. I haven't seen you so well and happy in a long time."

Cathleen gazed at him with love shining through her tear-filled eyes. He almost reached for her, but then remembered their audience. After a moment of silent exchange, Cathleen cleared her throat and looked at Bridget. "You're right. I've felt lost and heartsick for weeks, but my husband's arrival changed everything."

"I got new friend." Sammy interrupted the adult conversation and pointed to the little boy who appeared a few years older.

"I'm happy that you found a new playmate, and I understand you will be bringing him home with you."

Sammy bobbed his head up and down as he and Joey returned their attention to the toys.

"Do you want to play with my blocks, Papa?

Ben gave Annie to Cathleen and sat on the floor with the two boys. "I'd love to play with you and Joey. What are you building?"

"We make wall to keep bear out."

Ben hadn't thought about the impact the bear attack had on the children. Obviously, Sammy hadn't forgotten that scary day.

"That's one bear you don't have to worry about, Son, and if any of his friends show up, Mr. Jim and Mrs. Myriam will make sure they don't harm us. You were a brave boy, and I'm proud of you. Have you enjoyed your time in Boston?"

Sammy deserted his wall and jumped to his feet. "We go to park and feed ducks. They like us."

Ben had never seen his son so animated. His excitement sounded a lot like Cathleen's when she told the children stories. Sammy's list of activities stopped when a maid brought their supper to the door. Ben and Cathleen joined the children at a low table. Though Sammy was too excited to eat, his friend attacked a chicken leg with such gusto, the grease smeared the lower half of his face.

"Look at Joey, he's enjoying his fried chicken."

Not to be outdone, Sammy picked up his own piece. "Me eat bear," he growled. Ben raised an eyebrow at his wife. So much for changing the subject.

Cathleen glanced at the clock on the mantle and frowned. "I hate to leave the children so soon, Bridget, but my mother will expect Ben downstairs for dinner. She's probably wondering what happened to him."

Turning her attention back to Bridget, "Could you finish feeding Annie for me?"

After they hugged the children, they left the nursery with Cathleen leaning heavily against him. "Do you feel strong enough to go downstairs with me?"

"Yes, I think I should. I don't want my mother to eat you alive." Cathleen squeezed his arm and chuckled.

Taking their time descending the stairs, Ben stopped midway and grimaced. "I hate to tell you, but I was so anxious to see you when I arrived, I completely ignored your mother. Pray she'll forgive me."

Cathleen snuggled into his side and shook her head dramatically. "Tsk, tsk, but this won't be easy. She already considers you a con man for stealing me away. Now she'll think you're an uncouth cowboy."

"You are teasing. Aren't you?"

"Not much, I'm afraid." Ben groaned and held his stomach as if in great pain.

"Stop worrying. Just be yourself and that western charm will win her over in no time."

They continued to the foyer where Ben considered rushing out the door instead of facing his mother-in-law in the parlor. His lack of manners a few hours before would put him at an uncomfortable disadvantage for the remainder of the evening—an evening he'd prefer to spend alone with his wife.

"Come in, children. Ben hasn't met your mother. Eugenia, this is Cathleen's husband, Ben Sorenson. My wife and your mother-in-law, Mrs. Eugenia Doyle."

Ben moved toward the woman and took her hand. "You are lovely, Mrs. Doyle, just like your daughter. I must apologize for rushing past you when I first entered your home. Mr. Doyle's telegram left much to my imagination, and your daughter's welfare has been my only concern since I received the message. Please forgive me."

The woman scrutinized him from head to toe. He'd done the right thing when he purchased a new suit before leaving Chicago. From what he knew of Mrs. Doyle, he suspected she put considerable emphasis on appearance.

"I should kick you out of my house, Mr. Sorenson, but your arrival seems to have done wonders for our daughter. I don't know how you managed to get her out of the bedroom, but here she is, dressed for dinner and never looking better. I'm happy to see you up and about, Cathleen."

"Thank you, Mother. Ben said the telegram indicated I needed him, and I did. Thank you, Father, for knowing me so well."

Mr. Doyle embraced his daughter. "Understanding the needs of my wife and daughter has taken me a while, but I'm gradually putting my priorities in order."

"Dinner is served, madam."

With Jensen's announcement, the family moved toward the door. Mr. Doyle pulled his daughter's hand into the crook of his arm, leaving Ben behind to escort his wife. The woman frowned and hesitated before taking the offered arm. Her body felt as stiff as a frozen piece of bear meat.

"I can forgive you for your ill manners on arrival, but I don't appreciate your luring my daughter away from her family," she whispered as they made their way through the foyer.

Ben smiled down at the woman while giving her arm a soothing pat. "I understand your concern, Mrs. Doyle. I don't know how I would live without her myself. She is a remarkable young woman, and I'm fortunate to be the recipient of her love."

"Her money would entice anyone." Mrs. Doyle fumed between clenched teeth and jerked away from him. When she reached the seat opposite her husband, Ben pulled out her chair. After seating her, he walked to his own place across from Cathleen. His wife's lips puckered into a sympathetic pout. A foot with a soft slipper slowly massaged up his leg. Looking across the table at his naughty wife, he chuckled at her mischievous grin. She knew how to get his mind off the long, dreaded evening ahead.

# Chapter Twenty-two

Since Ben's arrival, Cathleen felt more energized every day. On nice days, they bundled the children and went for walks in the park or strolled through the downtown area to see the storefronts decorated for Christmas. The children's faces beamed when they saw the animated figures in Macy's window display. Even Annie clapped and giggled at the colorful movements.

During nap time, the parents caught up on a few neglected issues. Ben understood Bridget's predicament and agreed to sponsor Joey until his sister reached the legal age. They also went over the copy of house plans he'd sketched from memory on the train.

"I should be there supervising the work, honey. I don't want you to come home to an unfinished house."

"You told me you hired expert carpenters and left Dan in charge. You can't deny his competence. He'd let you know if a problem arose." Cathleen brushed off his concerns and changed the subject.

"I realize we haven't discussed this, but I would like to stay through Christmas. My parents need more time with us. By then, the house should be far enough along." When he started to object, she hurried on. "Don't even think of going home without us. If you feel uncomfortable here, we could move into Grandmother's house."

Ben shook his head and gave her that appealing grin. "What am I to do with you, Mrs. Sorenson?"

"Just keep loving me." Cathleen felt moisture building in her eyes as she put her head on his shoulder. The warmth from the logs crackling in the fireplace in no way compared to the warmth she felt in her husband's arms.

Cathleen sat up straight when she heard the door to the library open and watched her mother rush into the room. "Look what came in the mail, Cathleen. An invitation to the Kennedy's Christmas Ball. We received an invitation a few weeks ago, but this separate invitation addressed to the two of you arrived in today's post."

The woman handed the richly engraved invitation to Cathleen while giving Ben a cold shoulder. Though her mother had grudgingly accepted her marriage and even Ben's children, she still resented her daughter's choice. Nor had she forgiven her for running away.

"You two look rather cozy. Do you think you can handle a large social affair, Mr. Sorenson?"

"No problem, Mrs. Doyle. I look forward to dancing with my gorgeous wife." Ben rubbed his hands together as if he couldn't wait, but the hesitant frown spreading across his face gave Cathleen a hint of his true feelings.

"I suppose I'll need a new suit for the occasion."

Cathleen took her time opening the invitation and scanning the contents. "They didn't give us much time, but yes, we'll both need to do some shopping.

"I'll respond for us. Thank you, Mother."

Despite her boredom with Boston society, Cathleen would enjoy reconnecting with friends and introducing them to her handsome husband. But she wondered how Ben would react. She recoiled when she imagined the two of them sitting alone through the dances while overhearing snippets of gossip about their unconventional marriage.

Cathleen reprimanded herself for such negative thoughts. Since when did she care about frivolous gossip? Regardless of Ben's discomfort, her easygoing, kind husband would make the best of the situation if for no other reason than to please her and her parents.

The night of the ball arrived too soon for Cathleen. Only that morning she'd stood on a stool for the last fitting of her gown. Ben had picked up his dark tailcoat with matching pants and vest from the tailor. They'd argued over the choice. He had wanted something more versatile while she insisted he purchase the latest in tuxedos. Instead of hearing negative comments, she'd hold her head high and march into the Kennedy's ballroom on the arm of the most stylish man in Boston.

Right after they tucked the children in bed, Ben dressed in his new formal attire. Under protest, he waited downstairs in the library with her father. Cathleen had to force the man to leave while she dressed. From experience, she'd learned that he would be more of a distraction than a help. His idea of buttoning her dress involved kissing her bare back and shoulders, disheveling her hair and undoing what had already been done. The disgruntled man she shoved out the door would only be a temptation.

Before Bridget helped her into her corset and buttoned the string of pearl buttons cascading down her back, she'd need her mother's personal maid to style her hair. Meredith had perfected the Gibson-girl look which should go nicely with the dress she'd chosen. Excitement washed over her as she rushed about the room.

A few months ago, she would have dreaded such an event. She hadn't appreciated being on display for all the eligible bachelors in need of an advantageous match. Now, she couldn't wait to enter the fray with her handsome prince knowing he had eyes for her alone. She giggled just thinking about the envious stares.

"What has you in such a happy mood, Miss Cathleen?" Meredith stood in the doorway with a tray filled with brushes, pins, ribbons, and an array of decorative combs. "It wouldn't have anything to do with that fine-looking husband I passed in the hallway, would it?"

Cathleen couldn't stop another giggle from escaping her lips. "It does, Meredith. I'm very happy. Mr. Sorenson is the best thing that ever happened to me."

"I understand, but if we don't get busy, he's going to wonder what happened to you. Sit down while I tame those curls into a style that will make the other women jealous."

Ben watched the clock on the mantel and tried to concentrate on an article in the *Boston Globe*. He and his father-in-law had exhausted every subject from politics to the economy. *What could be taking the women so long?* Though he enjoyed Mr. Doyle's company, he felt anxious about the evening and would rather be alone with his wife. Cathleen relaxed him like a long ride on the open range. She didn't seem to have a worry or negative thought in her head.

*Where was she?* Ben couldn't take another minute of this impossible waiting. He placed the newspaper on the side table and stood.

"I suppose this is new to you, Ben—waiting for hours for the women to make themselves presentable."

Ben chuckled. "You read me well. I have the patience to wait for cowboys to return with a batch of steers or for a stubborn calf to be born, but little for sitting around waiting for someone to make themselves beautiful. As far as I'm concerned, your daughter is pretty enough without all the primping."

Mr. Doyle chuckled as he glanced at the clock and stood as well. Ben walked into the foyer and let his gaze drift upward along the curved stairway. He caught his breath. Cathleen beamed down at him in a vision of gold ruffles and lace. The light from the electric wall sconce cast her in a mystical glow. He wanted to scoop her into his arms and take her to their bedroom where he would kiss every inch of her gorgeous body. She must have read the direction of his thoughts because just as his foot hit the first step, she held up her hand and shook her head. Satisfied that she'd waylaid his plans, she made her way down the stairs.

Cathleen held out her hand and smiled as he kissed her palm and continued up her arm through the maze of ruffles and lace. "Enough! Do you want to destroy what Meredith and Bridget took hours to accomplish? I would like to walk into the ballroom looking half-way decent, if you don't mind."

"I don't suppose I could talk you into staying home?"

"Don't tempt me. We need to do this for my parents. Introducing us as a couple is important to my mother. Please try to understand."

"I do understand, but you look too good. I'd rather not share you with anyone else, especially those wolves you mentioned."

"You have nothing to worry about, Ben Sorenson. I rejected them ages ago in favor of a very good-looking cowboy." They laughed at her tease while Ben kissed low on her neck.

"Later." Ben groaned, remembering the times he had to pour cold water over his head to resist his tempting wife. He'd been a cowardly fool then, denying himself months of pure pleasure. Now he'd have to suffer hours of torturous look-but-don't-touch.

Reluctantly, Ben pulled Cathleen's hand through his arm and escorted her into the foyer. Staring off into the distance, Jenson stood like a hall tree waiting to help them with their wraps. Cathleen's parents met them at the door, and moments later, they were in the new Cadillac heading to Ben's first Christmas ball. He'd have preferred horse and carriage, but he'd refused to compromise when his wife wanted him to wear dress shoes. A cowboy didn't wander into the unknown without a fine pair of leather boots.

Following a congenial trip through the receiving line, Ben led his wife toward the ballroom. As they walked under the archway, he heard a catch of breath and a soft, "Oh, Ben." The crystal chandeliers cast a warm glow on the multicolored gowns waltzing across the dance floor. Scattered about the room were elaborate Christmas decorations with gold and white glittering against green sprigs of holly, spruce, and mistletoe. The far corner held a towering Douglas fir groaning under the weight of handblown glass ornaments. When he looked over at Cathleen, her eyes twinkled in anticipation of his reaction. He laughed and gave her hand a squeeze.

"What do you think, Ben?"

"The room or my intriguing wife? Personally, I'd rather be on the ranch, riding Prince and galloping after you and Lady. May we leave now?"

Cathleen pinched the inside of his arm. "Not before I show you off to Boston society."

Ben growled at her, and then noticed the other participants. Heads turned and every eye fixed on them as they worked their way across the crowded room. Guests leaned toward their neighbors with gloved hands covering their mouths. Fingers pointing in their general direction made Ben wonder what the observers found so intriguing. The thought of him being their target made him want to grab Cathleen and run for the exit. Instead of a magical Christmas ball, he felt as though he'd been thrown into the corral with a herd of angry bulls.

"Why are you so uptight, Ben? They're just anxious to see the man who wooed me away from Boston."

"More like they're out for retaliation. Look at all those disappointed mamas whose sons you rejected."

Cathleen laughed at him.

"So, you think throwing me to the wolves is funny, eh?"

"Stop being such a coward, Ben. Smile and make me proud."

Ben pasted on a fake smile until he took another look at his wife. "Honey, you are so beautiful. I feel like the luckiest man in this room. No wonder I see envy dripping from the pores of every single male present."

"Thank you, Ben, but the single women are the ones who concern me. You are one handsome cowboy."

"Dance with me, Cathleen." The orchestra finished a waltz and the singer began the words to a new song, "Let Me Call You Sweetheart." He'd only heard the lyrics a few times, but he liked what they said. The music had an easy swing.

Cathleen stopped and pulled on his arm. "Are you sure you know how to dance anything besides the do-si-do?

Ben chuckled and gave his wife a reassuring squeeze. When they found a vacant spot, Ben placed her right hand in his left. With his other hand he touched her shoulder. Pleased relief replaced Cathleen's suspicious frown as they joined the other dancers.

"Who taught you to dance like this, Ben Sorenson?"

"I wasn't always a rancher, Cathleen. Before I left home to attend the university, my mother made sure I learned basic etiquette along with the popular dance steps. She didn't want me to be embarrassed amid the social scene of the city. I argued with her, but my father remembered his own years in Boston and took her side of the argument."

"Remind me to thank your mother. The woman amazes me with her perception."

Waltzing with Cathleen felt as if they had practiced for hours. They circled the room as a single unit, allowing the music to carry them into their own little world. Waves of passion passed between them as Ben gazed into those compelling green eyes. A look of longing stared back, urging him to devour her. Dancing with Cathleen set his entire body to tingling.

As the last notes faded, Ben felt a tap on his shoulder. "May I cut in?"

Ben didn't recognize the tall fellow, but his wife did. He felt her body weaken against him and watched as the blood drained from her face.

"I'm sorry, but I believe my wife needs a breath of fresh air. Please excuse us."

"So, you're the one she chose over me. Whatever were you thinking, Cathleen?"

"Let's just go, Ben."

Cathleen pulled at his arm as Ben continued to glare at the intruder. He wanted to smash the smirk right off the arrogant face. If he guessed right, he'd come face to face with the cad who sent his wife fleeing Boston a few months before. Ben would have enjoyed a few moments to gloat over his good fortune if his wife hadn't taken off without him. Rather than embarrass Cathleen or her parents, he rushed to catch up and escort her toward the patio door.

As they passed her parents, Mrs. Doyle stopped them with a touch to his arm. "What's wrong, Cathleen? You look like you've seen a ghost?"

Ben seated Cathleen in a chair where she could feel the cool air coming through the open door. He knelt next to her and grabbed both her hands. Rubbing her knuckles with a gentle circular motion, he watched the strength return. She straightened against the back of the chair and looked at her mother with a faint smile lifting the corners of her mouth. "I'm fine, Mother. Just a visit from my horrific past."

Mrs. Doyle looked past Ben and gasped at the man she spotted in the crowd. "William, you'd better deal with Mr. Stanwick before he upsets Cathleen further. Ben looks frustrated enough to cause a scene."

A different version of his mother-in-law emerged, and he caught a glimpse of where his wife inherited her fortitude. Mrs. Doyle put her arm around her daughter and whispered loud enough for him to hear. "You don't have to worry, honey. Your father will take care of that awful man. If he doesn't, I'm sure Ben will."

Mrs. Doyle smiled warmly at Ben. She placed her hand over his and gave it a tight squeeze. Ben stood in time to see his father-in-law walk out of the ballroom—one arm over the intruder's shoulder and deep in conversation. In that moment, Cathleen's father reminded him of his own father who believed that most conflicts could be solved with understanding and forgiveness. Since he knew little of the original problem, he figured his interference would do more harm than good. He headed to the refreshment table.

"Well, well, well. If it isn't the handsome Mr. Sorenson. Dance with me, Ben." A familiar voice stopped him. Cathleen wasn't the only one subject to visits from the past.

"Miss Hillsboro, I'm happy to see you looking beautiful as always. Where's that rich husband your parents insisted you marry?"

Audrey waved her hand as if swatting a fly. "Oh, you mean Roland Devonshire. How could I marry someone like him when I'm in love with you?"

"That's been almost five years, Audrey. If you loved me, you'd have accepted my proposal long ago. Despite my anger, and the hurt you and your family inflicted, I must say, you did us both a favor. It took a while to get over the rejection, but I finally realized that your parents were right. We didn't suit. I am now happily married with two young children. Though my wife, Cathleen, came from Boston, she doesn't mind being married to a cowboy."

"You married Cathleen Doyle? But she only left town recently to avoid an entanglement with Geoffrey Stanwick. I thought you left Boston ages ago to marry your childhood friend."

Ben gave Audrey a wide smile. "I did. Lana passed away after our second child was born. I've been blessed with two good wives since you rejected me. Please thank your parents for doing us both a favor. If you'll excuse me, I need to attend Cathleen."

Audrey's face turned a few shades of red as Ben backed away and hurried to the punch bowl. A few splashes of sticky punch later, he returned to Cathleen and her parents.

"Looks as if you ladies could use a drink."

After Ben distributed the cups, he used his handkerchief to wipe the stickiness from his hands. Mr. Doyle stood nearby looking completely at ease—not at all like a man who'd just confronted a scoundrel. "I trust your little meeting went well?"

"Without a hitch. Our Mr. Stanwick has his sights on greener pastures. He didn't make himself clear as to why he needed to harass my daughter, but I made certain he won't bother her again."

Mr. Doyle rubbed his chin, giving himself time to think before he continued. "Actually, I feel sorry for the young man. Only a few months ago, I tried to arrange my daughter's life the way his parents are using him. Thank goodness, Cathleen didn't let me succeed. I'm not sure young Stanwick has the strength of character to resist the unethical schemes proposed by his father."

Mr. Doyle studied his wife. "Excuse me, Ben. I need to spend some time romancing my wife. I do believe I'm falling in love for the first time. Thank you for your wise example."

Ben watched Cathleen's father lead her mother toward the dance floor. The orchestra shuffled and then followed the conductor in the opening stanza of "Silver Bells."

"That's a pretty sight." Ben gestured toward her parents who gazed at each other as though they were the only couple on the dance floor.

"Would you like to dance with me, Mrs. Sorenson?"

"Nothing would please me more."

# Chapter Twenty-three

Cathleen stretched under the heavy quilts while waiting for Ben to undress and join her. They'd left the ball earlier than they'd planned, but neither couple felt the need to linger. A feeling of satisfaction came over her when she rehearsed the evening. Mr. Stanwick had temporarily blindsided her, but she'd recovered, and in the process realized a precious truth. During that unstable time after her grandmother passed, she'd felt alone and abandoned by the people who should have loved her. Now, she knew those same people would stand with her no matter how difficult the situation.

About midway through her reminiscing, she remembered her husband's encounter with Audrey Hillsboro. Though Audrey was a few years older than Cathleen, she knew of her and her family. She must have met Ben when he attended the university. She seemed like a nice enough young woman, but Cathleen didn't like the way she mooned over her husband. *Could Audrey be the one who rejected him?*

Ben finally came to bed and pulled her into his arms. She gave him a push and shivered as his feet massaged her legs. "Get away. You're cold as an iceberg."

Ben laughed and held her tighter. "The idea is for you to warm me, my lady." He kissed her with a fierce passion and nuzzled into her neck. "My plan is working already."

"Not as much for me. Tell me how you happen to know that Hillsboro girl?"

"Jealous, are you?"

"How could I be jealous when I'm the one warming your cold feet?"

"Good point. But I do want to explain. During my second year of college, I thought I was in love with Audrey Hillsboro and asked her to marry me. Her parents, however, didn't think me good enough for their daughter. Not wanting to go against her parents, Audrey rejected me in favor of a wealthy man they had planned for her."

"I figured as much, but the last I heard she remains unmarried. I wonder what happened to the other man."

Instead of Ben giving Cathleen the answer Audrey had given him, he shrugged. "I'm not sure what happened, but I guess she's enjoying her independence."

"I'm glad we don't have to see her again. I don't appreciate the way she looks at you. Doesn't she know she lost her chance long ago?"

"If she didn't before, she knows it now. Could we think about something else? Perhaps something that resembles love?"

"Is this the same man who slept on the floor all summer to keep from being with his wife?"

"That man was a fool. Sorry I took so long to realize what I'd been missing."

Cathleen moved closer and let her fingers brush through the curls at the back of his head. She released a long breath and tweaked his ear. "I'm glad you finally came to your senses."

The next day, after they'd taken the children to the park, Ben and Cathleen retired to their bedroom. Ben had picked up the mail before he came upstairs, and nearly choked when he saw the amount of money Cathleen had spent on furniture. "What's the matter, Ben? You're giving me the silent treatment, and I don't like it. Did you receive disturbing news from home?"

"No, nothing like that. I'm trying to come to terms with this receipt for the furniture you ordered. I hate that you paid this bill. Though the amount means little to you, the total, including shipping, represents more than I would need to run the ranch for a whole year. I don't have that kind of money and probably never will. My pride would prefer you settle for what I can afford, but I know that's not fair. Pray for me to get over this thorn of a wealthy wife."

"Oh, Ben. Sometimes I wish I had come to you empty-handed. When I took the train west, I hoped to find a husband who would love me for the person I am—not the way I looked, or the amount of money left me by my grandparents. I never considered you would resent my inheritance. My paying for the furniture wasn't meant to demean you or make you feel inadequate. I want to contribute to some of the expenses of our new home. Please use the money as you would income from the ranch. My grandmother's gift belongs to both of us.

"As for the furniture, I want our home to be comfortable and welcoming. Though I could have chosen expensive artwork and rich furnishings, I purchased only the basic pieces needed for each room. I chose well-crafted and durable furniture that will last a lifetime. The walls will remain bare until we find something that appeals to both of us."

Cathleen paused a moment and tapped her chin thoughtfully. "What do you think about selecting pieces from some of the local artists who specialize in western culture and scenery?"

"I like that idea, but are you sure cowboys and sunsets will match the furniture you selected?"

"You'll have to wait and see."

While his wife smirked at him, Ben stared at the bill in his hand. "I hope the chairs aren't too fine to sit on."

Cathleen looked adorable when she placed a finger on her chin and tilted her head to the side. "You aren't going to let that invoice ruin our Christmas, are you?"

"No, and I'm sorry for making such a big deal over it. I love you, and I don't want anything to come between us. Forgive me?"

Ben opened his arms, and Cathleen melted into them and chuckled. "What's so funny?"

"Just thinking about how you've stretched yourself since you married a wife with almost no useable skills and immensely naïve to the dangers lurking about the ranch. Now, you're forced to swallow your pride and let her contribute to the family budget. Poor, poor man."

Ben lifted her off her feet and turned her around. He let her slide downward until her forehead touched his own. "Do you have any idea how you make me feel? All the stretching in the world couldn't keep me away from you."

"That's good to know. While you're in an appreciative mood, could we talk about Christmas for the children. I purchased a few items, but I want your approval. I know you don't want to overindulge them, especially when there are children with little or nothing." Ben groaned at the way she dismissed his romantic mood and turned her attention toward a piece of paper on her desk.

"I bought Sammy a stuffed bear he saw in the window of Macy's Department Store. He can't stop talking about the 'bear who tried to eat him.' I've had to interrupt his exaggerated story several times with less emphasis on the danger. Bridget's little brother thought the tale a great adventure and couldn't wait until he arrived in the Wild West to 'kill himself one of those bears.'"

"So why would you want to increase Sammy's obsession by buying a toy that would be a constant reminder of the incident?"

"I'm trying to improve the bear's reputation. I read an article in a magazine about the lovable stuffed animal. The idea came from a cartoon of President Teddy Roosevelt after he showed mercy to a captured bear. This little animal is the latest rage in toys. After I saw how Sammy reacted to the cute stuffed animal, I returned the following day and bought him one for Christmas."

Cathleen pulled the stuffed brown bear out of the wardrobe and held the fuzzy toy in front of her face. "My name is Teddy. I'm going to be Sammy's new best friend. Instead of wanting to shoot me, he's going to love me."

Ben laughed at the squeaky muffled voice coming from behind the toy. "He looks more like a cuddly puppy than a dangerous bear. Do you think this is a good idea?"

"Every time my parents endure another of Sammy's bear stories, they are more convinced than ever we should stay in Boston. I want him to love the wildlife in Wyoming, not be afraid of it. We don't have to shoot every bear we see."

"I know you think bears are beautiful creatures, but when they come down from the mountains, make a meal out of my cattle, and threaten my wife and children, I plan to shoot them. Not sure I want the children thinking they're a mere toy."

"That was a scary experience for all of us, but Sammy's obsession frightens my parents and puts unrealistic ideas in the minds of other little boys. Wouldn't a cuddly teddy bear make the incident less frightening? I'm surprised he doesn't have nightmares. Besides, the bears who visit the ranch are only looking for something to eat."

Ben shook his head and wondered if he'd ever convince his wife of the dangers lurking near their home. He hoped the peace and security she felt wouldn't be the death of her.

"Do you have any ideas for Annie or Bridget's little brother?"

"I found a zoetrope reel I thought might interest Joey. The viewer brings animals to life when you look through the hole and turn the lever. The boys will both enjoy playing with the toy. I also bought a wooden train and track for Sammy. He loves his toy cars, but since our trip to Boston, he now is obsessed with trains. For Annie, I purchased a soft doll and some colored blocks. Some of the books from the nursery here will go home with us, but I bought a few new ones as well. Do you think that's enough?"

"I would have preferred one gift for each child, but they can share most of them. Perhaps we should buy Joey a BB gun. The boy looks old enough to handle a gun and Sammy's tale about shooting bears has obviously pricked his interest. What do you think?"

Ben watched Cathleen squirm and look away. "Honey, I know you don't like the idea of guns. But in the area where we live, they are a necessity. A gun is no different than any other tool used on the ranch. Shotguns, rifles, and even revolvers are the best defense against danger. Besides, when we tire of feasting on beef, wild game makes a delicious substitute."

Cathleen turned up her nose. "I can't say I'm excited about the variety of meat or the idea of guns, but I'll trust your judgment. I'll leave Joey's gift to you. I suppose this means Sammy will also be wanting a gun in a few years."

"Unless you want him to be an outcast among his friends. When I'm away, he'll be the man of the house and expected to protect his mother and sister. Our neighbors might not be around when the next bear pays a visit."

"Please say you'll give him a few years before you hand him that kind of responsibility."

Cathleen ground her teeth in exasperation. The two of them would never agree on the need for guns. She didn't want dangerous weapons around the children, but she had to admit their usefulness in the skilled hands of Jim and Myriam when the bear attacked her and the children.

Not wanting to continue the argument, Cathleen changed the subject. "We should do something special for Bridget's uncle and aunt and their children. They suffered along with their niece and nephew when his brother and sister-in-law passed away."

"But Cathleen, a man takes pride in providing for his family; I doubt Mr. Fulcher will accept charity. You said he resisted the check you gave him to help with his move. Suppose we give him a bonus and let him shoulder the responsibility for his family's Christmas."

"What if he saves the money for another business venture instead of buying gifts for his family? I don't want the children neglected."

"My dear wife, you can't control the lives of others. We give the bonus and leave the decision for how it's spent to him. Perhaps Bridget will throw a few hints her uncle's way."

Cathleen left her comfortable chair by the fire and moved into the matching Queen Anne with her husband. "Why are you contradicting almost everything I suggest? What happened to my easygoing husband?"

Ben hung his head. "I don't mean to be contrary, but Boston seems to bring out the worst in me."

"I want to go home right after Christmas, Ben. Neither of us belong here. The visit with my parents has been great, but I miss the ranch and our privacy. Would you make the arrangements?"

"Where did that come from? I thought we were arguing about the Fulcher's."

"You settled the problem with their gift. You're the one who brought up Boston. I don't like to fight with you, Ben, and if you aren't happy here, we need to leave. Besides, I have this yearning to go home."

"What happens if the house isn't finished in time?"

"The house will be ready. If not, we can always stay a few days with your parents."

"What happened to wanting your privacy?"

"Good point." Cathleen pulled Ben's arms around her and snuggled into his chest. He kissed the sensitive spots behind her ear and down her neck. She pulled his head up and touched her lips to his. They had more privacy in her parents' home than she'd ever have in Laramie, but that didn't keep her from longing for their life in Wyoming.

A light knock interrupted them. Cathleen stood, caught a few wayward strands of hair and finger pressed the wrinkles in her skirt. Ben groaned, "And I was about to move us to the bed."

"You are naughty, Ben Sorenson. Our babies are probably awake, and we promised to play in the garden. Let's go."

Cathleen expected Bridget and her brother to have a hard time celebrating their first Christmas without their parents.

Much had changed for them in one short year—difficult changes that could have a lasting impression on a young boy. Cathleen wanted to make this festive season special for them.

Despite his sadness, Joey bubbled with excitement every time someone mentioned Christmas. He jumped and cheered until Sammy also caught his enthusiasm. On Christmas morning, the boys didn't bother to wake Bridget, but burst through Cathleen and Ben's door without warning. She wasn't prepared for the tackle they received from their son. Although Joey probably initiated the wake-up call, he stood near the door waiting for his friend to do the damage.

"Merry Christmas!" Sammy yelled in her ear.

Ben groaned, pulled Sammy off her and engaged him in a tickling match that did more damage than the initial attack. "Settle down, boys. Why don't you and Joey tiptoe back to the nursery while we get dressed? Try not to wake Bridget and Annie. We'll come get you in a few minutes."

By the time they arrived in the nursery, Bridget had them all dressed and waiting. Ben followed the boys down while Cathleen took Annie. When the girl didn't follow, Cathleen turned around. "What's the matter, Bridget? Aren't you ready to celebrate Christmas?"

Bridget dropped her head and studied her hands. "It's not that I feel unwelcome here. You and Mr. Sorenson have been so good to Joey and me. Even your parents treat us as family. The problem is that I don't know what's expected of me. I miss my parents. With them, I had no question about where I belonged. Now, I'm not so sure."

Cathleen touched the girl's shoulder and forced her to look into her eyes. "Since I didn't make myself clear before, I will try again. I love you like a little sister, Bridget. Little sisters are expected to celebrate special holidays with their families. Thank you for staying with the children last night while we attended the Christmas Eve service with my parents, but today we want you with us. We will exchange gifts and then eat breakfast together. Later this afternoon, Winston will drive you and Joey to visit your uncle's family. Please relax and enjoy your time with us."

Bridget hugged Cathleen despite the protest from an unhappy Annie squeezed between them. "Forgive me for feeling a bit like Annie, trapped between two different worlds. In one position, I follow orders and accept payment for a job I love. The other finds me thrown into an upper-class family where my best friend treats me to shopping trips, shares her secrets and helps me make decisions about the future. Though I feel loved and accepted, I still long for a family of my own. Perhaps when we travel West, my role will become clearer."

As the two women, walked arm in arm down the main staircase, an idea popped into Cathleen's head. It took her with such force that she stumbled and nearly pulled all three of them down with her. After chastising herself for being so careless with Annie, she resumed making plans. Dan needed a wife and a family. Though a bit young, Bridget would make the perfect bride. Cathleen couldn't wait to head West and set her plans in motion.

The last present had been unwrapped and the children ushered into the dining room for Christmas brunch. Talking her mother into including everyone turned into a surprise for both women. Her mother stared with her mouth agape when her daughter first suggested they include the children and staff. Cathleen continued defending her position long after her mother had smiled and nodded in agreement.

"If the children don't join us, Bridget will be left out, and if you invite her without including the other servants, they will feel slighted."

"Cathleen, stop talking. I agree. Last year, I would have been appalled at such an outrageous suggestion, and I can't guarantee that this new practice will continue, but you and your father have convinced me to accept Bridget and her little brother. Besides, some of our staff have been with us since your father and I first married, and a Christmas brunch seems like a good way to express our appreciation. Though convincing Jenson and Mrs. Murphy won't be easy."

On that point her mother had been right. Even Mrs. Thomas, the cook, was heard to say, "It ain't proper, I tell you. Having everyone sitting down together like one big happy family. They might get away with such out West but wait 'til the servants in the other big houses get wind of such goin's on."

Cathleen knew about the servants' gossip mill. Any news out of the ordinary traveled at lightning speed to every household in the city. By evening, every society matron would have received news from their staff about the Doyle's outrageous Christmas brunch. Her mother would be mortified.

Over brunch, Sammy showed the guests the teddy bear he received for Christmas. Unfortunately, the bear generated comments which led their son into his dramatic version of how the bear tried to eat Mama. Cathleen hated to admit her error, but Ben had been right about the gift. She cringed when she realized the bear story would spread even faster than her mother's unconventional brunch.

With a twinkle in his eye, Ben reached across the table and patted her hand, patronizing her. "What's the matter, honey? Are you afraid I might say 'I told you so?' I wouldn't think of being so cruel, but I'm fairly certain your mother will be relieved when we board the West-bound train."

Ben chuckled as he released her hand and sat back in his chair. Cathleen wanted to kick him under the table and wipe the smirk off his face. When he fluttered his eyebrows up and down, she couldn't help but return a cheeky smile. She could never stay angry with a man who managed to turn the makings of a disaster into tantalizing fun.

By the time the children were taken to the nursery for their afternoon naps, Bridget and Joey had left to visit their family at the house. Ben took Cathleen's hand and led her into their bedroom.

"I have a present I wanted to give you in private." After joining her on the loveseat before the open fire, he put a hand in his pocket and pulled out an unwrapped velvet box. Placing the gift in her hand, he closed her fingers over the small box.

"I found this in Chicago and planned to give it to you when you returned home. The day I left, I rushed into the barn office to get cash for the trip. When I opened the safe, this little box caught my eye, and I couldn't leave it behind. Now I know why."

Cathleen gazed into her husband's eyes and saw adoration and love beaming back at her. He rubbed his hands on his trousers and covered her hands with his larger ones. "Cathleen, would you do me the honor of becoming my wife?"

"What? I'm already your wife. Remember that hasty little ceremony the day I arrived?"

"I know, and I'm embarrassed when I think about that shoddy wedding—no ring, no music, no flowers and no marriage proposal. Would you give me a second chance?"

"The day I arrived in Laramie had to be one of the worst days ever for me. I boarded the train in Boston with such high expectations. I had packed a beautiful wedding dress, complete with veil and silk slippers, thinking I would marry the prince of my dreams. Nothing turned out the way I'd imagined. My reluctant groom only wanted a mother for his children. I felt hopeless until you touched your lips to mine—my first real kiss."

"If that was your first kiss, what gave you the idea to open your mouth? That little gesture hit me like a hot poker."

Cathleen laughed at Ben's confusion. He scratched his head and waited for her to stop laughing enough to answer. "When your father said you could kiss your bride, I enjoyed watching you squirm and wondered how you'd escape the age-old tradition. I didn't expect you to kiss me.

"My mouth opened with a shocked 'Oh' when I realized what you were about to do. The moment your lips met mine, a heat coursed through me, and I felt as if something powerful connected us. Along with a gang of butterflies, hope stirred within me, and my disappointments vanished. I wanted to dance about the room. But moments later, my hopes were crushed when you pushed me away and rushed out the door."

"We did connect, honey. Even before that passionate kiss, the wall around my heart began to crumble. The way you looked when I walked into the kitchen and saw you with the children. You weren't what I expected from a Boston socialite. You were real, and love danced in your eyes when you looked at Annie and Sammy. As for my departure, you don't know what it took for me to walk out that door. The feel of you in my arms and your breath in my mouth set me on fire."

Cathleen tingled from head to toe as she listened to Ben recall the day they were married. He would have saved her a lot of anguish and grief if he had explained himself that mortifying day.

Ben fidgeted with the box he held. "You never answered my question."

Watching her husband's expression, she touched her finger to his forehead and traced the worry lines. "You had me from the moment I first saw you standing by the barn door. Yes, I love being your wife."

Cathleen kissed him and then stared at the sparkling gold wedding band with diamonds circling the top half of the ring. "But you already gave me your grandmother's beautiful ring."

"I know, but I need you to have something from me." He placed the ring on her finger next to the emerald and then kissed each finger before pulling her onto his lap. Cathleen took another look and admired how the two rings caught the light and complemented one another.

"Thank you, Ben. They look beautiful together. How will I ever repay you."

"I wouldn't mind another one of those toe-curling kisses."

After the kiss, Ben touched his forehead to hers and gazed into her eyes. "When we've had time to settle into our new home, I would like for us to renew our vows with a nice church wedding—the one you had in mind when you first stepped off the train in Laramie. We'll invite your parents to come and stay with the children while we go on a honeymoon. Perhaps we'll take the train further west to California. Would you like that?"

"I would love to see the Pacific Ocean, but I'm not sure about leaving the children."

"They'll be fine with our parents. Sammy and Annie will enjoy the extra attention. Besides, they'll have Bridget."

"You're right. We should get away. But we need to go home first. I plan to pack our trunks tomorrow and leave as soon as you secure tickets."

# Chapter Twenty-four

Cathleen's father tried to charter a luxury private car for their return trip, but Cathleen wouldn't agree. When she fled Boston, she'd left in such a hurry the only seat available was in coach. She spent five miserable days on a hard seat—sleeping in an upright position, fanning away obnoxious odors, and enduring the miserable heat. That would never work with two small children, but she no longer belonged to a luxury kind of family. A small compartment with a sleeper would work fine.

Not knowing the condition of the house, Ben had asked Bridget and Joey to delay their trip west. They would stay in Boston and live with their aunt and uncle. Though Bridget expressed disappointment, Cathleen knew her concern was more for Joey. The little boy had been abandoned one too many times.

"But I want to go with you and Sammy now."

Cathleen looked to Ben to soothe the boys' feelings. "Just as soon as we have the house finished, Joey, we'll send you and your sister tickets. Besides, your aunt and uncle want to spend time with you before you take off. This will be your last opportunity to see them for a while."

Bridget put her arm around her brother and hugged him. Whatever she whispered in his ear must have worked, because he smiled and rushed up the stairs ahead of her.

Two days after the new year, Cathleen, Ben, and the children arrived at the Boston train station. A light snow fell on the platform and the wind stung her cheeks. Cathleen hugged her parents one more time before taking her husband's hand to board the train.

Together with her parents, they had chosen a date in late May near their first anniversary to renew their wedding vows.

Her parents seemed grateful for the opportunity to stay with the children while she and Ben spent a few days on the West Coast.

Her parents seemed old and sad as Cathleen watched them from her window seat. They clung to each other as they searched every window for a final glimpse of their daughter. The moment her father spotted her, she saw him alerting her mother. Smiles replaced the sadness, and they waved enthusiastically.

The scene appeared remarkably different from the last time she'd left Boston. Then, she had been running away from her parents into an unknown future. Now, too, she grieved the thought of leaving, yet Cathleen longed to return to the ranch she considered home.

"Mama, the train blew the whistle." Sammy climbed over her to watch the train pull out of the station.

"I heard. Wave to Grandfather and Grandmother. Do you want my window seat?" With the boy's bouncing and climbing she'd be a wrinkled mess before the train reached the suburbs.

Annie had fallen asleep in her father's arms, and he'd moved her to the bench seat next to him. Pulling down one of the beds would have been more comfortable for the baby but would allow little walking space in the small cubicle. Now, she understood why her father promoted the private parlor car.

The trip wasn't nearly as dreadful with Ben along. Of course, she wasn't sick or pregnant this time around. They took turns watching the children, visiting the dining car and sharing moments with other travelers over a weak cup of coffee. Newspapers and magazines were available, but after a few days of sharing with strangers, Cathleen preferred a quiet nook where she could immerse herself in *Anne of Green Gables* by L.M. Montgomery.

Ben laughed at her choice of the novel over a newspaper. "Why should I read the news when you'll inform me of anything worth knowing. Besides, I'm enjoying the adventures of Anne Shirley. She reminds me of myself at that age."

"How so?"

"Like Anne, I was rather precocious with a hint of mischief and didn't hesitate to speak my mind, regardless of the subject. At times, Mother didn't know what to think of me. That's probably why she allowed me to spend so much time with Nana."

"You don't seem to have changed much—still precocious and headstrong, I might add, and always with that hint of mischief."

Cathleen gave Ben a playful swat on the knee with her book as she scooted out the door. Never would she have imagined such a husband. He teased her in a way that made her want to dance for joy. She'd twirl down the aisle if her fellow passengers wouldn't think her uncouth.

She'd barely settled into her story when the porter stopped at her table. "We've just crossed into Wyoming, Miz Sorenson. We'll be making a stop in Cheyenne within the hour. Laramie's not much farther down the track."

As the dark-skinned man worked his way down the aisle, Cathleen's thoughts turned toward the ranch and the new house. The furniture they'd selected had been shipped, and she worried the house wouldn't be ready when they arrived. Staying in town didn't appeal to her. She'd fallen in love with the view from the cabin window and dreamed of similar views from her new home. In anticipation of leaving the train, she returned to the sleeping parlor to help Ben with the children and to gather their belongings.

They spotted Ben's parents standing stoically near the steps, looking anxious, as the train pulled into Laramie. Ben released Sammy who made a dash for his grandfather. Maggie, with tears in her eyes, reached for Annie. "My dear Cathleen. How glad I am to see you and my sweet grandchildren. I have ached every day for your return. Don't ever do this to me again." Cathleen reached around her mother-in-law to hug her with Annie squashed between.

Cathleen stepped back to straighten the hat she felt slipping. Maggie looked at Annie as if seeing her for the first time. "My, how you've grown, little one."

Annie frowned and reached for her mother. Expecting the baby to cry as she did with Jenson, Cathleen prayed Maggie wouldn't feel rejected. Instead of tears, Annie returned her attention to the older woman and ran her hand across her grandmother's wrinkled cheek. Upon recognition, she kicked her feet and began a conversation of happy blabber. The child never ceased to surprise her.

After Ben's father shook hands with his son and put Sammy down, he pulled the girls, including Cathleen into his long arms. "You stayed away too long, Cathleen. I thought you'd deserted us."

"How could I desert the courageous fellow who brought me to this beautiful place and introduced me to my amazing family? You'll never get rid of me." The kind man squeezed tighter until Annie squealed and pushed him away.

"How's my little princess? I see you're as opinionated as ever." He laughed while tickling Annie under the chin. Cathleen felt her eyes filling with tears when she remembered the similar emotional scene she'd left on the platform in Boston. So many changes in only a few short months—all for the better.

Ben put his arm around her and motioned toward Dan who waited by the wagon. He had the trunks loaded and looked ready to head back to the ranch.

"Why don't you ride with us in the buggy? The wagon will be crowded. Did you bring half of Boston home with you, Cathleen?"

She gave her teasing father-in-law an affectionate pat. "Of course. Can't wait to fill my house with treasures from my hometown. We don't mind riding with you, but are you sure you want to drive out to the ranch this late? It's almost time for dinner—I mean supper." She smiled at her own confusion.

"No problem. We'd planned to go home with you anyway. Maggie made a fine meal, so you wouldn't have to cook."

"That's very kind of you, Mama. Thank you." Reaching for her mother-in-law, Cathleen emphasized the name Ben used for his mother.

Sammy bounced up and down between his grandparents during the bumpy ride to the ranch. The excited child pointed out every rabbit, squirrel, chipmunk, bird, and even withered weeds hiding amid patches of snow.

"Did you see my bear?" The boy held the stuffed animal before his grandfather's face waiting for a response.

"Well now, that's about the finest bear I've ever seen."

"Mama says he's a good bear. Not like the one that tried to eat her."

Cathleen shook her head and sighed. Would the boy ever get over that unpleasant day? Ben and his Dad chuckled, knowing her attempt to erase all references to the "mean ole bear."

When she looked up from her embarrassment, Cathleen saw the welcoming, but faded sign—Hope Ranch. *Thank you, God, for bringing us safely home.* She gazed into the distance toward the small cabin she'd come to love. She wrinkled her brow at the buggies and wagons lining the lane and filling the yard.

"What's going on, Ben?" Her husband scanned the scene with similar confusion.

"I don't know, honey, but I bet my parents have an idea. Mama? Papa?"

"We aren't the only ones who've missed you. Our friends and neighbors insisted on welcoming you home with a covered dish supper."

Though exhausted, Cathleen had learned to appreciate the tight-knit community. The rough tables groaned with cloth-covered dishes. Women were busy making room for more while the men congregated in small groups and the children chased each other around the yard. A small group of Mexicans stood near the barn, looking misplaced and uncomfortable.

"It's about time you showed up." Jim and Myriam interrupted her concern for their employees. The tight hug from her friend let her know she'd been missed. "I thought you'd never come home. We need a few wash days to catch up."

After a good deal of laughter, hugs, and handshakes from those who'd gathered around the buggy, the group moved toward the food tables. Cathleen and Ben left their neighbors and went to greet their ranch hands. "Cathleen, I would like you to meet Pedro's family."

Cathleen reached her hand toward Maria. "Maria, estoy tan feliz de que finalmente estés aquí!"

Ben stared at her as if he couldn't believe the words coming from her mouth. "You speak Spanish?"

"Didn't I tell you? I also speak French and Italian."

"What did you say to her?"

"I welcomed her and told her how happy I was that she'd come. I should have said you are the one who'll be happy to get a decent meal."

Ben pulled her close and whispered in her ear. "You continue to surprise me, Mrs. Sorenson, but we have a problem. I am the only one on this ranch who doesn't speak Spanish. Do you think you could teach me?"

"Of course, and I'll teach our Mexican friends English if they want to learn."

Cathleen greeted the remainder of Pedro's family, including José and Isabella, and urged them to join her at the food tables. On the way, she looked around for the children. One of the Langland sisters held Annie while Sammy and Toby were exchanging kisses. Ben grabbed the boy's hand and stood next to his father.

The minister took little effort securing the attention of their hungry guests. All eyes turned to him when he hit a knife against an empty plate. After he said grace and motioned for

Cathleen to lead the way to the table, he mingled with their friends and neighbors.

The table overflowed with such a variety of dishes Cathleen hardly knew where to start. The hunger she'd felt earlier had left her when she noticed the obvious barrier between the town's people and their Mexican workers. They seemed hesitant to mingle and partake of the food. Had someone made them feel unwelcome or did they choose to stay on the sidelines because they didn't understand English?

Cathleen relaxed and turned her attention back to the table when she saw Jim and Myriam urging their Spanish friends to join the food line. She'd only taken small servings of about half the dishes before her plate overflowed with more food than she could eat. Looking behind her to check on Ben and Sammy, she eyed Ben's hefty plate compared to their son's sparse one.

"Do you think you have enough to eat?" Cathleen motioned at his plate. He shrugged and laughed while rearranging the food to make room for one more barbequed rib. The man certainly loved his meat.

Cathleen led Sammy to a table with benches and waited for Ben. The man took his time chatting with each person. Even the food wasn't compelling enough to lure him from the people. For her sake, he'd endured a few weeks in Boston among strangers. But here, he was home with his neighbors and friends. Looking at the crowd, she let out a slow breath and smiled at her own feeling of belonging.

With the bowls empty and the men rubbing their full stomachs, Ben's father tapped an empty platter on the table and cleared his throat. "I know Cathleen and Ben are exhausted from their trip, but before they leave us, I want to thank you all for coming. You represent some of the best people on God's good earth. We have been recipients of your generosity for years, but during the last few days, we've never felt so loved and supported.

"The new house would not be finished without your sacrificial contributions of time and labor. When my son and his wife understand the extent of your efforts, I know they'll want to make the rounds to thank you personally. God be with you as you return to your homes."

# Chapter Twenty-five

Cathleen cried when Dan unlocked the front door. Standing inside the entryway, she turned in slow motion to get a sense of the new surroundings. A well-built, spacious home welcomed her in every direction. Never could she have imagined such a place.

Through a glaze of tears, she looked at Ben whose smile matched her own. "Oh, Ben. When I came to you, I never expected or even wished for such a fine house. I know you built this for me and I'm grateful for the sacrifice. Thank you."

Cathleen hugged Ben and Annie who remained asleep on his shoulder. "How did I get so lucky?"

Following Sammy into the oversized dining room, Cathleen stopped to admire the way the light came through the sheer curtains. The furniture she'd purchased in Boston complemented the stained chair rail. A brass candelabra hung over the massive oak table which anchored a dozen chairs. The matching buffet occupied one side of the room while a server stood on the wall closest to the butler's pantry. A Christmas cactus in full bloom graced the center of the table.

"Wait for Mama, Sammy." Eager to investigate, the little boy ran through the butler's pantry and into the kitchen, bouncing with each new discovery.

Cathleen ran her hand along the open shelves in the pantry. One side contained a skimpy array of table linens, while the other held the dishes she'd purchased from the general store. Not wanting Sammy to explore alone, she walked on through to the kitchen. The large table in the center of the room reminded her of Ben's comment. "With the massive dining room, I don't understand why we need this large table in the kitchen."

Despite her mother's training, she preferred the casual atmosphere of the kitchen to the formal dining room. Even when Maria and her daughter were present, they would sit in the warmth and comfort of the kitchen. The formal area would be used for special occasions and guests. She dreamed of holidays when the ranch hands, neighbors, and family would come together for one big celebration.

"My chair." Sammy sat at one of the side chairs and patted the seat next to him. "You sit here, Mama."

"That's sweet, darling, but we need to finish our tour. You can't be hungry after eating all that chicken." She'd noticed an increase in his appetite lately and wondered how long before he'd be as big as his papa.

Sammy hopped down and led her by the hand through an open archway to the large room on the right. Dan guided them to the center of the room while drawing attention to the craftsmanship and skills of different workers. Cathleen watched the setting sun blend with the curtains framing the bank of windows. She'd chosen the fabric because of its resemblance to a painted desert. The effect rendered her speechless.

Recalling their late afternoon arrival, Cathleen had watched Dan drive the wagon with the luggage past the welcoming party without stopping. He hadn't returned to eat and visit until many of the platters sat empty. His late arrival explained the placement of the last-minute tables and lamps that traveled with them from Boston.

"Dan Riley, you are a good man. What would we do without you?"

"My pleasure, Mrs. Sorenson, but I didn't do any of this alone. I received a lot of help from your friends and neighbors. Ben's parents were great at making decisions on paint color or where a piece of furniture should go. If you don't like how we arranged the rooms, I'll be happy to change them."

"I couldn't have placed the furniture better myself. Looks as though I'm indebted to a long list of generous people—beginning with you. Please call me Cathleen. Ben and I consider you a dear friend." Cathleen touched Dan's arm lightly. "Ben told me about what happened between you and Isabella. Forgive me, but I can't be sorry. I have a feeling God has someone special for you. Just wait and see."

Avoiding eye contact, Dan shoved his hands in his pockets and mumbled. "Thank you. I'd appreciate your prayers."

Cathleen turned back to the great room and admired the stone hearth covering most of one end. Though the design lacked the formality and traditions of the East, the open beams and banks of windows brought the outdoors inside. Her mind already at work on the finishing touches, she envisioned blanket throws and rugs made by Myriam's relatives in Oklahoma, pottery and candleholders with Spanish influence, and pictures depicting western scenes.

Ben noticed Sammy's pull on her arm. "Could we move this tour upstairs? The children should have already been in bed."

The boy released her hand and took off toward the high stairway. "Don't forget what you learned in Boston about holding on to the rail." Sammy slowed down and complied with her request.

Arriving on the upper level, Cathleen waited for Ben to tuck Annie into her crib and pull the nursery door closed. He looked down at Sammy who'd lost most of his energy half-way up the stairs.

"Would you like a ride, little man?" The toddler reached for his father and once in his arms, rested his head on Ben's shoulder—a long day for such a little boy. Cathleen wished she could do the same as she felt her own strength waning.

Dan opened the door to the bedroom she would share with her husband and stood to the side for them to walk in alone. Cathleen traced the flower design carved into the bed post and noticed how well the green and rose drapes matched the counterpane. The room couldn't be more elegant if she'd designed it herself. She reached for her handkerchief to dab the tears from the corner of her eyes. Even the bed had been made with new, fresh linens.

Ben handed Sammy to Cathleen and walked downstairs with Dan. One look at the boy and she knew she couldn't put him to bed on clean sheets. Dirt and grease covered him from head to toe. Creamed corn and chocolate cake decorated his face and clothes.

"How did you get so dirty in such a short time? We need a basin of water, fast."

Sammy looked at her through droopy eye lids and snuggled closer to her chest. Her dress would be ruined, but the love from her son was worth more than many dresses. She tried a few doors before finding what she thought might be a toilet room with a pitcher of water. Stopping at the threshold, she couldn't proceed further. Ben had put running water in the house? A white porcelain sink sat in one corner of the room while a claw-footed tub occupied the space at the far end. Hidden behind a partial wall sat a toilet—an indoor toilet.

With no electricity, how did Ben manage such a feat? She tapped her chin wondering how she'd missed the running water when Sammy rushed her through the kitchen. If not for her son, she would have returned downstairs to see what else she'd missed. Regardless of the overlooked details, she recognized the thread of Ben's love meandering through every room.

"Mama, is this our house now?"

"Yes, Sammy. This is the house Papa built for us. Mama's going to wipe you off and put you to bed in your very own room."

"What about Annie and you and Papa?"

"Annie's already asleep in her room. Mama and Papa will be just down the hall. You're a big boy, and big boys need to have their own rooms."

Sammy gave her a sleepy smile and laid back against her chest. She pulled the chair from the dressing table close to the sink and turned on the shiny chrome and porcelain faucet. Using the washcloth she'd found on top of a stack of towels, she wiped his face, arms, and legs. Not as good as a soak in the bathtub, but at least he wouldn't soil the fresh linens.

Without the usual bedtime story, Cathleen tucked the little boy into the feather mattress with the blue and white quilt tight around his body. Teddy bear snuggled in his arms. She kissed Sammy's forehead and felt her chest expanding with gratitude. *Lord, watch over our little boy. Show us how to teach him your truth so that he grows into a mighty man of God.*

Leaving Sammy's door ajar, Cathleen heard Ben's stride on the stairs. She waited for him and grabbed his arm in a tight squeeze. "You didn't tell me we would have inside toilets. How did you manage the plumbing?"

"Seeing how you despised the outhouse, I researched alternatives to electricity and discovered farmers all over the area are using windmills. I'd seen them from a distance, so I had to investigate for myself. Didn't you notice the windmill on the hill between the house and the ranch proper?"

Cathleen shook her head, wondering how she missed such a sight.

"I suppose you also overlooked the elevated water tank. Because the tank sits high in the air, gravitational pull flows the water into the house. The well company drilled deep into an underground water supply which they claim will produce enough fresh, clean water for the whole ranch. Now, Maria wants Pedro to install indoor plumbing in their home too. What we men are forced to do to keep our women happy."

Cathleen hit Ben playfully before hugging his arm tighter. "I not only married a handsome man but a resourceful one as well."

Ben chuckled while lifting her off her feet, dancing her across the threshold and throwing her in a heap on their four-poster bed. "My pleasure, my curious and inquiring wife. Most women wouldn't concern themselves with how the water arrives, but not you. What a smart woman I married. You, my dear, are worth more than all the money in the world."

Ben shifted her on the bed while pulling back the covers. His face turned from teasing to that look of desire she'd come to love. He took his time removing each article of her clothing while kissing the exposed areas.

Amid thoughts of Ben's love, a dismal sadness swept over her. The choking sensation felt as if someone had pulled a heavy cord tight around her neck. Cathleen couldn't keep the soft whimper inside. Ben's kisses stopped and he looked into her eyes. "What's wrong, honey?"

"I try to forget, but at the most unexpected moments I remember the baby we lost. Instead of preparing for the exciting event, my stomach remains empty, filled with nothing but grief for my child. Why can't I get over this aching sorrow?"

Without expecting an answer, she went on. "Do you think we'll ever have another baby? You were with me in Boston for weeks and nothing happened."

Cathleen felt cold air hit her exposed body when Ben moved away and stood next to the bed. His expression changed from desire to anguish at her wounding words. "Oh, Ben, what have I done?"

She watched her husband shake himself and stuff his fears behind a sympathetic smile. Returning to the bed, he placed his head against her forehead. "I'm sorry, honey. I know how you grieve for the baby you lost and how you long for another, but my old fears keep rearing their ugly head. Please forgive me and pray that I can enjoy the oneness with you without dreading the consequences."

Cathleen sucked in her grief and cleared her throat. She prayed silently while removing Ben's tie and unbuttoning his shirt. By the time her hands touched his waist, the look of desire had returned. "Oh Ben," she whispered as she kissed his exposed chest and yielded to the love of her husband.

Cathleen awakened the next morning and reached for Ben. When she found only a cold empty impression in the feather mattress, she dressed and went down to the kitchen. Ben, Pedro, and Maria were sitting at the table clutching cups of hot coffee. She paused at the opening into the dining room and glanced at the cuckoo clock on the wall. Nine o'clock? "Is that the right time? Why did you let me sleep so long? Where are the children?"

"Sammy and Annie have had breakfast and are with Mariana. She took them for a walk before the storm."

Cathleen stared out the large window over the sink into a dreary day. The warm sun of the day before had disappeared behind a blanket of clouds. "Is it supposed to rain?"

"It might start out as rain, but the temperature is dropping fast. I expect heavy snow by mid-afternoon. Dan's coming soon to make plans in case the storm turns into a blizzard."

Ben stood and gave her a peck on the lips. "Good morning to you too!"

"Sorry, I can't believe I overslept." Cathleen apologized and greeted Maria and Pedro in Spanish. To warm her cold hands, she cradled the cup of coffee Maria handed her.

"So much has changed in the few months I've been gone. I don't know what to do with myself. Even our clothes were unpacked for us."

"I doubt you'll be looking for chores once the children are back inside. In the meantime, let me know if you need any ideas." Ben moved his eyebrows up and down accompanied by a quirky smile.

"Behave yourself, Ben Sorenson. We're not alone here." Cathleen could feel the blush rising on her face and noticed Pedro whispering the translation to his wife. Maria looked at her and smiled.

Dan arrived with Walt and Clint before Ben could tease her further. "That wind cuts right through a body. I'm afraid we're in for a big blow—I already feel the pain in my bones." Clint massaged his left shoulder and winced.

The other men agreed as they grabbed cups of coffee and pulled out chairs. Cathleen found her heavy coat inside a small closet next to the back door. "I'm going out to find the children."

As predicted, the storm moved in fast, and by sundown, the snow had blown onto the porch and banked against the front door. The wind increased in velocity and roared through the valley like a freight train. Even the rafters creaked with the forceful gusts. During the night, the first time Cathleen heard groaning in the vicinity of the fireplace, she sat up and shook Ben. "Ben, there must be an animal stuck in the chimney. Is there something we can do?"

Ben pulled her into his arms. "The sound is coming from the wind, honey. Try to get some rest. Daybreak will be here soon, and the storm should blow over in a few hours."

The morning dawned with little light and no relief from the wind. Noticing the empty space next to her, Cathleen jumped from bed and shrieked when her feet hit the cold floor. She made a mental note to purchase another rug as she tiptoed across the floor to find her slippers. Choosing her warmest robe, she pulled her hair into a loose bun and went over to the window. She strained for a glimpse of the distant mountains. Her beautiful view had disappeared into a white veil.

When she found the children's rooms vacant, Cathleen made her way downstairs and into the large room adjoining the kitchen. She lingered inside the doorway long enough to take in the domestic scene. Ben lounged in a comfortable chair facing the fireplace with Annie cuddled in his arms. Sammy sat on the floor surrounded by a stack of colorful blocks. Her head jerked toward the musical tweets when the colorful bird hopped out of his house and cuckooed eight times.

"Why did you let me oversleep again today? You must be starving."

"Good morning, my dear. Since you were restless during the night, I thought you might need the extra sleep. Besides, you appeared so peaceful when I left, I didn't want to disturb you. How do you feel?"

"I'd feel better if this awful wind would cease. The constant roar makes me jittery."

"Stay where you are. We have a surprise for you." Ben put Annie down and walked her toward her mother. When she was a few feet away, he released her. Cathleen started crying when the baby toddled into her arms.

"What have you done with my baby? Oh, Annie, you are growing too fast. Before long, you'll be too big to snuggle."

Annie kicked and made happy baby sounds as Cathleen moved toward the open fireplace. The heat penetrated the back of her thick robe while the little girl's body warmed her front. She hugged Annie and swayed back and forth until she heard a loud noise coming from the basement.

"What in the world? All night the rafters have creaked as if we're harboring a family of squirrels. Now, there's banging in the basement. These weird sounds are enough to drive a person insane."

The news stories about women losing their lives in blizzards seemed irrational when she first read them, but after one night, she could see how the continuous wind might cause a person to lose their sanity. Some of those who survived chose to return East instead of enduring another endless winter of confinement and howling winds. If not for Ben and the children, she'd leave at the first thaw.

"That's just the furnace working overtime to keep the radiators hot. Watch the children while I check the pressure gauge and replenish the coal."

Cathleen put Annie on the rug next to her brother while Ben headed for the stairs. Feeling chilled, she stood before the fire until the back of her robe felt hot enough to scorch. Turning to give equal time to the front, she chuckled at the picture forming in her mind—a juicy pig roasting on a spit.

"What would you like for breakfast?" Cathleen asked Ben when he returned.

"Pancakes, Mama!"

"That's a great idea, Sammy. Why don't you come help me make the batter and I'll make some blueberry syrup from the canned fruit Mrs. Myriam gave us? How does that sound?"

Sammy hopped up and started for the kitchen.

"Hold on there, little man. What do you do when you finish playing with your blocks?"

Sammy's shoulders slumped as he stopped and turned around with one hand on his hip. One stern look from his father halted the expected whine. By the armloads, the toys were soon returned to the storage box in the corner.

Though the meal took longer to prepare, and flour covered most of the workspace and floor, Cathleen didn't mind. The time spent with Sammy was well worth the trouble. In Boston, she'd missed the teachable moments that presented themselves while cooking or doing chores with the children.

"Okay, fellow. You did a great job. After I wipe some of this flour off you, you can let Papa know the pancakes are ready."

Three days later, Cathleen awakened to an eerie silence. Though she welcomed the quiet, her ears were accustomed to the constant roar, and a strange feeling came over her. She turned on her back and heard paper crinkle beneath her.

Cathleen sat up and pulled out a note. The early-morning sun projected enough light to read Ben's scribbled handwriting.

> Dan and I have gone out with the men to investigate the damage from the storm. Be back soon. Love, Ben.

Never one to linger, she hopped from the bed and rushed to the window. Using the sleeve of her robe, she cleared the fog enough to see through one of the panes. The bright morning sun reflecting on the brilliant white blinded her. After her vision adjusted, she saw the mountain range visible in the distance against miles of drifted snow.

# Chapter Twenty-six

The blizzard of 1911 wreaked havoc on the cattlemen in and around Laramie, Wyoming. Hope ranch was no exception. When the snow began to melt and the creek ran free of ice, thousands of carcasses were discovered huddled together in ravines or near the creek bed. With the snow warming the ground, the smell of rotting flesh permeated the area. Wearing bandanas over their nose and mouth, Ben and the men spent several days burying the dead bodies in mass graves. Cathleen refused to open the windows until the job had been completed and the air again smelled crisp and pure.

The first time Ben rode in from assessing the damage, tears spilled onto his beard as he described the devastation. "I don't know why God allowed such a terrible loss. I hate having to borrow money at the bank. Maybe I'm not supposed to be a cattleman."

Stunned speechless, Cathleen watched Ben collapse onto his desk and sob like a baby. Before she could respond, he raised his head and looked around the large room. He let out an angry roar and slammed a tight fist at the stack of bills on his desk. Cathleen shrunk back lest he take his anger out on her. Thank goodness, the children weren't in the room to see such rage coming from their father.

"If I hadn't spent so much money on this house, I'd have a reserve to get us by until next year. One good year, and I spend money as if we had an endless supply."

Cathleen had heard enough. Her courage returned as she leaned over and smacked both hands solidly on the desk in front of him. He jerked back as if she'd slapped him. "Ben Sorenson. You are way too young for senility. Think about what you're saying.

"Yes, what the blizzard did was devastating and many will have to take out loans to survive, but the Sorenson's will not be among them."

Instead of smiling as Cathleen hoped, Ben rocked back in his chair, glowering. Before he could blast her further with his anger, she continued her own tirade.

"Are we going to have another argument over that joint account that sits unused down at the bank? Stop being ridiculous. For the record, you don't have a loan, much less need an additional one. Not only do you have money for our ranch, but God has provided us with the means to help our neighbors and friends."

Ben sat back in his chair with a blank expression on his face, staring at her as if hearing the information for the first time. He scratched his beard and ran his hands through his hair until the short curls stood on end. He waited so long to respond she wanted to hit him over the head with his stack of bills.

"Say something before I lose my temper."

At last, the man came to his senses. His wet eyes danced, and a smile relaxed the corners of his mouth. "Once again I've been put in my place by my smart, rich wife."

"Don't you say another word, Ben Sorenson. How many times do I have to remind you that when you married me, you also married my money? You are lying to yourself if you continue seeing us ruined."

"I don't know what's wrong with me, Cathleen. The death and destruction I've seen almost made me give up. I've ignored and resented your money for so long, I must have thought it had disappeared. Now that you've reminded me, I don't know whether to be resentful or grateful."

"I'm going to be honest with you, Ben. Your resentment of my inheritance makes me wonder if you don't also resent me."

Ben reached for her. "I could never resent you, honey. Please forgive me."

Cathleen pushed him away. "But you resent who I am. You continue to guard yourself against that bad experience with Audrey in Boston years ago. God sent me here when I desperately needed you. Why can't you accept the gift God wants to give you? He brought me to you because he could trust you. You are a man of integrity who will use the money with wisdom and discretion."

Her husband glanced down a moment before speaking. "In my heart I know you're right, but my head wants me to be the sole provider for my family. This position of feeling secure about finances will take some getting used to. Perhaps we should talk to our neighbors before making a visit to the bank. I like your idea of using the money to help other ranchers."

Cathleen came around the desk and sat on Ben's lap. "I will be patient with you, but I refuse to hear any more whining. You sounded a bit like our three-year-old." She tweaked his cheek and rested her head against his heart. Ben ran his finger down her face and across her lips. Desire surged in the pit of her stomach, and she responded to his kiss. He picked her up and carried her up the stairs to their bedroom. She didn't mind the argument if the debate ended in the arms of her passionate husband.

Cathleen loved spring in Wyoming. Cold nights kept the radiators hot, but with milder days, she opened the windows. Multi-colored birds flocked to the small tree Ben had planted outside the kitchen window. Honking geese flew in perfect formation as they made their way north.

Together, she and Ben had prayed about which families in the area could use financial assistance. Not wanting to injure their neighbors' pride, they offered interest-free loans. Cathleen and Myriam worked with Maggie to provide food and clothing for struggling families. The absence of cash reserves left growing children without clothing and shoes, and several families had overdue accounts at the mercantile and bank. Mr. Jacobson wasn't too pleased with his loss of interest revenue, but Ben reminded him that unless someone provided the funds, some of the ranchers would lose their property.

Ben and Jim left for Texas in April to restore their own herds and to purchase cattle for those who couldn't make the trip. Ben's prize bull had survived the blizzard but drowned when the fast-moving creek swelled from the snow run off. Both ranchers needed to purchase additional heifers. Ben had worked several years to establish his herd, and even though he had the money, regaining his losses would also take time.

Cathleen planned their wedding ceremony for late May in case the men were delayed in returning. In addition, she didn't want another snowstorm interfering with her plans. Her parents were arriving the week before the wedding, and she also didn't want their train running into a storm.

One day in early May, Dan returned from town with a fat letter from her parents. A single page was all Cathleen had come to expect from them and wondered what warranted such a lengthy message. She itched with curiosity as she sliced open the envelope and began to read.

Dear Cathleen,

We look forward to our visit with you and your family. Like you told us from the beginning, Annie and Sammy stole our hearts. We can't wait to reunite with them and celebrate the renewal of your vows. Along with you, I felt cheated at not getting to participate in your original wedding. Have you hung your dress as I suggested?

The news I'm about to share can be taken either way. I hope you will understand, but Bridget has decided to stay in Boston. Since you left, Winston has been courting the girl, and they are engaged to be married. Your father had to fire his accountant, and Winston has been helping him with his books. According to your father, the young man is a whiz with mathematics. He still drives us on occasion, but his main job will be working as your father's accountant. Your father hired a professional to teach Winston the new system.

I've surprised your father with my recent interest in his affairs. I regret all the time I've neglected him while giving my undivided attention to worthless, unproductive pursuits. I resented him instead of getting to know him. After all these years, your father and I have fallen in love.

Cathleen read the two remaining paragraphs with tears flowing down her cheeks. For years, she had longed to see her parents engaged in a loving relationship. Thank God they were still young enough to enjoy their new-found love.

The letter from Bridget explained the thickness of the envelope. Her friend expressed regret at not leaving Boston as planned, and asked Cathleen's forgiveness. She thanked Cathleen for rescuing her from the threat of poverty. After the first few sentences, the girl abandoned further feelings of remorse and gushed over Winston and the love he had for her and Joey.

Though happy for Winston and Bridget, the announcement tasted bittersweet to Cathleen. Since Maria and Mariana did most of the cooking and housework, she didn't need, nor did she want, a nanny for the children. What she longed for was the companionship of her friends. Sammy talked about Joey every day and couldn't wait for his arrival. She didn't know how to tell him the sad news. They would both grieve the loss.

Besides, Cathleen had picked out Bridget for Dan. How could she have been so wrong? She shook her head to clear her useless thoughts. Those looks Winston gave the girl when she first arrived should have been clue enough for Cathleen. They were perfect for each other, and she'd have to get over the disappointment for Dan. Thank goodness, she hadn't mentioned Bridget to him. She brushed off her mismatching and breathed a prayer for their ranch foreman. God hadn't disappointed her when he sent her to Ben, and he wouldn't disappoint Dan either.

After days of cold damp rain, Cathleen opened her eyes the morning of their wedding to bright sun shining through the window. A warm breeze blew the sheer curtains in a pattern that resembled a dance. She jumped from bed and twirled to the sound of Bach's "Prelude in C Major" playing in her head.

The music stopped at the thought of her grandmother—the one person who would not be with her on this day. If not for her prayers, Cathleen wouldn't have had the courage to board a train to the unknown and give herself to a stranger.

Returning her thoughts to her parents, she remembered the fervent prayers of her grandmother for them. God had used Cathleen's departure to shake her father out of his lethargy and restore her parents to her. Though she would miss Nana at her wedding, she had two sets of loving parents to stand with her on this special day.

Instead of the Bach symphony, a song of thanksgiving and praise took its place. She dressed as if going to church and packed a small bag. As her mother had suggested, her wedding dress had been hanging in a closet at the parsonage since she first returned from Boston. The week before, Maria went to town and helped Maggie press out any remaining wrinkles. This day, her dream for a church wedding would be realized.

Ben and the children went into the church with her father while she and her mother took the small portmanteau and met Maggie at her front door.

"I'm so excited, Cathleen. Look at this beautiful day God has given you. I can't wait for my son to see you in that gorgeous gown."

After hugs and greetings, her mother-in-law sat Cathleen on a chair in the kitchen. The table held an array of brushes, hair pins, and two matching pearl-colored combs. "These are lovely, Maggie. Are they yours?"

"The combs are my gift to you. I found them in a catalog not long after you came to us. They match the pearls on your dress."

Cathleen fingered the pearls while Maggie styled her hair into a fashionable coiffure. "We'll add the combs after you're dressed. They will help hold the veil in place."

She looked at her mother whose eyes were glassy with tears. "Are you all right, Mother?"

"I'm not sure. Though I've longed to see this day, I feel terrible about the way I tried to force you into an arranged marriage. Thank the good Lord you're as stubborn as your father. I am so happy that you found Ben. You raised a fine son, Maggie."

"With God's help, I did, but your daughter couldn't be more perfect for him. His father and I fell in love with her from the first day she came."

"Okay, ladies, I don't think my veil will fit if you keep singing my praises."

The women laughed as Cathleen's mother held the dress for her. The cream-colored silk skirt fell in folds from the tight waist and lengthened in the back to form a trail of silk fabric. Miniature lace rose buds, dotted with small pearls formed the front panel of the bodice. Cathleen wept when her mother pulled a strand of pearls from a velveteen pouch.

"These belonged to your grandmother. She asked me to give them to you on your wedding day. I'm sorry you didn't have them for your first ceremony."

Cathleen giggled to break the serious moment. "Grandmother's pearls were not all that was missing that evening." She didn't say it aloud, but that knee buckling kiss had been the only redeeming moment. Maggie grinned along with her while her mother looked confused.

"It's a long story that my mother-in-law can explain while Ben and I are on our honeymoon." Maggie laughed again as she handed her a pair of short white gloves and a bouquet of spring flowers.

A knock sounded on the door and Mr. Harvey only stuck his head through the small opening. "You ladies about through primping? The reverend sent me to fetch you."

Cathleen climbed the steps to the church holding the train of her dress over one arm. When Harvey opened the double doors, her breath caught. The small sanctuary overflowed with people, many standing around the sides. Candles twinkled from standing holders on each side of the altar, along with baskets of wildflowers. All heads turned toward her, but the only one she saw stood at the front beside his father.

Never could she have imagined such love shining from a person's eyes. Her father pulled her hand to his arm and ushered her down the aisle to meet her husband.

"I know she's already yours, Ben, but I want to officially express my approval by giving you her hand." Her father lifted the short veil and kissed her damp cheek.

"You're beautiful," Ben whispered as he took her gloved hand.

"And you are my handsome cowboy."

They listened to the sacred words as if hearing them for the first time. That hurried exchange in the cabin sounded fake and insincere in comparison. Honesty and mutual love filled the words with meaning and spiritual significance. Cathleen felt God's approving presence not only in the words, but in the prayers and communion they shared.

"And now, my son, you may kiss your bride."

Ben held her face and looked into her eyes. "I am one blessed man."

When their lips touched, Cathleen melted against her husband and felt the oneness of their spirits pulling them together. Unlike their first kiss that reeked of sexual desire and uncontrolled passion, this mutual submission held the promise of eternal love. Cathleen had found her prince who would love her forever.

# Chapter Twenty-seven

Cathleen and Ben boarded the train the next afternoon for California. They were both exhausted from Sunday's celebration and a morning of rushing about preparing for the trip. She told herself repeatedly the children would be fine with Maria and her parents, but she still hated to leave them behind. They had played such an important role in her marriage to their father. If not for his children, she and Ben would have never married.

"What's wrong, honey? Are you worried about the children?"

"Not worried—I'm sure they'll be fine. I was thinking about how our mutual concern for the children had brought us together. When I understood that marrying you would mean that I would be the mother of two young children, I wanted to catch a return train to Boston. I didn't feel qualified, nor did I want the responsibility. My parents had neglected me, and I didn't want the opportunity to neglect someone else's children.

"You should have been in the room when your mother thrust Annie into my arms. I expected us both to be crying before someone rescued me, but the sweet baby surprised me. Instead of tears, she reached her little hand toward me and ran her fingers through my hair."

Ben's face lit up like a proud papa. "Our Annie has a way about her. When her mother died, I blamed the baby and refused to even look at her. But when my mother gave me a stern lecture and insisted I hold her, I fell in love. That woman seemed to know what we both needed—a touch of Annie."

"Yes, your mother has been a lifeline for both of us. She must have recognized a mothering tendency in me that I didn't know existed. At first, I was afraid to be alone with the children, but you were a pretty good teacher once you stopped running for the barn. Now I love being a mother and hate being separated from them."

"I know this isn't easy for you, but the trip will be good for us." Ben placed her head on his shoulder and kissed the side of her hair. "We are all thankful that you didn't run away, even when I treated you with such contempt. You are one courageous woman, Cathleen Sorenson."

"My grandmother insisted that I possessed my father's stubborn backbone, but I'm convinced her prayers gave me the courage to follow through with my commitment. When I stopped whining over my disappointments, the children became my greatest motivation.

"Speaking of children, I have a gift for you. I waited until now because ..." Cathleen looked out the window from their private sleeper and wondered how she should tell him. Ben raised his eyebrows in question.

"You'll understand once you know what the gift is." She looked into his eyes and prayed for more of that courage.

"We're going to have another baby, Ben." Cathleen bit her lip and waited for his reaction.

Instead of the worried look she expected, a smile started at the edge of his mouth and spread into his eyes and cheeks. "You couldn't have given me a more wonderful gift."

"I couldn't? I thought you'd be upset."

"Even a month ago, such an announcement would have paralyzed me with fear and dread, but while Dan and I were in Texas, we talked about how much you wanted another child. When I confessed my fears to him, my ranch foreman gave me a stern lecture that exposed my selfishness. Fear, he said, meant that I had not given God complete control of my life. He pointed out a few verses from the Bible on trusting God in the face of fear and told me I not only sinned against you, but I also sinned against God. You wouldn't believe how much his words changed my thinking."

"I knew I liked that man. What Scriptures did Dan give you?"

"The one that made the greatest impact was from Psalm 56, "What time I am afraid, I will trust in thee" (56:3). Reading those words from King David reminded me of the king's story when he faced the giant Goliath. Because God had given him courage against the wild animals attacking his father's sheep, David knew that he could also deliver the giant into his hands. I thought to myself, if God gave my wife the courage to fight off an attacking drifter, overcome a cantankerous woodstove, tackle mounds of laundry, and scare the daylights out of a hungry bear, he would surely give her strength to bring a child safely into the world."

Cathleen couldn't hide the joy shining through her tears as she touched the small baby forming in her womb. "Oh, Ben. God has freed you to share my happiness."

"Yes, he has, but I must confess something that has been on my conscience since you told me about losing the baby in Boston. Though I felt relieved when I realized you weren't talking about Annie, I also felt relieved that you wouldn't be in danger of dying in childbirth. I should have been as concerned for the child in your womb as I was about Annie and Sammy.

"God has forgiven me, but I must ask you to forgive me as well. I don't want to ever again treat life so callously."

"I suspected as much. Your reaction seemed a bit forced—more relieved than grieved while I was devastated. I appreciate your concern for me, but I'm glad that God has now freed you to love our unborn child."

Ben pulled her under his arm and placed his head against hers. His large hand covered the hand that embraced their tiny baby. "I never could pretend around you."

"No, you're fairly transparent, but I happened to think—" Ben's lips met her open mouth and she melted beneath his passionate kiss. Not remembering what she intended to say, she looked into his eyes and chuckled at his ability to so easily distract her.

Instead of more romance as she expected, Ben leaned heavily against her shoulder. Without moving a muscle, his body relaxed with a long sigh. "You're tired, Ben. All the rushing around and preparing for the trip has sapped your strength. Why don't you rest on the other bench while I read?"

Ben looked about confused before he answered. "I hate to desert you so soon, but with my tired body and the motion of the train, I can't keep my eyes open. Guess I'm more like my daughter than I realized."

He released a frustrated sigh and accepted the pillow she offered. When he'd curled his large frame on the undersized bench, Cathleen covered him with a light blanket. She knelt on the floor beside him and kissed each of his drooping eyelids before planting a lingering kiss on his lips.

"Are you tucking me in or trying to wake me up?"

Cathleen tweaked his nose and stood. "Get some rest. I'll wake you in time for dinner." Cathleen grinned at her use of the eastern title for the evening meal.

Grabbing a book from her portmanteau, Cathleen returned to her place by the window. But neither the view outside nor *The Heritage of the Desert* by Zane Grey succeeded in distracting her from watching Ben. Soft snores drifted from his slightly open mouth while his unruly hair fell in curls off his forehead. The man had stolen her heart almost from the beginning. Despite his quick temper and stubborn ways, his humility and his readiness to admit failure made him easy to love. Who would have thought such a fine man would need a mail-order bride?

Grandmother had been right when she said God had a plan for her life—a plan more wonderful than she could ever imagine. Tears of gratitude ran down Cathleen's cheeks as she rehearsed God's involvement in bringing her to Ben. Even the horrible things they'd experienced became steppingstones to the life they now shared.

Cathleen looked out on the landscape where the green pastures had given way to a barren land. The setting sun had begun painting the desert in bright hews, more brilliant with each passing mile. The changing colors reminded her of the naïve young woman who had boarded a similar train in Boston over a year ago. That girl had such high expectations, unaware of how much she needed to change.

All the knowledge she'd learned at her grandmother's knee hadn't prepared her for survival as a frontier woman. Since stepping off the train in Laramie, she'd faced difficulties that would make the average society girl retreat in fear. But, with courage and strength from God, she had stayed the course. The skills she'd learned, the people she'd met, and even the obstacles thrown across her path had all contributed to making her a better person. As she gazed out toward the horizon, she wondered what surprises God might have planned for her future.

Cathleen looked down at Ben and marveled at the way he made her feel. Though he continued to sleep peacefully, he had turned on his back. One long leg hung over the end of the bench while an arm dangled off the side. Even in sleep, he stirred her emotions and filled her with longing. She shivered and drew her shawl tighter as she remembered the cad in Boston and how close she'd come to accepting a loveless marriage. Looking back toward the colorful scene flashing outside her window, she whispered under her breath, "Thank you, God, for the hope I have in you and for leading me to this fine Wyoming rancher—the man only you could have chosen for me."

# About the Author

Claudette Sharpe was raised on a dairy farm in South Georgia. While attending Lee University in Cleveland, Tennessee, she met and married a fellow student, Charles Renalds. They moved to fast-paced Northern Virginia where she worked at the Pentagon. Five years later, she left to become a housewife, mother, and Christian education volunteer. As their children grew older, she accepted a full-time position as Director of Children's Ministry for Church of the Apostles, Fairfax, Virginia. When Claudette retired in 1994, she had time to indulge in her love of reading Christian fiction, and her desire to write surfaced when she and her sister compiled their mother's biography.

Claudette's writings are included in compilations by the NVCWF (now the Capitol Christian Writer's Fellowship): A devotional, entitled "Treasures of the Sea" was published in Whispers, 2015; "My Proverbs 31 Mother," in Characters We Know and Love, March 2016; and in Short Story Revival, April 2017, her submission, "A Touch of Regency," sends the reader back in time with a love story set in England. In June,

2018, NVCWF published an anthology entitled Legacy. Her submission, "The Legacy of Prayer," describes the impact her grandmother's prayer had on her family. *By the Sea* is her debut novel. She and Charles live in Haymarket, Virginia.

# Claudette's Other Novel

*By the Sea*

Made in the USA
Columbia, SC
18 June 2020